The sign said: PLEASE STOP.

It was nailed to the top of a broom handle.

Andy Farmer stood inside the fence where his driveway met Dog Creek Road and waved the sign, which was a piece of cardboard with black block letters, as the mailman flew by in his green pickup truck.

The mailman stomped the gas when he was just short of where Andy Farmer stood frantically waving the PLEASE STOP sign, and as he looked back to read the message, he threw his head back and laughed, knocking off his straw hat.

He laughed, honked, and waved.

A few dozen yards north, a pint whiskey bottle sailed out of the right window, and some letters flew out the left window.

The mailman moved out of sight, still honking.

Books by Jay Cronley

Funny Farm
Cheap Shot
Quick Change
Screwballs
Good Vibes
Fall Guy

FUNNY FARM

Jay Cronley

BALLANTINE BOOKS ● NEW YORK

All rights reserved under International and Pan-American Copyright Conventions. Published in the United States of America by Ballantine Books, a division of Random House, Inc., New York, and simultaneously in Canada by Random House of Canada Limited, Toronto.

Library of Congress Catalog Card Number: 85-47599

ISBN 0-345-33530-9

This edition published by arrangement with Atheneum Publishers, Inc.

Manufactured in the United States of America

First Ballantine Books Edition: November 1986

Once there was a writer who dedicated a book to a spouse. It was a real sweet dedication. Unfortunately, the spouse divorced the writer shortly before the book hit the hands.

It's no wonder you see a lot of books dedicated to unexplained initials.

What the heck, this is for CONNIE.

IT WAS THE GREATEST MOMENT OF ANDY Farmer's life, but he didn't want to get *too* excited and drop dead.

He was a little fat.

He was going to start exercising the first thing in the morning so he wouldn't have to tiptoe around anymore, wondering how his heart was doing. He felt odd, worrying about his health. Usually, "fix health" was far down on his list of things to do some month. It was hard to believe there was nothing else to worry about.

He stood beside the new cherry-red MG—it had only 930 miles on it, mostly from the drive in—as some clean air blew on his face. It was the kind of breeze that made a person want to roll up his sleeves and fool around in the dirt.

He looked up at his new place in the country, the MG purring at his side, and couldn't believe any of it.

It was the third of May.

If this was an average spring day out here, Andy Farmer was sorry they hadn't left a few hours earlier— the weather was *that* perfect.

The temperature was around sixty-five.

He had stopped at the mailbox near the dirt road that ran in front of the house and the surrounding twenty-five acres. The large white house, which was square, was at the top of a gentle rise. There was a knoll behind the house that was about thirty feet higher than the rest of the land. In the fall, deer trotted from the thick clump of trees to the right to the pond on the other side of the house, passing within a few yards of the front porch. The pond was full of clear water and contained, according to the realtor, catfish as big as a man's leg. About halfway between the dirt road and the house, there was a 250-year-old cottonwood tree where, again according to the realtor, some desperadoes—train robbers for the most part—had been hanged.

Living on land first settled by native Americans beat living in a glass building owned by Arabs.

Tiny purple wild flowers were blooming all around.

They had been here twice before, feeling the soil and checking for termites, while they were deciding where they wanted to spend the rest of their lives. They had fallen in love with this area a couple of years ago, during a cross-country driving vacation. The sky was big. The land was cheap. There were no yellow cabs. Life was too short to waste on routine, they decided. The farther away from people, the better. They wanted more than a change of scenery. They wanted a change of heart.

They had been here in the summer and in the fall, but this was the first time they had seen the sky so richly blue, it looked like the background for a Disney cartoon.

Andy Farmer felt lucky to be alive, but without the jitters that accompany the close call that *usually* makes you feel lucky to be alive. He felt lucky to be alive because of the beauty that surrounded him. It was as though he had been reborn without first having met the devil at the bottom of the barrel.

"Look at that," he said to his wife, who sort of wished he hadn't. Elizabeth wasn't feeling all that well. It was five minutes until noon. They had been on the road since a quarter of five, after breakfast in a place called Mitch's Café, where they had omelets with black chili inside. And although the new red MG cornered superbly, hugged the road like the center stripe, and got great mileage, it would never be mistaken in terms of comfort for a four-door Lincoln, or even a horse with a smooth gait. The MG was a little noisy and a little rough, and Elizabeth was a little tired and hungry.

Even though they had stopped, her body still tingled.

Still, she was glad to see her house, so she got out and stood next to her husband and took in some of this good air. She didn't have room for much more. She had already taken dozens of deep breaths during the 370-mile drive this morning. Her husband had repeatedly slammed on the brakes so he could admire cows standing by fences, gnarled trees standing starkly against a pink morning sky, ungnarled trees standing majestically against an azure midmorning sky—farms, birds, rabbits, you name it, he had admired it.

The house *was* gorgeous.

"You think you could reach in and grab us a fish out of the pond?" Elizabeth asked. She was hungry for some *real* food. "I'll cook it on a stick."

Andy Farmer was so anxious to get at his house and property, and have a look at the two ducks that came with the place, he almost left his wife standing by the mailbox.

Elizabeth threw a dirt clod at the MG and yelled, "*Hey!*"

THE HOUSE WAS SEVENTY-FIVE YEARS OLD.

It had high ceilings and thick walls.

It had been put together before union rules dictated how many nails could be struck per hour. When this house was built, the only union that mattered was between the builder and his God.

The rooms were big and bright.

All the floors were wooden, except in the kitchen at the back of the house. The floors there were tile. The fireplace was enormous. There were jog-in closets upstairs.

They inspected every inch of their new place, opening drawers, flicking tiny spiders out, thumping woodwork, blinking at the perfect condition of the house, right down to the shine on all the windows.

"The Musselmans must have been infirm," Elizabeth guessed of the former owners.

"They were claustrophobics, that's for sure," Andy Farmer said with regard to all the space and windows.

A quick tour of the house and toolshed out back took an hour or so. Most everything was as it should have been. The water had been turned on, and some garden equipment—a new soil tiller, some rakes, hoes, shovels, and clippers—had been delivered by a store in the nearest town, Redbud, and locked in the shed. There was also a rod and reel in there that had evidently been forgotten by the former owners, who had been transferred.

Even the old bomb shelter—a cement room in the ground near the knoll—was spotless.

There was only one minor problem, and it was funnier than it was worrisome.

The telephone was a little screwed up.

They had requested that a beige wall phone be installed in the kitchen next to where the new refrigerator would go. Once the furniture was arranged, they would make a decision about the locations of other telephones. The request for the beige wall phone had been submitted in writing to the Great Plains Telephone Company, along with a $30 deposit. But instead of a wall phone, somebody had hooked an old black table-model unit to a two-foot cord behind the front door, which was solid oak. To use the old black telephone, a person had to get down on his or her hands and knees; then if somebody came in through the front door unannounced, the person on the telephone might be knocked out.

Andy Farmer lifted the receiver and said there was a dial tone, which was all that really mattered at this point.

They had made such good time on the last leg of the trip, they still had more than an hour to kill before the movers were due. After everything was unloaded, they'd zip into Redbud, which was only thirty-two miles away, for an old-fashioned, home-cooked dinner.

Elizabeth said that she could hardly wait.

Andy Farmer decided to walk the property lines, then maybe paint their names on the mailbox out front.

Elizabeth was feeling better with her feet on the ground, not four inches above it as they had been for the last eight hours, and she guessed she'd have a look at the area between the house and the pond and decide on the best place for their garden.

CROCKER, THE DRIVER OF THE MOVING VAN THAT CONtained the Farmers' furniture, had a headache.

"There's no meat on this cheeseburger," he said to the waitress at the truck stop on the interstate.

"You're kidding," she said.

Crocker raised the top half of the bun to show the waitress that there was nothing on his cheeseburger except lettuce, tomato, onion, and mustard.

"This isn't some trick to try and get a free meal is it?" the waitress wondered, looking around for the meat patty.

"It's a simple attempt to eat," Crocker said.

"Excuse me, but I've got a problem too," Mickey, Crocker's assistant, said.

The waitress frowned.

"I ordered a fish sandwich."

"And?"

"I got a hamburger."

The waitress picked up the hamburger in front of Mickey and put it on Crocker's bun.

"My compliments to the chef," Crocker said.

"That's me," the waitress said. "Thanks a lot."

She returned several minutes later with a slice of cheese for Crocker's hamburger and a fish sandwich for Mickey.

"You ever hear of Dog Creek?" Crocker asked her.

"You fixing to make some comment about the quality of the food here?" The waitress drew back a pot of coffee.

Crocker squinted.

He had been told by his doctor to watch his blood pressure, so Mickey took over. "We're delivering some furniture to a party on something called Dog Creek Road." Mickey looked at a couple of maps that were spread under his fish sandwich. "It's supposed to be around this far west of here." He held the thumb and first finger of his right hand four inches apart.

"There's nothing west of here," the waitress said.

Crocker played with his spoon.

"There has to be *something* west of here," Mickey said.

"There's a damn road on the other side of this place," Crocker said without looking up.

"It goes to Bookerton."

"*That's* something," Crocker said.

"A matter of opinion," the waitress said, wandering off.

A truckdriver in the next booth said he thought Dog Creek Road was more north than west.

Mickey said that would make sense if they turned one of the maps upside-down.

One map was a state highway map that had been marked with a huge X, below which had been written: *Make left here.*

But the X was so large, you couldn't tell which of three possible roads you were supposed to take.

The other map was homemade. It had been drawn on poor quality paper with a Magic Marker. The lines had bled together. Various landmarks had turned into big blobs. As far as Crocker could tell, they were supposed to make a left here, proceed to a barn and make a right, travel approximately fifteen miles to a lake or crater or city, and make another left.

That would be Dog Creek Road.

"I'd like to get my hands on the person who made this map," Crocker said, folding the homemade mess in half. He handed it to Mickey. "Take very good care of it. It could be the evidence that gets me off the hook at a manslaughter trial."

On the way out of the truck stop, Crocker bought three packages of Tums.

He pointed the moving van west and rolled slowly over some deep ruts. These ruts, Crocker told Mickey professorially, dated back to the days when dinosaurs roamed the land, dragging their tails through the mud.

ELIZABETH DECIDED THAT THE BEST LOCATION FOR the garden was between the house and the pond. This was obviously the spot where the previous owners had their garden, as the soil was still broken in places. The new garden was going to be roughly twice the size of the previous effort—around twenty-five yards square— so even though the wind had picked up some, and it was on the chilly side of pleasant, Elizabeth got some twine from the toolshed and began laying out the southern border of what would become their vegetable patch.

It was a lucky thing.

Had she been laying out the northern edge—the right side as you stood in front of the house looking toward Dog Creek Road—her husband might have been wounded, or even killed.

Elizabeth was on her hands and knees, pinning

the twine onto the dirt with sticks—it beat sitting around listening to her stomach rumble—when she noticed a small wisp of something on the horizon to her left.

This wisp became taller and wider, fast.

Elizabeth got up and dusted herself off.

At first she thought it was a wisp of smoke, and she thought it was a long way off. After you've spent twenty years living in a city, surrounded by tall buildings, it's hard to judge distances in wide open spaces. Whereas Elizabeth was decent at guessing how long it might take a cab to cover a city block, she had no idea how long it would take a wisp on a wide open horizon to reach her husband, who sat near the road painting their name on the mailbox. And as a result of her inexperience in judging the speed of an object moving through clear air, she almost waited too long.

The wisp turned out to be dust.

It was being kicked up by a green pickup truck that was veering from one side of the road to the other. As the pickup truck came into view, it looked like a big animal sniffing around for a bone.

"Honey," Elizabeth said, brushing her hands off on her jeans. *"Honey!"*

The wind was blowing from the right—against the truck.

Andy Farmer, the mailbox in his lap, continued with his painting, oblivious to the problem bearing down on him.

The truck popped out of the far ditch like a pinball out of a lucky hole, rocked from side to side, bounced over a rut, then swerved toward where Andy Farmer sat facing in the opposite direction.

Elizabeth dropped the twine and began running. It was a tough run because the yard was full of rocks. Elizabeth found that she couldn't enunciate while running, waving, and dodging rocks, so rather than attempt a sentence, she screamed and pointed at the wall of dust that was about to engulf her husband.

Andy Farmer's mind was elsewhere. He was thinking about what kind of dog he was going to buy to run the fields with. He was also thinking about a name for their new place. Naming your acreage was a little corny; but Star Route 2, Dog Creek Road, didn't exactly suggest an image of birds chirping. This property was no hollow or crest or brook. It was a rolling plain. One possibility was The Dells, as in Farmers in the Dell. It was too bad a dell was a gorge cut by a river. Elizabeth had suggested that Grandstaff be included in the name of their property, since Andy Farmer's grandmother, Mildred Grandstaff, had made the move possible when she left her grandson $80,000, $50,000 of which had been used as a down payment on the house and twenty-five acres. But about the only thing Grandstaff went with was Grandstaff Estates, which sounded like a low-cost housing development. Something like The Meadows would suggest a logo—a sketch of the sun setting behind the knoll out back, perhaps—which would go on all their stationery.

Andy Farmer's concentration was interrupted by the green pickup truck. He heard a scream and looked left and saw a grill—the truck was *that* close.

Help, he thought.

Elizabeth didn't know what to do, so she pulled up just short of the barbed-wire fence that extended along the front of their property, placed her palms against her cheeks, and screamed some more.

Andy Farmer pushed himself backward into a ditch containing rocks, sticks, and a few small things that crawled. He hit the back of his head, and the black paint he had been using on the mailbox splashed on his neck.

The right rear tire of the green pickup truck slipped into the ditch and spun near where Andy Farmer was trying to hide.

Elizabeth kept screaming.

The truck ran over the mailbox and dragged it north a couple of dozen yards. The mailbox came loose, skipped end-over-end a few times and sailed into a field on the far side of Dog Creek Road.

The truck didn't slow down, but continued to weave from one side of the road to the other.

Elizabeth put her glasses on and squinted, trying to get a tag number. But all she saw was something white sailing out of the driver's window several hundred yards down the road.

She peeked over the barbed-wire fence into the ditch.

"The bastard didn't even honk," Andy Farmer said. "Help me up." He was on his back.

"I think not," Elizabeth said.

"Why?"

"Your neck. It's all . . . bent."

Andy Farmer took his chin off his right collar bone and slowly looked up at his wife.

"Is anything broken?" she asked.

"I don't think so."

"Well, it wouldn't matter one way or the other,

would it," Elizabeth said, looking left and then right, wondering how many days it would take an ambulance to arrive from somewhere.

She then crawled under the barbed-wire fence and stepped into the ditch and helped her husband out. He had dived onto some ants, and Elizabeth brushed a few of them out of his hair.

"Stick your tongue out."

He did.

"It's black."

"I swallowed some paint."

"How was it?"

Elizabeth's stomach growled.

THE MOVERS STOOD BESIDE THEIR VAN WITH THEIR backs to the wind.

"What *is* all this stuff?" Mickey asked.

"Oats, weeds," Crocker said sourly. "Who gives a goddamn."

They were surrounded by some kind of knee-high grain or growth that extended as far as the eye could see.

"What is it people do out here?" Mickey said, trying to unfold the homemade map.

"Live," Crocker guessed.

"You're kidding."

Mickey held the map close to his chest so it wouldn't blow away, then glanced around for landmarks. They were looking for a barn to the left and a road to the right. The last twenty minutes, they hadn't passed so much as a pile of bones.

"When did we get this map?" Crocker asked, looking at the foundation of what might have been a barn. There were a couple of cement slabs off to the left.

Mickey checked a notebook. He said that the homemade map had been delivered to the loading dock twelve days ago.

"Well, for Christ's sake, that explains it," Crocker said, smiling without really meaning it. "The goddamn barn has obviously blown away since the map was made."

Crocker's point was that nothing could survive in this kind of wind for twelve days. He walked a few yards to his right, onto some bare ground that *might* have been a road. He looked for tire tracks. He looked at the sun and scratched his chin. Crocker didn't know where in the hell they were. But he was certain that they were in some *part* of hell.

"We need to get to a phone and call Washington, D. C.," Mickey said. "The neutron bomb has hit out here. We need to let somebody know."

Crocker stretched. "We're taking this trail west."

"We who, you and the truck?"

"HERE COME THE MOVERS," ELIZABETH SHOUTED TO her husband, who was in a field on the west side of Dog Creek Road, retrieving what was left of the mailbox. Andy Farmer had found everything except the red flag you turned up when you had something to be mailed and wanted the carrier to stop.

He picked some burrs off his jeans and looked up the road in the direction Elizabeth was pointing.

He didn't see any movers.

He saw a kid on a bike.

"Very funny," he said.

"Maybe he's an advance scout," Elizabeth said, buttoning a jacket around her neck. "I'm freezing."

The kid on the bicycle was named Toby, and he was thirteen. His hair appeared to be about six months. It was long and shaggy. He wore a sweatshirt, jeans with holes in the knees, tennis shoes, and a dusty ball cap. He rode right up to the Farmers, stopped, and put the kickstand down as though his arrival had been expected. The bicycle on which Toby rode was not in the best of shape, and appeared to have been made out of old plumbing.

"Hello," Andy Farmer said.

"Lo." Toby shuffled his feet and removed a notebook from his back pocket. "Your name Crabtree?"

Andy Farmer frowned.

"No," Elizabeth said. "Are you hungry?"

"Yeah."

"That's too bad," Andy Farmer said. "We haven't got any food. Yet."

Toby shrugged. He said his name was Toby Hall, and he studied his notebook some more. "Your name Fairchild?"

Andy Farmer shook his head. "We're the Farmers."

"*Where?*" Toby asked. He looked left and right several times.

"Here," Andy Farmer said.

"*What* farmers?"

"Andy and Elizabeth."

Toby looked at the ground and shook his head.

"Farmer is our *name*," Elizabeth said. "Not our occupation. We're Andy and Elizabeth Farmer."

"We're going to farm a garden, though," Andy Farmer said.

"My sister has been keeping the notebook while I had the mumps," Toby said. "She got everything on the wrong page. She thought you lived over on Dead Horse Mountain Road."

Andy Farmer said no, they lived right here.

"Oh." Toby walked to his bicycle and rummaged through a bag tied behind the seat.

"The poor little guy is selling something," Elizabeth whispered. "I want you to buy it. Buy *two*, bless his heart."

"Got any candy bars?"

"Nope."

Toby shuffled back to where the Farmers stood and handed them a card. The card was addressed to Occupant, Star Route 2, Dog Creek Road. It advertised a dress sale in town. All winter clothing was marked down 90 percent.

"Your mom own the dress store?" Andy Farmer asked.

Toby rolled his eyes and shook his head no and took a couple of deep breaths. He seemed to be painfully shy. He straightened the bill on his ball cap several times, probably wishing he could type so he could put all this stuff on a piece of paper and *hand* it out. Eventually, he began his explanation.

"Junk is a dime."

"What kind of junk?" Andy Farmer asked.

"Give him a dime," Elizabeth said.

Andy Farmer gave Toby a dime.

"Real names are a quarter, dollar a day, maximum."

"Give him a quarter."

"What kind of names?" Andy Farmer asked.

"Brother," Toby said. He took off his ball cap and banged it against his right thigh. Dust flew. He picked up a rock and tossed it at a tree on the other side of Dog Creek Road. "*These* names." He held the bag open. And Farmer reached inside and removed some of its contents.

"They're *letters*. This kid is stealing *mail*."

Elizabeth said, "You shouldn't do that."

"He's stealing *welfare checks*."

Toby grabbed at his bag, missed, and said, "Damn."

Elizabeth took the bag from her husband and told everybody to calm down. She was certain all this could be straightened out with a couple of telephone calls. There was probably a logical explanation why Toby was carrying mail on the back of his bicycle. Had there been an accident involving the mail carrier? Toby hadn't actually *stolen* the mail, had he?

"*No*, lady," Toby said, shaking his head. "I'm delivering it."

Elizabeth dropped the sack of letters.

Andy Farmer looked at the card advertising the dress sale. It was postmarked a week ago Tuesday.

"What the hell is going on here?" Andy Farmer asked.

"I've been trying to tell you for *days*. Junk is a dime."

"Junk mail," Elizabeth said.

Toby nodded. "Names are a quarter."

"Letters with our names on them," Elizabeth said.

"Thanks, lady," Toby said.

* * *

TOBY AND HIS FATHER LIVED THREE MILES SOUTH AND a half a mile east on Indian Road. His father drove a bus—when his back wasn't bothering him—and made grain alcohol every month or so. The last tub had blown the roof off the garage and got some splinters in it. But all you had to do was strain it. Because of the splinters, a pint only cost $1.50.

"You want some, leave a note in the mailbox," Toby said. "You *got* a mailbox?"

"A man just ran over it and almost killed my husband," Elizabeth said.

"Green truck?"

Elizabeth nodded.

Toby nodded.

They had moved up the hill, and now sat on the steps leading to the front porch.

Toby took a deep breath and continued with his explanation; the next time somebody new moved in, his sister, who loved to talk, would do this part.

He was their mailboy. Tuesday, Thursday, and Saturday, except when one of them was a holiday, he followed along behind the green truck, which was driven by a man named Petree, picking up cards and letters and packages. Petree was the regular mail carrier. He drank a lot, and was a mean old bastard to boot. When somebody moved into a place on this end of Dog Creek Road, Petree had to swing about eight miles out of his way to deliver a simple postcard. And that made him mad. So rather than stop to deliver something, which was hard on his truck, Petree simply threw mail out of his window whenever the urge hit

17

him. The way Toby heard it, Petree didn't get mileage money for extra driving.

"My God," Andy Farmer said.

Packages were $1.50 each. "Some of the damn things are *heavy*," Toby said, in case the $1.50 sounded like a lot. "You ought to see some of the places I have to stomp into to get packages."

"The Waterford crystal," Elizabeth said. She had ordered a vase from Ireland and had requested that it be sent to their new address.

Toby shrugged and said if something was broken, he still had to collect. "You want something mailed, leave it in a paper sack Thursday morning. My dad goes to town every Saturday. Mailing something is two bucks a sack."

Elizabeth rubbed her eyes and wondered if it was too late to call Ireland and cancel the order.

Her husband told her not to worry, he'd write the Postmaster General in Washington if the regular carrier wouldn't listen to reason.

"Who's that?" Toby asked.

"He's in charge of all the mail in this country."

"Well," Toby said, putting his sack of letters back behind the seat on his old bicycle, "you'd probably be better off calling him instead of writing." Toby grinned at his joke. "You people get a lot of mail?"

Andy Farmer nodded.

"Good, the Musselmans didn't get hardly any." Toby pushed up the kickstand on his bike. "They got more mail after Claude Musselman dropped dead than when he was alive."

"I thought he was *transferred*," Elizabeth said, scooting closer to her husband.

"Not until after he was dead," Toby said. "I wouldn't get too close to this road between one and four in the afternoon. By the time Petree gets to this spot, he's usually drunk."

Elizabeth tucked a dollar into Toby's shirt pocket. "It's a tip."

"I'll start looking for your vase real good, lady."

Toby got onto his old bicycle and pumped away.

Andy Farmer gave his wife a hand up from the porch steps.

"There's a piece of genuine Americana," he said, putting his arm around his wife as they watched Toby ride out of sight.

He told her not to worry about the alcoholic mailman who threw letters and packages out of his window. He'd have a visit with this Petree and get things resolved.

"I thought Americana was older," Elizabeth said. "I thought it was like a fifties movie."

"No, it's the simple life."

"Oh," Elizabeth said, wondering if things like being starved also fell under this broad heading of Americana.

THE MOVING VAN SAT AT A FORK IN THE MIDDLE OF the prairie.

Dirt roads went straight and to the right. Both were similarly worn, and you couldn't tell which might lead to another human or which might lead nowhere.

Crocker sat with his eyes closed. His breathing was labored.

"You want me to flip a coin?" Mickey asked.

Crocker took faster and shorter breaths.

"Don't you dare black out on me," Mickey said.

Crocker opened his eyes and took the microphone from their citizens band radio off its rack. He pressed a button and said, "Has anybody ever heard of something called Dog Creek Road?"

He released the button. There was some static, followed by, "This is Red Rover, come again please."

Crocker rubbed his face with his left hand. He squinted at the CB radio and said he was a mover from New York looking for an address on Dog Creek Road.

"What's your handle there, stranger?" the voice said.

"None," Crocker said.

"Come again?"

"You need to get yourself a handle," Mickey said, "We could think of one in ten seconds. They *love* nicknames out here."

"My name is Crocker," Crocker said into the microphone. "C-r-o-c-k-e-r."

"Your *what*?"

"Tell him it's your handle, tell him it's Crock Pot or something like that."

"My *name*."

"What's your *handle*?"

Crocker despised the CB. He appreciated hearing about highway conditions and the locations of speed traps; but he was not about to waste his time communicating in some sort of corn-pone pig-Latin jibberish.

"I haven't got a handle, I've got a name," Crocker said into the microphone.

"But, you've *got* to have a handle," Red Rover said.

"Or what," Crocker said. "You won't tell me where the best grits are?"

Mickey looked out his window and shook his head.

"I don't talk in rhyme," Crocker said. "Now have you or have you not heard of Dog Creek Road?"

"*Everybody* has a handle."

"Hillbilly son of a bitch," Crocker said.

"Ten-four, Hillbilly Son Of A Bitch, welcome to God's Country. Now what was it you were looking for?"

"Hillbilly son of a bitch is not my handle," Crocker said. "It's a description."

"We don't need your kind around here," Red Rover said.

"Stay out of the east," Crocker said.

He hung up and went straight.

THE MOVERS WERE NOW AN HOUR LATE, AND ELIZA-beth was not pleased.

She sat on the ledge in front of the huge fireplace in the living room, a can of warm diet pop and half a Baby Ruth candy bar at her side. "Let me get this straight," she said. "We can't go eat, is that what you're telling me?"

"Not now, no," Andy Farmer said. He stood at the front window. "If we went to eat, we'd miss the movers."

"*What* movers?"

"You're just tired."

This *just tired* business was starting to lose some of its effectiveness, Elizabeth thought.

"They probably took a wrong turn," Andy Farmer guessed.

That was a possibility—about a fifty-fifty chance,

but Elizabeth had her own ideas about the movers. Elizabeth thought the movers had stolen their furniture, most of which was new, and their artwork and china and silver, and had bolted for Mexico.

"They'll do anything for money at those border town. You can get a root canal for seventy-five cents. You give a guard our new television, he'd wave an MX missile through. What we should have done was meet the movers in the nearest town."

Elizabeth's point here was: This place was a little hard to find, particularly the first time.

"There's no need to bitch."

Elizabeth said she wasn't bitching. The circumstances simply made her words sound evil.

ANDY FARMER GAVE THE MOVERS FIFTEEN MORE minutes, then he went to the MG for a copy of the contract. All he had to do was call the movers' home office and find out what the hell was going on.

"If they were lost, why would they call the home office?" Elizabeth wondered. "Why wouldn't they call us?"

"You need to calm down."

"Where?" Elizabeth asked, looking around the empty living room, which was getting cold. The heating and cooling unit wasn't scheduled to be turned on until next week.

Andy Farmer said he was getting tired of the sarcasm.

Elizabeth told him that he continued to mistake simple, God-fearing questions for bitching and sarcasm.

22

Andy Farmer spread the contract, which had the home-office telephone number across the top, beside the old black table-model telephone behind the front door.

He began dialing.

"When they're late, you get a rebate."

"Terrific."

Andy Farmer stopped dialing.

"I mean it. *Terrific*."

Andy Farmer finished dialing the movers' home office and folded the contract and put it in his windbreaker pocket.

The call rang twice.

An operator cut in and said, "Okay, deposit two dollars and sixty-five cents."

Andy Farmer grinned and said, "Do *what*?"

"Deposit the change."

"Sorry," Andy Farmer said, hanging up.

He told Elizabeth he'd gotten the wrong number. She nodded.

THE NEXT TIME HE DIALED THE MOVERS, THE SAME thing happened.

Roughly.

The call rang twice.

The operator cut in and said, "Deposit two-*seventy*."

Andy Farmer licked his lips and cleared his throat and held the black table-model telephone up, expecting to see some loose wires hanging out the bottom.

"Huh?" he said.

"Put the two-seventy in the slots," the operator told him.

"What . . . where?"

"The coin slots."

"Listen, there's some mistake. This isn't a pay phone. This is a table-model phone in my living room."

"Hold on."

The operator went off the line.

"There's a problem," Andy Farmer said to Elizabeth, who had leaned against the fireplace, her eyes closed.

"I heard."

"But they're fixing it."

"Terrific."

"Do you know another word?"

"Good."

ON THE OTHER END OF THE CALL, MILLIE POCK, Operator five, sighed and opened her Instruction Manual to page seven. She sat at a new computer, next to Operator one, Gretchen Honneycutt. There were no Operators two through four on this particular shift. The management at Great Plains Telephone thought that having an Operator five suggested a big staff and the kind of activity that would fill a customer with confidence. It was called creative marketing.

Operator five, Millie Pock, squinted at a paragraph on page seven that said if a dot appeared on the computer screen, you were getting a call from a pay phone. To find the charges, you hit a bar, which was blue.

Operator five hit the blue bar and the screen flashed: Toll charges, $2.70.

Operator five sniffed.

Great Plains had gone computer three weeks ago. Only the operators who had worked with the company twenty-five years got to stay on, and they were sent to computer school. Operators five and one had returned from computer school just yesterday and were, according to District Manager Woolcott, making a smooth transition from the dark ages to the world of tomorrow.

Sure they were.

On this shift alone, which was only forty-five minutes old, they had received calls bound for Walrus Point, Alaska, Second Creek, Wyoming, and Houston, Texas.

"This guy says he's not at a pay phone," Operator five said.

Operator one looked at the screen and said, "Either he's lying or you screwed up."

"You still there?" Operator five said into her headset.

"Sure," Andy Farmer answered.

"The computer says you owe us two-seventy."

"Listen lady, this isn't a goddamn bit funny."

Elizabeth opened an eye.

Operator five put the call on a squawk box.

"... and there's no goddamn place to put any money because this isn't a pay phone."

"You don't have to take that," said Operator one.

Operator five agreed and hit a bar, disconnecting the call.

Andy Farmer slammed the receiver onto its base, sending a plastic chip in Elizabeth's direction. She ducked. It hit the wall to her left.

"They think this is a pay phone."

"More Americana," Elizabeth said.

* * *

ANDY FARMER PACED AROUND THE LIVING ROOM, but the only thing he could think of was *more* calls.

Call three:

Two rings.

"Deposit two-ninety."

"It was two-*seventy* a few seconds ago, for the love of Christ."

Disconnected.

Call four:

"Deposit two-seventy."

"Lady, I beg you, don't hang up. We just bought the Musselman place out on Dog Creek Road. We just got here. Our furniture is missing."

"We're tired and hungry," Elizabeth said from the fireplace.

"And I'm trying to call New York to see where everything is. *Please* help me."

"We've got new computers," Operator one said. "We haven't got all the bugs worked out yet."

"*Bugs*. There's the Creature from the Black Lagoon hanging from our damn wires."

Disconnected.

Call five:

"I'm his wife, Elizabeth Farmer. Everything he says is true."

"Hon, all I can do is what this computer lets me."

"Don't hang up on him. He's only tired."

"Tell him we don't have to listen to people cuss us."

"I will."

"And keep warm, there's a cold front moving in."

"Hi," Andy Farmer said, getting back on the line.

"Sir," Operator five said coolly.

"Help us find our furniture. Help us make a call."

"What I think you need to do, *sir*," Operator five said, flipping through some pages in her manual, "is report trouble on the line to the business office."

"I'd *love* to do that."

Elizabeth sat back by the fireplace.

Andy Farmer gave her the okay sign.

"There's a temporary service number you can call on Saturday," Operator one said. "It's a little shop around the corner."

"That's great news. We appreciate it. Now hook me through to the emergency repair shop."

"Deposit thirty cents."

The base of the black table-model telephone was split down the middle.

Call six:

Andy Farmer put his shirttail over the receiver to disguise his voice.

"Deposit two-seventy. Five."

"Please make the call collect."

"Name?"

"Jones."

"Hold."

The call rang through.

"Edwards, loading dock," somebody said.

"Will you accept a call from a Mr. Jones?" Operator five asked.

"Well," Edwards said.

"It's about our stuff," Andy Farmer said loudly.

"Be quiet," Operator five said. "You can't converse until the charges are accepted."

"I've got to tell him what the call is about so he *will* accept the charges."

"Hush."

"You bastards haven't shown up with our stuff. Our name is Farm..."

Disconnected.

Calls seven through twelve: He made up area codes and numbers, trying to reach *anybody*. Each time, an operator cut in, wanting money. Call twelve was incoming. Andy Farmer jumped on it. It was from London. It had missed Toronto by more than a thousand miles.

After that, the black table-model telephone behind the front door went dead.

"A MERCY KILLING," ANDY FARMER SAID, STANDING over the phone.

Elizabeth rose from her seat by the fireplace and put her arms around her husband's neck.

He was depressed.

"I wanted everything to get off to such a great start," he said.

"It's still early. Relatively."

"It's important to start off with some good memories, you know?"

Elizabeth said everything would be all right—the movers would probably arrive any second. One thing was *not* all right. She was truly starved. "Why don't you get that fishing pole out of the shed and go to the pond and catch us a big catfish. We'll cook it on a clothes hanger, like a marshmallow."

"That's a *hell* of an idea," Andy Farmer said, brightening.

Elizabeth grabbed the front of her husband's windbreaker. "Hurry, for God's sake, *hurry*." She shook him, then winked and kissed him on the cheek.

"I'll dig some worms out of the garden."

"Perfect."

"The first thing we put up is the bed. We make love all night."

"Once the movers leave, sure."

Andy Farmer went to catch their first dinner, which was a lot more charming than eating in town.

Elizabeth curled up beside the fireplace and slept forty-five seconds, until a mosquito bit her nose.

THE MOVERS STOOD FACING COOPERMAN'S BRIDGE, which was wood and had three levels. You went up a ramp, across a flat part, then down a ramp similar to the first.

Hopefully.

Cooperman's Bridge was built in 1928 and named for Maurice Cooperman, the first person to crash through the railing and fall onto the jagged rocks below. Maurice had sailed through the railing not ten minutes after the bridge was opened for business. Fortunately for Maurice, the construction workers were still packing up their hammers and nails, and they rushed down the bank and dragged him to safety. He broke a few bones.

All told, approximately seventy-five vehicles had fallen off of, or crashed into, Cooperman's Bridge, which doesn't sound like many in nearly sixty years; but the figure becomes much more alarming when you consider that only a few dozen people use the bridge regularly, regularly being once a month.

In the last five years, the only improvements had been a coat of paint and a VERY NARROW BRIDGE sign. The last time the highway department was out, a traffic counter was placed in the level portion of Cooperman's Bridge. During a ten-day period in the peak of the tourist season—around the Fourth of July—eight vehicles and nineteen animals, probably cows, crossed the bridge.

Crocker had been a mover eighteen years.

He had survived the rush hour in Los Angeles, where vehicles moving less than sixty miles per hour were considered legally stalled. He had driven heavy loads of furniture down icy peaks in Colorado. He had even driven some furniture to a crazy old man who lived in the Louisiana swamp. That time, Crocker's van had to be ferried to an island where snakes as big as railroad ties hung from the tree limbs. But in all the years Crocker had been driving a moving van, he had never seen anything as disgusting as Cooperman's Bridge.

It was an insult to his intelligence.

"Don't take it as a challenge," Mickey said, blowing on his cold hands. "Take it as an omen."

"You would think," Crocker said, shielding his eyes from the sun, "it's more likely something is straight ahead, since we haven't passed anything alive in an hour. You would think it's nearly impossible to drive a couple of hours without coming to something in this day and age."

"Day and age doesn't apply out here, Crocker. Nothing's changed since fourteen hundred. At least we *know* some humans are behind us. Somewhere."

Crocker turned his attention from the bridge to

the dirt road they had been on. It was narrow. There had been no place to turn around for many miles.

"I'm a hell of a backer," Mickey said.

Crocker looked at the bridge. "Climb up there and check it out. One of us has to check out the top, one of us has to check out the bottom."

Mickey looked at the tall weeds and rocks and God only knew what else underneath the bridge, then handed Crocker his billfold and watch. "You see Sally gets this with my love."

"You've got my word on it," Crocker said, putting Mickey's valuables on the hood of the truck.

Mickey went up the ramp on his hands and knees. "There's cracks in this thing three inches wide," he said, crawling onto the level part. "Hey Crocker, you know these wooden guide-ruts for the tires?"

Crocker was checking the bottom of the bridge. Casually. He was still standing on the dirt road. He was leaning left and looking at a half dozen posts the size of telephone poles that went from the bridge into the muck. "Yeah."

"The guide-ruts *move*, Crocker."

"Jump up and down."

"*What?*"

"Stomp the bridge."

Mickey tapped his toe; rocks fell through the cracks.

"*Harder.*"

Mickey jumped an inch into the air. He knocked a piece of rotten wood onto the rocks. He tiptoed to the far side and reported, if such a thing were imaginable, that the other ramp was steeper than the first. "And you know this railing on both sides of the bridge?"

"Check it."

"Well, Crocker, it's not railing. *It's termites holding hands.*"

Crocker told Mickey to return to the truck. He didn't have to tell him twice. Mickey jumped off the up ramp. Crocker caught him.

"We're going over it," Crocker said.

"Not me," Mickey said, "I wouldn't go over it on a skateboard."

"If your number's called, there's not a damn thing you can do about it, you understand what I'm saying? You can't screw with fate."

"Fate? *Fate?* Fate is where you get hit by lightning. This is like the electric chair."

"This is almost religious," Crocker said, dragging Mickey toward the truck.

ANDY FARMER HAD A BITE NOT FIVE MINUTES AFTER he put a worm from the garden on the end of his hook and tossed it into the center of the pond.

He used a piece of Styrofoam he found in the toolshed for a bobber.

The Styrofoam held the worm a few feet off of the bottom of the pond.

When the piece of Styrofoam dipped beneath the water, suggesting a catfish was playing with, or had swallowed, the worm, Andy Farmer yanked the fishing rod over his head.

Only nothing happened.

"Damn," he said, wishing Elizabeth were on the far bank with a camera. But on the other hand, it would be a lot of fun, surprising her with a substantial catch his first time out.

The catfish Andy Farmer had hooked was a big one, so big, in fact, it overwhelmed the tiny rod and reel he had found in the shed. There was no way to reel the fish in conventionally—it would rip the guts out of the reel and snap the rod in half—so Andy Farmer dropped the rod and reel and started to haul in his catch hand over hand.

The fishing line cut into a couple of Andy Farmer's fingers and caused them to bleed slightly; but more important, the catfish remained in the pond, obviously tangled around a log or something like that.

Andy Farmer hadn't done much fresh-water fishing and didn't know what he was supposed to do now. He wrapped more fishing line around his knuckles and walked to his right yanking every so often. After he had walked ten or fifteen yards, he was able to drag his catfish a foot or so nearer the shore.

He was not *about* to lose this fish, even though they would both be around another day. He was going to wade into the damn pond, shoes and all, if that became necessary. Before he did that, however, he yanked the line as hard as he could and almost fell over backward.

And *it worked*.

Andy Farmer's prize catch came free—it erupted from the water like a missile fired from a submarine—and flew straight for his head.

It happened so fast, he was not able to focus on what he had caught until it was several feet from his face, moving at a high rate of speed.

He had not caught a catfish.

He had caught—he recognized it as he ducked—
a snake.

Which flew over his head.

"Jesus," he said.

It was a big snake, at least four feet in length and
easily as big around as a garden hose. The snake had
not been hooked through its mouth. It had been hooked
through its back and was wiggling from both ends.

The snake landed near the two ducks that had
come with the place; they ran for it.

Andy Farmer was too frightened to do much of
anything.

He was worried about passing out and having the
snake crawl up his pants.

After the snake flew over his head, he whirled
around and backed up, pulling the snake along after
him.

When Andy Farmer had dropped his rod and reel,
a lot of fishing line had come loose on the ground; and
as he backed up, much of this line became tangled
around his ankles, calves, and knees.

The snake seemed to be coming at Andy Farmer
faster than he was backing up, so he turned and ran,
which was a mistake, because he pulled the snake
right along behind him, like a wagon. He ran first for
the front porch, then decided this might upset
Elizabeth; so he swerved right and ran past the 250-
year-old cottonwood tree. He ran for the road as fast
as the fishing line wrapped around his legs—and now
his stomach and arms—would permit.

The snake bounced along behind, gaining ground,
it seemed, each time Andy Farmer looked over his
shoulder.

Once he began running, there was no way for him ever to stop, so he made a left at Dog Creek Road and ran into the near ditch, hoping to knock the snake off the hook on a rock. That didn't happen, so Andy Farmer ran until the fence stopped, made another left, and entered a field full of all sorts of goddamn things— burr bushes, shrubs, small trees, mail—it was all in this field.

His plan was to run until he or the snake died.

About fifty yards into the field, the fishing line went slack. Andy Farmer turned and back-pedaled a few yards until he could see the end of the line blowing in the breeze. The snake was stuck in a bush.

Relieved, Andy Farmer collapsed.

But he couldn't collapse long because snakes were probably like cockroaches. If there was a four-footer in the pond, there were probably six-footers in the weeds.

Andy Farmer got to his feet and cautiously approached the bush and the snake, which flicked its tongue repeatedly. He found a big rock and dropped it on the snake.

Ugly things were under the rock.

He walked home, wiping blood from his hands onto his jeans. Upon his return, the ducks were on the far side of the pond. The male had lost quite a few feathers and was quacking.

Andy Farmer went to the MG and looked up the snake in one of the many nature books he had brought. The snake he had caught in the pond appeared to be a harmless water snake, harmless unless you resented the bastards flying at your face. Some people, the book

35

said, kept water snakes as pets. These people, Andy Farmer guessed, were gluttons for punishment.

He decided not to tell his wife this latest nightmare.

CROCKER BLEW PERSPIRATION OFF HIS NOSE AND inched the moving van up Cooperman's Bridge.

Mickey rode with his hands shielding his face.

Crocker drove with his head out the window so he could see what he was about to hit. He got the cab of the moving van to the flat portion of the bridge and stomped the brake. He took a deep breath to prepare himself for the tricky part. He was going to have to move the cab slightly right while bringing the van with the furniture straight up the ramp. The flat part of the bridge, for some insane goddamn reason Crocker couldn't relate to, angled slightly to the right.

"I think it's warped," Mickey said.

"Here we the hell go." Crocker leaned out his window and let the clutch out.

The truck jerked forward.

The bridge creaked.

Crocker turned the steering wheel an inch to the right and asked his assistant how much room he had to work with on that side.

"Oh," Mickey said nonchalantly, "about forty-five feet."

His answer was followed by the sounds of wooden railings crashing onto rocks.

"You knocked some stuff off, *bad*," Mickey said. There was nothing left on his side except one rotten post.

"Don't panic," Crocker said.

He tried to back up a foot or two. This attempt was greeted by a *thump* and more sounds of wood crashing onto rocks and into pools of stagnant water that had typhoid written all over them.

Their situation was this:

They couldn't go forward or backward. They were stuck. The cab was pointed at the right side of the bridge and the back of the van was pointed at the left side. Further movement in either direction would benefit only the undertaker.

Crocker turned the truck off, set the emergency brake, and looked around for something to punch.

"Feel that," Mickey said, his eyes wide. "Crocker, we're moving. We're *swaying* in the wind."

Sure enough, Crocker focused on a tree on the other side of the bridge and felt himself, Mickey, and the truck rocking slowly back and forth.

"Maybe we'll only be pinned under the wreckage with broken legs," Mickey hoped.

Crocker told his assistant to quit whining. They were going to get out of this alive. They *had* to, so they could discuss matters with the person who had done this to them.

THEY COULDN'T GET OUT OF MICKEY'S DOOR, AS IT was suspended over the side of the bridge.

They had two feet of bridge to work with on Crocker's side, so they slithered out his door and crawled headfirst underneath the truck.

It was rough going under there, with all the splinters and grease.

They pulled themselves ahead on their stomachs and scrambled down the up ramp to safety.

"By God we *did* it," Mickey said, hugging Crocker.

"It's cold," Crocker said. "It's cold, it's almost dark, we've got no food, and we're lost."

"You're right, we're still fucked," Mickey said.

"ARE THEY COMING?" ANDY FARMER ASKED.

"Not unless they're driving with their lights off," Elizabeth answered.

She stood at the front window with binoculars. She took the strap from around her neck and put the binoculars on the window sill, trapping a mosquito beneath one of the lenses.

"There's no need to be a smart-ass."

Elizabeth shrugged. It was simple. It was a quarter after eight. It was dark out there. The movers weren't coming unless they were driving with their lights off. Nothing was coming. Except mosquitoes. Elizabeth thought mosquitoes liked *warmer* weather. She didn't know they were so active when it was twenty degrees.

"It's fifty," her husband said.

"What I think has happened here," Elizabeth said, swatting a mosquito near her face, "is that we've settled on their ancient burial grounds, and they're mad as hell."

Andy Farmer, sitting on the ledge in front of the fireplace, frowned.

Elizabeth leaned against the window sill and frowned back.

"So the fish weren't biting."

"No."

"You try to grab some with your hands?"

Andy Farmer looked at his hands, which still had some blood on them. He opened one of his books about the first pioneers who settled this area.

After a minute, Elizabeth asked if the story he was reading were a good one; she had to keep talking to take her mind off how bad she felt.

"The pioneers came out here in wagons that had yardsticks for springs."

Elizabeth nodded.

"They slept under the stars, ate wild berries, bathed in icy streams, and shaved with pieces of broken glass."

"And lived to an average age of twenty-nine," Elizabeth said.

Andy Farmer closed the book.

Elizabeth said she was sorry but one of the reasons she couldn't help being a smart-ass was because of the large mosquito bite under her left eye, which had started to throb and burn and swell. It made her mad.

Andy Farmer walked across the living room and looked at where the mosquito had bitten his wife.

"You get used to it," he said.

"You build up an immunity?"

"No, you get used to looking all deformed like that."

He returned to the fireplace. They sat quietly a while before declaring a truce on smart-ass remarks.

Their plan was to think positively.

CROCKER GRABBED HIS LEFT SHIN AND SCREAMED, "Goddamn, a *rat's* got me."

"Oh no," Mickey said, crawling away.

They were in a dark ditch. They had crawled into

a ditch near Cooperman's Bridge to get out of the wind and catch some sleep before setting out on foot at dawn for help.

Once the rat had Crocker, Mickey's strategy was to get away from his boss in case there were any more rats. But Crocker thought that was a lousy idea. He grabbed Mickey's foot, turned on a flashlight, and told his assistant he was not running anywhere—he was going to track down the rat and catch it in case it had rabies.

The movers' union was going to love this.

"*Listen*," Crocker said, pointing the light at some tall weeds. "It's over there."

Mickey took the flashlight and walked toward the sounds of weeds rustling. Crocker watched the light bounce around. His assistant appeared to be running or dodging.

"Come back here, you," Mickey yelled, deep in the weeds.

"Attaboy," Crocker shouted.

After a couple of minutes of shuffling around in the weeds, Mickey returned with his catch. He had it by the tail. It wasn't a rat. It was an armadillo, a hard-shelled creature that looks something like an army helmet. It's a harmless animal whose role in the scheme of things is to keep hot dog and hamburger buns picked up from along the sides of this nation's highways and byways.

"They're like teddy bears," Mickey said, holding the armadillo at arm's length to show Crocker.

"You're *sure* that's what got me?"

"Goddamn Crocker, this isn't the San Diego Zoo. Yeah, it's what got you."

Mickey shone the light on Crocker's left shin. It was red, but the skin wasn't broken. Mickey wanted to put the armadillo on the dirt road, then follow it to civilization. Wherever it took them would be more civil than the ditch.

Crocker told Mickey to toss the armadillo into the weeds.

They decided not to try to sleep in the ditch anymore.

They stood in the road near where the moving van hung stuck, still swaying in the wind.

Mickey held a cigarette lighter under his chin for warmth. He wanted to start setting things on fire to signal their position, the truck, for example.

"Be quiet and let me think," Crocker said.

"*Think?*"

Crocker paced in small circles.

"Think about *what?*"

Mickey was thinking about scratching his will on the dirt road with a stick.

"About getting out of this mess."

"You're kidding." Mickey began pacing beside his partner. "You actually think there might be a way out? *Tonight?*"

"Don't know." Crocker stopped pacing and shone his flashlight at the bridge and the truck.

"Whatever you do, Crocker, don't shine that light under the bridge at this time of night."

"It just might work."

"What might?"

Crocker walked to the edge of Cooperman's Bridge and put his foot on a board and pushed. The board gave some.

"Does what you're thinking have anything to do with the bridge?"

Crocker shone the flashlight on the back doors of the van.

"Count me out," Mickey said. "I resign. I quit."

Crocker looked over his shoulder and smiled and said, "You have to give two weeks notice."

"Swell. Fine. Great. It'll take longer than that to get the truck loose. I'm as good as resigned."

"IN A BED," ELIZABETH SAID. "WE PLANNED IT IN A damn *bed*."

"But there is no bed," Andy Farmer said. "The bed was only window dressing anyway."

They were talking about sex again.

It had become obvious that the movers weren't going to arrive anytime soon, and Andy Farmer was grasping at straws, trying to think of a way to save at least part of their first day at their new place in the country.

Elizabeth stood in the middle of the living room with her hands on her hips.

Her husband stood by the fireplace, grinning and unzipping his windbreaker.

Elizabeth took a good look at her husband and wanted to simultaneously hug and murder him. He wanted things to go *so* well. He simply wouldn't take several no's from God as an answer. He looked great, and Elizabeth despised him for that. Except for the bloody hands, he appeared to have just gotten up from a nine-hour sleep. Elizabeth had told him that she enjoyed sex a lot more when she wasn't numb with cold; but he just grinned. She thought things over one more time and concluded that the road to blissful sleep led right through him.

So she took her flannel shirt off, threw it to the floor, and said, "All right, let's get this over with."

Andy stepped out of his loafers.

Elizabeth kicked her jeans at the roof.

As she stood in the middle of the living room, wearing a bra and panties, freezing, something flew from the overhead light fixture and landed on the nape of her neck.

Andy Farmer saw the thing fly out of the light, but didn't have time to tell his wife to duck; it flew very fast.

Elizabeth thought a bat had her.

She screamed for help and reached behind her, trying to knock what had her away. As Andy Farmer moved across the living room to help, Elizabeth turned and ran, as though her husband and the thing on her neck were in this together. She ran from the living room through the dining room and into and out of the kitchen, appearing next in the hallway by what would become the writing room, which overlooked the pond.

She cried and continued to swat at the thing that clung tightly to the nape of her neck.

Andy Farmer picked up his windbreaker and chased his wife down after she made two more laps around the living room. He caught her by the front door and trapped the thing that was on her back, pinning it to the floor.

It wasn't a bat.

It was only a praying mantis, which looks menacing because of its long legs.

Once her back was safe, Elizabeth wilted in her husband's arms. He carried her to the far end of the living room, away from the overhead light fixture, and propped her in a corner.

It didn't appear that they would be making love anytime soon.

Andy Farmer dressed his wife and went to the MG for one of the books that explained insects. He opened it to page thirty-two and showed Elizabeth the picture of a praying mantis—in color—and read her the paragraph about how they were harmless to humans. They even ate mosquitoes, which was a little-known fact that caused Elizabeth to smile slightly. Furthermore, praying mantises kept snakes fat and happy by serving as dinner.

Andy Farmer was sorry he had read the part about how snakes ate praying mantises—Elizabeth's good eye opened at that reference—and he quickly closed the insect book.

He tossed the praying mantis outside, removed the glove from the overhead light and showed Elizabeth there was nothing else up there—much, but what was left was dead. Then he put his windbreaker around her shoulders and told her to get some rest, he'd watch for the movers.

"It's too late for them, honey," Elizabeth said weakly.

"I didn't mean it the way you think," Andy Farmer said, trying not to wince when he looked at his wife's puffed eye. "It's almost time for them to come *tomorrow*. If they're going to come at all."

He opened the book full of stories about pioneers. Elizabeth groaned.

* * *

"Easy," Mickey said, shaking all over. "Easy."

Crocker nodded.

As a show of faith in his great idea, Crocker did the dangerous work. He stood on the bridge. He stood on the up ramp, his feet spread for balance, at the back of the moving van.

He stood there and unloaded some things.

The back of the moving van was about twenty yards from the dirt road. If the up ramp collapsed with Crocker on it, he'd miss the rocks in the creek; he'd fall only fifteen feet onto a bunch of rusty fenders.

Mickey stood with one foot on the dirt road and one foot on the up ramp.

He took things from Crocker and tossed them onto solid ground.

But for the heavy stuff, Mickey had to creep onto the ramp and help Crocker lift.

Mickey hated being on the bridge.

But they were so lucky, it was hard to complain much.

They were lucky because the box marked "Bedroom" was by the back door. And the bed, a new brass bed, was along the truck's right wall, not two yards from the door.

It was also a lucky thing Crocker was strong and could lift headboards weighing seventy-five pounds off the floor of the truck and over his head, easy as you please. Before Crocker became a mover, he'd wrestled professionally on the north-eastern circuit as the Viking. He had maintained much of his powerful frame and was able to throw things from the back of the truck—

things like boxes of sheets and wool blankets—effortlessly.

It took them no more than thirty minutes to unload what they needed.

They needed the new brass king-size bed, which still had a $1,200 price tag on one of the legs.

They didn't need the box spring, which was too heavy, anyway.

They needed the mattress.

Crocker couldn't toss the mattress to the dirt road. He and Mickey had to carry it over their heads down the up ramp. Mickey guessed they looked something like a high-wire team as they tiptoed toward the dirt road, stepping carefully around the rotten boards on the bridge.

They also needed some bedding.

They didn't exactly *need* pajamas and robes, but once they had them—they were in with the sheets—they certainly didn't *return* them.

They put them on.

Mickey put on two pairs of pajamas.

Crocker bundled himself in three warm, fluffy robes.

Once the brass bed was hooked together and made, they climbed in, shone the flashlight around, and laughed.

They put some rocks in the empty boxes and put the boxes behind the top of the bed to break the wind.

It wasn't the St. Regis, or even the YMCA, but it was a considerable improvement after the ditch.

Mickey was used to sleeping on the right side, and claimed that spot.

"Thanks, Crocker," he said. "There's no doubt about it. You saved our lives."

"You work in this business long enough, you learn how to survive," Crocker said.

"No kidding, we'd have frozen to death. Things would have eaten us. Boy, this is really something. The sun comes up, one of us wraps ten wool blankets around him and goes for help, that's that. Hell, I'm not this comfortable in my own apartment."

Crocker didn't reply.

He was sound asleep.

ELIZABETH DOZED FITFULLY AT FIRST.

Each time she opened her eye, she expected to see a trainer standing over her, fanning her with a large white towel. She didn't feel as though she had been dozing. She felt as though she had been knocked out.

She woke up once and said, "What do we do if we get a bad tooth?"

"See a dentist in town," Andy Farmer said.

After Elizabeth dozed off the third time, Andy Farmer made another swing through his new house, inspecting more cabinets, arranging furniture in his mind, planning a lawsuit against the movers.

A person could sleep *anytime*.

After most of a day here, the minor problems were few:

Talk to the mailman.

Get something to stir into the pond, some compound, in case there's another nonpoisonous snake or two in there.

Get the telephone fixed.

Small potatoes, all.

The phone was still at it.

The dial tone had returned; moreover, when Andy Farmer picked up his receiver, two people were having a conversation about the best way to make meatloaf so it didn't crumble. There was no indication which time zone this call was taking place in. Andy Farmer tried to speak to the people talking about meatloaf, but they couldn't hear him.

He smiled and hung up.

After some more peaceful roaming through the house, he went outside to sit on the knoll behind the house and watch his first sunrise.

He listened to an owl.

The breeze was a bit chilly, so he turned his back to it.

He waited for the horizon behind the house to start glowing.

This had to beat looking at the world through the peephole of an apartment door.

DOYLE SMOOT HAD BEEN UP MOST OF the night with his sister Lucy, who had the gout, and he was tired. Lucy lived in Coalton, fifty-five miles away.

It was difficult to tell whom the gout tortured more—the person who had it or the person sitting up with the person who had it.

"You've got to either lay off the pies or move closer to me so I can take care of you easier," Doyle Smoot had told Lucy at around 2:00 A.M.

Lucy was a very religious person. She didn't believe you caught the gout at the bottom of a pie pan, or that it was a virus. She thought you got it because you hadn't been praying enough.

"Then Lucy," Doyle Smoot had said at around 2:30 A.M., "the next time your toes swell up on you, call the preacher, not me."

Lucy prayed aloud most of the night.

Doyle Smoot read the newspaper.

Some would say—one of the men Doyle Smoot ran over, for instance—that fatigue and age (Doyle Smoot was seventy-six) were contributing factors in the accident.

But as Doyle Smoot said, once everything had settled into the mud under Cooperman's Bridge, "It wouldn't have made a damn if I would have been a sixteen year old with perfect reflexes who had just slept ten hours."

And, after various measurements had been made at the scene of the accident, everybody pretty much agreed that not even a seven year old with twenty-twenty vision—a seven year old on a tricycle—could have stopped in time.

DOYLE SMOOT WAS ON TOP OF THE BRASS BED BEFORE he knew it.

The bed had been set up just over a mound in the dirt road.

Nobody had put up flares or reflectors; the only thing Doyle Smoot saw that glowed were a couple of eyeballs.

When he first saw the bed, he thought he was seeing things.

But after he blinked, he was no more than forty yards from it, and going about thirty-five miles an hour.

He pumped the brakes, which were a little soft, and flashed on his brights.

Somebody in the bed *sat up*.

"God bless America," Doyle Smoot said, his instincts taking over.

Actually, it was a good thing Doyle Smoot was in the truck instead of somebody with better reflexes, but less experience.

Doyle Smoot had driven these roads sixty years. He knew their every rut and crater, and he also knew what you are supposed to do when you come upon something standing, or *sleeping*, in your path. You're supposed to go straight. For one thing, it didn't make a lot of sense to risk an expensive piece of machinery on something like a mangy coyote. For another, ninety-nine times out of a hundred, what's in the middle of a country road will jump sideways.

Doyle Smoot had come upon all sorts of things on the backroads of Matson County—wild turkeys, pigs, deer—and although he had never come upon a bed full of people, his instincts prohibited him from swinging the steering wheel right or left. He was aware of the deep ditches on both sides of the road and, in the split second before he plowed into the bed, could just see himself missing it by one inch and winding up with a broken neck as a result of a twenty-foot plunge into a creekbed.

It wasn't that the people in the bed *deserved* to be run over.

But it was close.

As it became painfully obvious that there was a brass bed in the middle of the road by Cooperman's Bridge at sunup, Doyle Smoot hit the horn, flashed the lights again, gripped the wheel tightly, pumped the brakes, and steered into the skid.

His Dodge pickup truck skidded in a clockwise rotation.

Its left rear fender hit the foot of the bed, and Doyle Smoot had to look over his shoulder to see what the hell was going on.

When the back of the truck smashed into the bed, Mickey was diving headfirst for a ditch. The force of the collision propelled his feet over his head. It looked like he had been caught by a hurricane-force gust of wind. He disappeared into some tall weeds.

Crocker was sitting up with his mouth open at the moment of impact. He appeared to have been caught in the wrong bed with his drawers down.

The mattress buckled upward and shot Crocker into the air.

He came down on top of Doyle Smoot's Dodge pickup truck, then bounced into the truck bed, then bounced out and onto the dirt road.

Doyle Smoot doubted his insurance agent was going to believe this; then his forehead hit the steering wheel.

"ARE YOU *BLIND*?" CROCKER ASKED.

"Me?" Doyle Smoot was as mad as Crocker. "Am *I* blind? What do you think this is, *indoors*? You see a *roof*? This is the outside, for Christ's sake. You think this is a land run?"

"What's a land run?" Mickey asked.

Everybody was very upset until it dawned on them that they were all lucky to be alive.

Crocker had landed on his head. *Three times*.

Mickey suffered cuts and abrasions and was covered with what he hoped was mud from a pool of water near where the ditch ran into the creek. This mud had a very stale odor to it.

Doyle Smoot had a big knot on his forehead.

The brass bed that had cost $1,200 was but a memory.

The headpiece had been knocked loose and had bounced end-over-end toward Cooperman's Bridge. Most of the brass rods on the headpiece had been knocked out. The frame was mangled and broken in half a dozen pieces. The mattress had ripped apart at its middle, spewing stuffing and springs all over the place.

"You people should have your heads examined," Doyle Smoot said, once he had surveyed the wreckage.

"We'd like that very much," Mickey said.

"It was a good goddamn thing the bed was there," Crocker said. "You'd have missed the bridge by twenty yards."

"I'd have hit it dead center. I could drive across it in my sleep."

"*Write that down*," Crocker said. "It's evidence."

"I said *could*, not *was going to*," Doyle Smoot said.

After a while, Doyle Smoot inspected the homemade map and admitted even *he* couldn't make a damn bit of sense out of it. Then they set about restoring order. The battery had fallen out of the Dodge pickup, and both trucks were inoperable. The nearest person lived a mile or so up the creek. Doyle Smoot volunteered to hike there and call some people.

"Run," Crocker said.

Ten minutes, it seemed, after Doyle Smoot had gone for help, Crocker shouted, "Hey!"

"Yeah," Doyle Smoot shouted back.

"Dear God, he's only walked fifty feet, it's going to take him a week to get anywhere," Crocker said.

SEVERAL HOURS AFTER DOYLE SMOOT HAD LAST said "Ouch" after twisting an ankle on a rock, some people arrived with rescue equipment. Jeff, a sheriff's deputy, became very confused about whom to cite for what kind of violation. You would think that being run

53

over in your sleep qualified a person for some kind of restitution, but Jeff couldn't find anything in the state highway laws that covered it. The way it looked, you had to be *in your house* before the person who ran over you could be ticketed.

"Look up hit and run," Crocker said solemnly, his head and neck still killing him.

"I didn't hit *them*, I hit the bed," Doyle Smoot said. "And I didn't run."

"Right," said Doyle Smoot's insurance agent, a man named Fox.

He arrived just before the tow trucks and almost went into a trance.

"No, we don't cover beds," he kept saying.

"Maybe my homeowners' policy covers beds," Doyle Smoot suggested. "Another thing, somebody's got to pay for the shoes I ruined walking for help."

"No," Fox said. "No, *their* insurance is going to have to cover most of this."

"You think *our company* is going to pay for the shoes of a man with twenty-four hundred vision?" Crocker said.

Mickey said they should all go in together and sue the state because of the lousy bridge.

Jeff wrote Crocker a $50 ticket for blocking a road with a bed. Crocker examined the citation carefully and excused himself. He walked into some bushes and returned without the ticket, zipping up his pants.

It took the tow-truck people two hours to get the van back onto solid ground.

Hydraulic jacks were placed under the truck, and its vulnerable edges were realigned onto the center of the bridge. This dangerous work was performed by a man named Harold, who also rolled the van backward off Cooperman's Bridge.

Mickey had never seen a person so brave. He wondered if this Harold had a death wish.

"Sort of," Jeff, the deputy, said. "He has a death wish on a man named Cumby."

Harold was a convict. He was in the county jail serving a few months for slugging a man named Cumby in the mouth.

"We sort of lease guys out for work like this," Jeff said. "Knock a few days off their time, you know how it goes."

"Yeah," Mickey lied.

The bill for getting the moving van off the bridge and turned around was $450.

"You'll have to excuse me again," Crocker said, heading for the bushes with the bill and another evil grin on his face.

Mickey told everybody that Crocker had received a number of jolts to the head in the accident, and that the company was good for the charges incurred.

ANDY FARMER WAS SITTING ON THE FRONT PORCH making notes about his novel—in longhand on a grocery sack—when the movers finally pulled onto the property.

It was 10:00 A.M.

He stood up and said, "They're here," and looked inside the front door. Elizabeth was asleep by the fireplace. Andy Farmer opened and closed the door a few times.

Elizabeth woke up and ducked, simultaneously.

"They're here."

"Who?"

Elizabeth hoped some chickens were here—something to *eat*.

"The movers."

Elizabeth sat up and felt her bad eye. It felt like a marshmallow.

Andy Farmer turned, jumped the porch steps, and ran for the moving van, which was proceeding slowly up the hill. He ran with his fists doubled. He ran to the driver's window and yelled. "Where the hell have you incompetent bastards *been*?"

"Oh man," Mickey said.

"Did you hear that?" Crocker asked his assistant. He continued to roll the truck straight for the house. He looked straight ahead. Mickey noticed a vein sticking out on Crocker's neck.

"No," Mickey said. "I didn't hear anything."

"I'll have somebody's *ass* for this," Andy Farmer shouted, running beside the driver's door.

"Perhaps you heard that."

"You're a day *late*, damn it."

"Or that."

"I heard a little of it," Mickey admitted. "Now Crocker, you've got to use your head. Don't ram the house, it'll come out of your check."

Crocker stopped the moving van halfway between the large cottonwood tree and the house. He turned off the ignition. He set the emergency brake. He looked out of his window.

"Answer me," Andy Farmer said, wild-eyed. "Where the hell have you been? We had to sleep on the *floor*."

Crocker looked at his assistant.

"I don't know what to say, Crocker. Life goes on. Forgive and forget. Christ, I'm at a loss."

"Somebody *answer me*."

Crocker's answer took approximately three minutes.

First, he removed from his shirt pocket the homemade map with blue smudges all over it. He threw the map out the window. It hit Andy Farmer's forehead.

Next, Crocker got out of the moving van—without a word.

He walked to the back of the van and opened the rear doors and looked inside. He tapped a finger to his chin as though he couldn't figure out what to wear on an important occasion. He looked at a table, shook his head no, looked at a brass lamp, wrinkled his nose, then he smiled at a chair. The chair was leather, and it appeared to be new.

Crocker hoisted the large chair out of the truck and over his head in one quick and powerful move that made Mickey and Andy Farmer take steps back. He balanced the leather chair over his head like a wrestler holding an inferior opponent. He adjusted his grip along the base of the chair so it wouldn't fall to the ground and break. Once he had a firm grip on the chair, he smiled and walked in measured strides toward the house.

"That's better," Andy Farmer said. "That's a *lot* better. The chair goes in the writing room at the north end of the house."

Elizabeth held the front door open.

Crocker made an unexpected left at the porch and began moving in a powerful shuffle toward the pond. Mickey had seen this wrestling move a hundred times on television. It was where a villain got thrown over some spectators' heads into the sixth row. Crocker, although slightly out of shape, particularly his legs, was magnificent. As he approached the pond, the leather chair began tilting forward; then, Crocker quit stomping and started running. His timing was perfect. He reached the apex of his power as he came to the water's edge and threw the leather chair with a mighty groan. The chair, which weighed in the neighborhood of a hundred pounds, sailed ten feet and hit the water headrest first.

One of the ducks was four years old, the other was six, and they had been around. They had been chased by wild dogs, shot at by hunters, and they had been nearly run over many times by the mail carrier. But they had never experienced anything like these last dozen hours. First, one duck was almost hit by a flying snake. Now this. It was *unbelievable*.

The oldest duck flapped its wings and lunged for the far shore.

The youngest duck dived beneath the surface.

The chair sank in three feet of water.

CROCKER KEPT IT SIMPLE.

He opened some boxes of food and medical supplies and let everybody have his or her pick.

He explained why they were late while kicking the homemade map. He explained about getting stuck on a bridge that *moved*. He explained about trying to sleep with things that crawled.

"Here's your bed," he said, emptying a box that

was three feet square. The box contained nuts and bolts and a prong or two from the $1,200 brass bed.

He explained about getting run over while they slept.

He pointed at Andy Farmer and said he never wanted to see or hear from him again.

"This is no way to act," Elizabeth said, squirting some antibiotic on the mosquito bite under her eye.

Crocker said he felt bad about Elizabeth's eye. And, without furniture, he was sure her night had been uncomfortable.

"A praying mantis landed on my neck while we were trying to..."

"Do you *mind*," Andy Farmer said.

Crocker gave Andy Farmer a murderous look.

Andy Farmer closed his mouth.

"The things that crawled on me would have *eaten* the things that crawled on you, lady," Crocker said to Elizabeth.

He said he believed that Elizabeth was probably a very nice person; but he was in such a bad mood, he simply couldn't trust himself around anybody who had anything to do with this project. If it was all right, Crocker respectfully requested that Elizabeth stay out of his way, too.

Crocker's head and neck, and Mickey's back, hurt so much they weren't going to *arrange* a goddamn thing. They were, or had been, movers, not interior decorators. They would put things in the middle of rooms. They wanted to get away from here, fast.

Andy Farmer, his eyes wide, pointed at a second-floor window.

Crocker frowned.

"I think he's wondering about the furniture that goes upstairs," Elizabeth said.

"The master bedroom up there?" Crocker asked.

Elizabeth nodded.

"Well," Crocker said, smiling at Andy Farmer. "That's going to save a lot of time right there, seeing as how you haven't got a bed."

Andy Farmer sighed.

"End of discussion," Crocker said, going to the truck for some lamps.

Elizabeth and Mickey put Band-Aids on each other's face.

ANDY FARMER WAS BANISHED TO THE KNOLL BEHIND the house.

He sat there and pouted and watched ants crawl around in the grass.

Elizabeth, rejuvenated by four cans of Vienna sausages and some cookies that had been packed with the kitchen appliances, decided to stay out of the movers' way by turning over some soil in the spot where the garden would go—the spot where the previous garden had been. As her husband had said, the okra needed to be planted this week; so she put on some goggles and fired up the new soil tiller, which had cost $500 at the hardware store in town.

She made a neat row around the garden and had begun a second lap when the blade on the soil tiller hit something hard and sent a few splinters flying.

The force with which the blade hit the obstruction, which was buried about five inches beneath the surface, caused the motor on the soil tiller to quit.

Elizabeth pushed the goggles to the top of her head and got down on her hands and knees to see what she had clipped. Mickey was on his way back to the van after having put a couple of floor lamps in the living room. He had heard the *whack!* and asked Elizabeth if he could be of any assistance. He told her not to worry about Crocker. Crocker liked women and would loosen up as the day progressed.

Elizabeth was scooting dirt off what she'd hit.

It was all wood.

It was long.

"Maybe it's something valuable," Mickey said.

As they worked together, she told Mickey a little something about herself and her husband. He used to be a sports writer for the *New York Times*. She used to teach high school English. They inherited some money and moved here so her husband could write a novel. She was going to enjoy life, garden, and so on.

"Be quiet and get back," Mickey said suddenly, taking Elizabeth by the shoulders.

Dirt had been cleared from a two-foot section of wood.

Mickey started kicking the dirt back *into* the hole.

Elizabeth stood up and looked over Mickey's shoulder.

And screamed.

As Mickey tried to push Elizabeth away from the hole in the garden, she screamed louder.

Mickey finally picked her up and ran for the house.

"YOU BETTER COME DOWN," CROCKER SAID CALMLY. "Now."

He turned and walked around the house.

Andy Farmer had heard his wife scream, but he thought Crocker was throwing the silverware or something into the pond. He could tell from Crocker's expression that something terrible had happened, so he scrambled down the knoll feet first and trotted to the garden where the two movers stood at the edge of the hole looking at some wood on which the following was printed: HERE LIES CLAUDE MUSSELMAN.

This was burned into the wood. Below that was: HE CAN GO STRAIGHT TO HELL.

Below that were the dates detailing how many years Claude Musselman had lived.

"There's no nice way to tell you this," Mickey said. "There's a stiff in your garden."

Crocker looked at the cheap pine box, shook his head, then walked to the back of the moving van for more furniture.

As ANDY FARMER RAN INTO THE HOUSE TO CONSOLE his wife, who sat weeping in the dining room, *the telephone rang*.

Andy Farmer grabbed it. He didn't exactly *grab* it. He fell to his knees, pushed the front door closed, accidentally kicked the receiver off the hook, and picked it up.

It was somebody looking to buy some barbed wire in a community seventy-five miles away.

Thank God, Andy Farmer thought. "Where are you calling from?"

The caller said he didn't know what that had to do with buying some fence.

Andy Farmer begged the caller not to hang up. He explained the problem with their phone. "We're having an emergency here. We need help. We need something hauled off *fast*."

The caller said he lived in a town called Arimona that was thirty-five miles away as the crow flew.

"Only the last crow that attempted the trip died of boredom," the caller said.

"It's a *miracle*," Andy Farmer said to his wife. "It's *help*."

The caller said that, as a mater of fact, he and his brother did odd jobs from time to time. But they weren't cheap. The odder the job, the more it cost. "What have you got that needs hauling?"

Andy Farmer started to make up something, but decided on the truth at the last second. "A body. But it's in a casket."

"Okay," the caller said matter-of-factly. "That'll be a hundred and fifty dollars, cash on the barrelhead."

"It's a deal. Hurry. What's your name?"

"We're the Criterion brothers," the caller said, taking Andy Farmer's address. "One-fifty, plus expenses."

"*What* expenses?"

"Gas. Oil. Windshield-wiper cleaner."

"Okay."

"Fan belt."

"*What?*"

"We've got to put one on before we can come," the Criterion brother said.

THE CRITERION BROTHERS—TWINS—SCREWED HOOKS onto one end of the pine box and tied ropes through these hooks. They wore jeans, sweatshirts, boots, and ball caps. They were big, around six-two, and strong. They had a few cows, a few horses. They appeared to be in their mid to late twenties.

"What we're doing with our lives right now is piddling around," a Criterion brother said to Andy Farmer.

"Another couple of inches with that soil tiller," Mickey said, making a sick face, "somebody would have had a hell of a mess on his hands."

Elizabeth stood twenty yards from the garden with her hands over her mouth. She had stopped crying, but her color was bad.

"It's going to be okay," Crocker told her.

"Everybody wondered where in the hell old Claude went," one of the Criterion brothers said.

"You by any chance come across Claude's aunt yet?" the other Criterion brother asked anybody.

"Aunt, what aunt?" Elizabeth took several steps toward what one of the Criterion brothers had called a "daisy garden."

As the Criterion brothers secured the hooks on the pine box, they explained the Claude Musselman story.

He died last summer right here in the garden, hacking weeks when it was 107 degrees. Claude requested that his remains be cremated and spread over the land he loved so much—from the knoll behind the house. That was fine with Claude's wife, Eula. But before she could get Claude in a vase, the will was read in attorney Marion Corey, Jr.'s office. Claude left Eula the house and land and accessories, and he also left his wife some insurance money, roughly $20,000 and the savings, about $7,500.

He also left a woman named Freeburger $10,000.

"You know," the Criterion brother telling the story said, "I saw Claude's truck parked in a field or two around here, but hell, I thought he was fishing or something. Who would have thought at his age he could have kept up with Donita Freeburger."

She was thirty-eight and worked in a town called Cedarville that was forty miles away.

Claude was sixty-nine.

The news that Claude had left a girlfriend ten thousand dollars was all over the county within a few hours. Eula was madder than she was heartbroken.

"It's face," a Criterion brother said. "Having the last word is pretty important around here."

"It's pretty easy to get the last word on a dead man," the other Criterion brother said, securing the ropes to the truck.

After Eula received her inheritance, she tried to *divorce* Claude, but attorney Marion Corey, Jr. told her there wasn't any way you could divorce a dead man.

"Everyone thought that would be the end of it," a Criterion brother said.

"But Eula was only getting warmed up," the other Criterion brother said, nodding at the pine box.

Rather than spread Claude's ashes over his beloved land, Eula had obviously stuffed him in a cheap box and planted him in the garden he hated so much.

The aunt one of the brothers had mentioned was named Hazel, and she stood about five-three. She had spent some time here, prior to Claude's passing.

"You don't think the woman buried the *aunt* somewhere around here, too," Andy Farmer said quietly.

"Jesus," Crocker said.

"Who knows," one of the Criterion brothers said.

"Claude, he also had a donkey, a goat, a bunch of stuff, so keep your eyes open, mad as Eula was. I wouldn't play around in any soft dirt."

"What's going on down there?" Elizabeth asked.

"Nothing," her husband said.

"I'd guess whatever she buried is in the garden here," a Criterion brother said.

"Yeah," his brother agreed. "I wouldn't try to grow anything with deep roots."

THEY PULLED CLAUDE MUSSELMAN OUT OF THE ground and shoved him into the back of the truck.

The bill was for $210, a bargain in anybody's book.

Andy Farmer wrote the Criterion brothers a check.

"I want it paved," Elizabeth said, pointing at the hole. She moved her finger right and left. "I want it paved from the pond to the tree all the way up to the house. I want it *all* paved."

"There's no need to overreact," Andy Farmer said.

Elizabeth whirled around and walked into the house.

The Criterion brothers visited among themselves about where to take Claude Musselman. Bartow's strip pits was probably the best bet, they guessed.

"There's stuff there you wouldn't *believe*," a Criterion brother told Andy Farmer, winking.

Strip pits are deep holes that have been filled with water, once the coal has been mined out of the earth.

The brothers told Andy Farmer the story about the café that disappeared the same night the water level in one of the strip pits went up two feet.

"Probably a coincidence," a Criterion brother said innocently.

"Somebody threw a *café* in a *strip pit?*"

"We were playing cards at the time," a Criterion brother said.

The café was only a trailer owned by some people from Detroit who had moved in three years ago. They put their trailer-café two blocks from a diner that had been in Redbud twenty-eight years.

"This county is a tough market for outsiders," a Criterion brother said, accepting the check for $210.

Elizabeth came from the house carrying four new sheets and some long nails you used on cement. She took a deep breath and nailed the new sheets into the ground over the hole in the garden.

"How much would it cost to pave this whole area?"

"Oh, about six thousand dollars," a Criterion brother said, handing Elizabeth a business card.

"I'll call you," she said; then she remembered the telephone. "No, I'll write you." She frowned, remembering the mail carrier. "Why don't you just stop by the next time you're out this way."

THE MOVERS WORKED ALL DAY AND DIDN'T NICK A thing.

They put everything exactly where Elizabeth wanted it, and even helped unload a few kitchen boxes.

They left at 6:00 P.M.

"Well," Crocker said.

"Well," Mickey said.

"Thanks," Elizabeth said.

"What the hell is going on out there," Andy Farmer

said from the front door. If the movers thought they could destroy valuable furniture and chase a property owner up a hill, they had another think coming. Letters of protest and demands for damages would beat the movers home.

Crocker and Mickey stepped forward and hugged Elizabeth.

"Very touching," Andy Farmer said, joining his wife by the new sheets nailed over the garden. The movers rolled the van down the incline.

Crocker turned right onto Dog Creek road and stopped.

Mickey waved.

Elizabeth waved back.

"You haven't heard the last of this," Andy Farmer shouted.

"You know," Mickey said, "it *is* kind of pretty out here, don't you think? Clean? Quiet?"

"If you have to ask, forget it," Crocker said, moving the van north.

Andy Farmer and Elizabeth watched the truck move out of sight.

"Thank God it's *over*," Andy Farmer said.

He walked away.

"Where are you going?" Elizabeth asked.

"To rope the leather chair and drag it out of the pond," Andy Farmer said over his shoulder.

Elizabeth nodded; but it sure didn't *sound* like it was over.

THE SIGN SAID: PLEASE STOP.

   It was nailed to the top of a broom handle.

Andy Farmer stood inside the fence where his driveway met Dog Creek Road and waved the sign, which was a piece of cardboard with black block letters, as Petree flew by, left to right, in his green pickup truck.

Petree ducked behind his steering wheel and moved by slower than he had the day before; still, he dipped into the far ditch several times with his left front tire.

He stomped the gas when he was just short of where Andy Farmer stood frantically waving the PLEASE STOP sign, and as Petree looked back to read the message, he threw his head back and laughed, knocking off his straw hat.

He laughed, honked, and weaved.

A few dozen yards north, a pint whiskey bottle sailed out of the right window, and some letters flew out of the left window.

Petree moved out of sight, still honking.

"Fine, you son of a bitch," Andy Farmer said, removing the sign from the broom handle. "You're not dealing with an ignorant hick here."

He folded the cardboard and put it in his back pocket and studied the immediate terrain in great detail, searching for a strategic point from which to wipe Petree off the face of the earth.

Elizabeth worked on a small garden spot—a *very* small garden spot—with a *hoe*, over by the clump of trees south of the house. She hacked at an area about five yards square. Granted, they would get no more than a couple of tossed salads a year from this minigarden, but the ground near the clump of trees was hard as a rock and obviously hadn't been tampered with in many years.

4 Out at the City Park in Redbud, next to the swimming pool, Perry Cooper stood at the bat.

It was the seventh and last scheduled inning of the annual North-South spring softball game, the highlight of the picnic, which was open to the public.

The game was tied, which made everybody nervous.

There was a lot at stake here.

Five kegs of beer were at stake, for openers. There was also some pride at stake, although not much, because nobody was all that good at softball. But the beer was important.

The score was tied 0–0, which was a little hard to believe because few players on either team could catch much. But hardly anybody could hit a tether ball tied to a pole, either.

Except for Perry Cooper, who was big and strong. He was at least six feet tall and he weighed more than two hundred pounds.

He could hit.

He had blasted one to left field and he had ripped one to center—earlier in the game—but both had been miraculously caught by stumbling opponents. The drive to center had hit a tree and dropped straight

71

down, or it would have wound up in the shallow end of the swimming pool.

Perry Cooper was a garbage man and he was black. He would love nothing more than to send one into orbit to defeat some white people who didn't know the meaning of the word Baggie.

"Throw it, damn it," Perry Cooper said to the pitcher, a high school kid named Hugh, who blinked and drew a little back within himself.

"There's no cussing an opponent until after the game is over," a fan cheering for the North yelled.

Basically, the game was Black versus White.

But it wasn't that everybody in Redbud didn't get along. Everybody shared the bathrooms over by the swimming pool, and they shared the softball and the bases.

With one out in the bottom of the seventh inning, and a count of one ball and two strikes on Perry Cooper, and with everybody scooting their aluminum folding chairs close to the mesh screens by the foul lines, Hugh the pitcher tossed the softball toward home.

Hugh pitched a high one.

"Bull," he said.

"I got it," Marion Corey, Jr. said. He wasn't a very good catcher, but a Corey had been catching for the North team for as long as anybody could remember, so there he was.

As a rule, catchers don't say, "I got it," of a pitch.

Since the pitch went *so* high, Marion Corey, Jr. stepped forward and stood on home plate to grab it.

At the same moment, Perry Cooper swung his big bat, which, as it whistled through the air, looked like an oar.

Perry Cooper's swing made a *swoosh* sound; then there was a *crack*.

A sick silence fell over the crowd.

"Oh, Lord," a woman in a folding chair said.

Perry Cooper looked down. He had hit the back of attorney-at-law Marion Corey, Jr.'s *head*.

Hard.

It had sounded like lightning hitting a tree trunk.

The pitch then hit Marion Corey, Jr. on his left calf and rolled to the backstop.

"*Run*," somebody on the South team said.

According to the rules of softball, a batter was not out when he swung at a third strike unless the catcher caught the ball; and Marion Corey, Jr. certainly hadn't caught *this* third strike. Moreover, there was some doubt among those sitting near home plate that Marion Corey, Jr. was still alive.

He lay motionless a few seconds, then began twitching.

That caused more of Perry Cooper's teammates to yell, "*Run!*"

Since there was always the possibility that Marion Corey, Jr. was just stunned, or even playing possum, Perry Cooper loped toward first base using long strides that ate up five or six yards at a whack. As he touched first and bore down upon second, he didn't know if he was a hero or a murderer.

"Get the damn *ball*," the wife of a player in the field shouted.

Hugh, the kid-pitcher, stood petrified on the mound. The third baseman, a service station attendant named Marcus, sprinted for the softball.

Marcus got to the ball just as Perry Cooper thundered around third and headed for home. Perry took off his baseball cap, slung it aside and set his sights on the plate.

Marcus picked up the softball and set his jaw.

The crowd again fell silent as Perry Cooper and Marcus ran as hard as they could and threw themselves at home plate with no regard for anybody's body—theirs, or Marion Corey, Jr.'s.

Perry Cooper slid into home feetfirst, catching Marion Corey, Jr. in the ribs. Marcus dove for home plate headfirst catching Marion Corey, Jr. in the groin with the softball.

The fans gasped as the bodies banged against each other.

The umpire, a man named Hardcastle who owned the bank, waved at the dust, squinted down at home plate and said, "God all *mighty*."

Then he said, "You're *safe*."

Marion Corey had been knocked five yards toward the grandstand on the first-base side of the diamond.

"The *hell* he's safe," the man playing first base said. His name was Moss. He removed a copy of the rules of softball from his back pocket and argued, as eloquently as was possible under the circumstances, Rule 10.b, which said, roughly:

If a batter swings and kills the catcher, it's called *Catcher Interference*, not *Ring Around the Rosy*. According to the rules of softball, the batter is awarded first base and the game is delayed at that point until the injured party is scraped up and a replacement found.

So they sent Perry Cooper back to first base and they put Marion Corey, Jr. in the back of an old station wagon and drove him to the nearest hospital with all the modern equipment, the hospital in Jefferson, which was fifty-two miles away. They put Marion Corey, Jr. into the station wagon like a bag of groceries and Troy Hardeman, who had once been a stock car driver, set off for the hospital in Jefferson, running over second base and a couple of curbs before he was off City Park property.

There were those who thought they would never see Marion Corey, Jr. again, not necessarily because he had been mortally wounded, but rather because Troy Hardeman would get lost and wind up stuck in the middle of some field.

It was depressing when the station wagon disappeared behind some trees in center field, with Marion Corey, Jr.'s legs dangling lifelessly out the back window. There had been a Corey practicing law from an office opposite the Town Square for seventy-nine years.

The Coreys were like *landmarks*.

Nobody was paying much attention when the game resumed and Perry Cooper stole second and third, then came home when a pitch hit the new catcher, a ten year old named Molly on the top of her head.

Even Perry Cooper's teammates were subdued after the alleged victory.

"You people owe us one *lawyer*," somebody on the North team yelled.

There was a lot of arguing.

The captains of both teams met at home plate and came to a compromise before everybody went home.

If Marion Corey, Jr. died, the game would be replayed from the point where he was struck on the

Jay Cronley

head, with a more competent replacement at the position of catcher.

If Marion Corey, Jr. recovered, the score of 1–0 in favor of the South would stand.

AFTER A WEEK OF UNPACKING AND HANGING PIC-
tures and arranging furniture, the Farmers had gone to town to take care of some business—like the mail and the phone—and have some fun.

They had arrived at the downtown area in Redbud at 4:00 P.M. on a Friday.

Downtown was closed.

All they found was an old guy named Coonfield. He was sitting on a bench in the middle of the Town Square, reading a newspaper. He said everybody was over at the park, watching the softball game. The Farmers thought that sounded like fun.

They had arrived at the picnic just as big Perry Cooper stepped into the batter's box.

After the incident at home plate, the picnic closed and everybody wandered off.

"What I'd like to know," Elizabeth said during the depressing drive home, "is why they'd take the lawyer to a hospital fifty miles away when there's one in the same town, not a mile from the park?"

"Maybe there's no hospital in town. Maybe they pretended they had a hospital so we'd sign the contract for the house."

"Is that a joke?" Elizabeth asked.

"Yes," her husband said.

He promised to find out why they hadn't taken

76

the attorney to the hospital a mile away, and get back to her.

Elizabeth wondered where a person shopped around here.

She was also concerned about a softball game being the highlight of the social season.

All in all, she hadn't had a very good time.

THEY BURIED CLAUDE MUSSELMAN ON Persimmon Hill at the Memorial Cemetery, two miles outside Redbud.

It was a lovely service, everybody agreed, made more dramatic by the scenic setting.

Persimmon Hill was the high-rent district.

It was the highest point in the cemetery and offered a spectacular view of a cornfield, particularly around October, when the colors changed.

Plots at the cemetery were priced according to location.

Maple Valley was inexpensive. In the rainy season, water tended to flood Maple Valley, and a couple of tombstones had even washed over onto Peaceful Glen, which was a flat spot that backed up to a field where cows grazed.

Persimmon Hill was where people who were somebody were buried; and a few relatives of prominent people buried on the Hill thought that it was in poor taste to bury a common farmer like Claude Musselman among them.

The management at the Memorial Cemetery thought otherwise, however. The service went so well— around 150 people showed up—that management decided to haul in ten tons of soil and extend Persimmon Hill to the west.

There was a strict building code on Persimmon Hill.

The deceased pushed up roses there, not daisies.

Pine boxes with words burned on top were prohibited.

Headstones less than three feet tall were prohibited.

Plastic flowers were prohibited.

Claude Musselman was laid to rest in style. His headstone was Italian marble with an eagle on top. Below his name and the years of his life was an excerpt from a story about fishing written by a man named Isaac Walton, a great fisherman, because Claude loved to fish. The excerpt was six lines at $9 per letter.

The only part of the service that was not top drawer was Rev. Cobb's speech. Rev. Cobb ran the First Baptist Church. He knew a captive audience when he saw one. People couldn't slip discreetly away from a funeral way up on a hill, so Rev. Cobb rolled up his sleeves and gave the devil hell, hardly mentioning Claude Musselman at all.

When it came time to send Claude Musselman off to his reward, Rev. Cobb had to look over his shoulder to see whom he was burying.

"Isaac Walton was a good man, a religious man," Rev. Cobb said. "Isaac Walton gave money to the church."

Sometimes Rev. Cobb made heaven sound like a country club.

Each month or so, he upped the greens fees.

Rev. Cobb's wife coughed at this point.

"And so was Claude Musselman, a good man," Rev. Cobb said, correcting himself.

He was to wonder later why the dead man's name had been printed in light-colored letters on the tombstone, and why some *fisherman's* name had been etched in black letters.

A funeral is a social event.

It brings together people who gamble and people who pray nonstop—opposites who would never be caught alive together under a common roof. A funeral gives small-town people a chance to dress up, to see who is swollen with alcohol, and to gossip.

It's something *to do*.

One reason Claude Musselman's funeral went so well was because he had been dead so long. When you bury somebody two days after he's dead, there is a lot of grief, a lot of wailing. But when you bury somebody who has been gone *ten months*, it's almost like a festival.

After Claude was dispatched, one of the mourners said she had received a card from Eula, and that she was fine and living a life of luxury in a condo near Fort Lauderdale—thanks to the windfall she had received as a result of selling the place on Dog Creek Road for three times as much as anybody in his right mind thought it was worth. A couple of people mentioned the writer who had bought the Musselman place. They wondered what this person was *really* up to. The Criterion brothers suggested that the man who bought the Musselman place might be a Mafia informer who had relocated here to get away from some guys who wanted him dead—but it was too early to tell.

The Criterion brothers had done their best to dump

Claude Musselman in one of Bartow's strip pits, as promised. But as they were preparing to pull onto Bartow's property, a sheriff's deputy had stopped them and said throwing bodies into a strip pit was unbelievably illegal.

The Criterion brothers were a little worried about how what's-his-name out on Dog Creek Road would react to this splendid funeral; but they were law-abiding citizens first and worrywarts second.

The relaxed atmosphere at the funeral was noticed by the owner and manager of the Memorial Cemetery, Louis Pickering.

On the way out, a number of people stopped at the office to browse through some headstones offered for sale. Several people contributed to the Tree Fund.

Pickering dispatched an assistant to the archives to see how long one of the dearly departed could be kept on ice before he or she had to be buried.

If they could hold off even a couple of weeks, the next of kin might be settled down enough to consider ordering a buffet.

PECK SOLD DOGS TO EVERYBODY IN THE county.

He lived in a tiny community called Echo that had been an oil boom town back in the 1930s. The town had dried up with the oil. Now, it was home for about eighty people and twenty or thirty dogs. It sat between a couple of hills like a ball in a glove. When the train stopped and blew its whistle, the noise bounced off the hills, consequently: Echo.

Peck sat on his back porch, wondering what to do with the Irish setter, which was nine months old. The dog was hyperactive. It jumped and barked nonstop.

"Maybe you should give it another shot," Peck's wife suggested.

"Shots cost money."

"So does feeding a dog five cans of food a day. Maybe you should let it loose."

Peck had paid $95 for the setter. He had it offered for resale at $200.

"The dog has papers," Peck said. "It stays."

He looked from the antsy dog to his grandson Rick, who had short arms and was having a difficult time holding a shotgun steady. Rick was twelve.

"Lock your wrist, boy."

Rick nodded, then pulled the trigger, and shot a

couple of limbs off a large elm to the right of the dog kennel.

Rick fell over backward and hit his head on the ground.

Cheeseboro, a neighbor, stuck his head out his living room window and said, "Goddamn you, stop that."

"Goddamn you back, Cheeseboro, get some earphones."

Cheeseboro had moved to Echo last month, after he inherited the small frame house next door from an aunt. He had moved from Minneapolis and didn't like guns. Peck had set Cheeseboro straight a couple of times already, and was going to do so again, if he didn't quit yelling.

Guns had always been important out here.

Long ago, guns served as a last bastion of defense against murderous bastards who came to steal. A lack of mobile law created a frontier of people who could knock a bottle off a post at forty paces. A gun was like a utensil. It was necessary. And, despite recent advances in the field of law enforcement, you still couldn't beat a good gun if a criminal was trying to get in a window at three in the morning, with the sheriff thirty-five miles away.

Unfortunately, every so often some kid learning how to shoot blew away his playmate or uncle, but these instances were rare; and the crime rate in most rural areas was very low.

Defending yourself and eating were traditions in the country, and that was that.

Peck showed his grandson how to relax his right shoulder so it would serve as a cushion. The kid shot the elm tree some more and, by the fourth try, managed to remain upright.

Having accomplished this, Rick got to go to his room and read some comic books.

Concerning the Irish setter, Peck's wife said, "Maybe what you should do is lower the price on that one."

"By God, now you're onto something," Peck said. "Only we don't *lower* it. There's nobody going to touch a dog on sale. We *raise* it."

The Irish setter, which had springs for legs, now cost $400.

This suggested it was rare.

ANDY FARMER COULDN'T DECIDE BETWEEN THE IRISH setter or the Dalmatian.

Both were magnificent animals, sound of tooth and coat.

The Dalmatian cost $200, the setter twice that.

Both had pedigrees.

"You can't go wrong either way," Peck, the dog man, said. "There's always the compromise."

"Which compromise?"

"You buy them both."

Peck grinned.

His wife did needlepoint on the back porch.

His grandson polished the shotgun.

The customer, this Farmer, had showed up not an hour after Peck had raised the price on the setter. During the preliminary browsing, Peck looked out of the corner of his eye and winked at his wife, like he was a genius.

Andy Farmer went to show his wife the Dalmatian again.

Elizabeth had retired to the car. As she had knelt to examine a spaniel, the kid had shot the shotgun at the tree. One of the things Elizabeth couldn't believe was the way people treated nature out here. In the city, people hung over a balcony twenty stories above the ground to get some sun on a lousy pot of ivy; out here, they shot two-hundred-year-old trees.

Strange, Elizabeth thought.

"Can it hear?" she asked, cracking her window a couple of inches, as her husband marched the Dalmatian around the corner of the house. This question was in reference to the location of the kennel, which was in the middle of a combat zone.

"Of course it can hear."

Elizabeth looked at the Dalmatian and said, "Boo." The dog didn't blink.

Andy Farmer squatted and said, "Good dog." The Dalmatian cocked its head.

"See."

Elizabeth shrugged. "You'll need to send up flares to get it home from a hundred yards away."

Before the gun had started going off, Elizabeth had liked the Pekingese, which sold for $250.

Andy Farmer didn't like the Pekingese at all. Its tongue was too long for its mouth, and it sat there looking like somebody was squeezing it.

"It's your house, your yard, buy what you want."

Andy Farmer said that Elizabeth had a wonderful way of screwing up a great day.

"Sorry," she said. "It's that kid with the gun. He gives me the creeps. I like them all, really." Elizabeth patted her husband's hand. "All except the Doberman."

According to the dog man, the Doberman was not for just anybody. It had recently bitten a burglar, about taking his leg off.

"It's a watchdog?" Andy Farmer had asked.

"I don't know about that," Peck had said. "Probably. The burglar the dog bit last week *owned* it."

Andy Farmer returned the Dalmatian to its pen. Then he inspected the Irish setter, which liked his hand.

"What's wrong with the Dalmatian?" he asked.

"Nothing."

"It's so much cheaper than this one."

Peck glanced at his wife, who grunted and kept needlepointing.

"It's just that there's a lot *right* with the setter here. Its grand-daddy was the best pointer in the country. When that dog was on point, you could have put a bottle of beer on its nose."

"Does it hunt rabbits too?"

"It don't hunt them," Peck said, spitting tobacco. "It *juggles* them."

Andy Farmer wrote Peck a check for $430—the extra was for the shots—and received in return a receipt and the Irish setter's pedigree. It had royal blood originating, according to the family tree, in Cork, Ireland.

"You got yourself one great dog," Peck said, shaking Andy Farmer's hand. "This check any good?"

* * *

THE DOG BEHAVED BEAUTIFULLY IN THE BACK SEAT OF the MG, which was the size of a drawer, rising from time to time to stick its head outside for some clean air.

Halfway home, it climbed onto Elizabeth's lap and rested its head on her knee.

"I like him," she said. "A lot."

His coat was auburn.

She wanted to name it something that related to the dog's coloring, possibly.

Andy Farmer said *kids* named their dogs colors; *Spotless* made more sense as a name than something like Rusty.

Elizabeth reminded her husband that this was a dog, not a relative, and she looked out of her window.

Thinking of a name for the dog was harder than hanging pictures, which had taken nine hours and had almost resulted in several fistfights.

They decided to wait until they knew their dog a little better, and then perhaps name it for something it did best.

THE IRISH SETTER STRETCHED, SHOOK ITSELF, AND sprang for the pond, where it barked twice at the ducks, who thought *this has to stop* and paddled for all they were worth toward the far bank.

The setter had a drink of water and sprinted down the hill past the cottonwood tree, its strides lengthening, its coat glistening in the sun, its ears pinned back.

"A hell of a dog," Andy Farmer said.

Jay Cronley

Elizabeth put her arm around her husband's waist and said, "It sure can run."

The Irish setter made a left onto Dog Creek Road, barely. It was moving so fast, its back feet skidded when it tried to stop, and it almost toppled into the far ditch. But it dug into the road with its two front feet, righted itself, began barking like crazy, and romped south.

"God in heaven," Andy Farmer said. "Hey. *Hey!*"

"Honey, it's running away," Elizabeth said. She squeezed her husband's arm.

"*Dog!*" Andy Farmer yelled.

"Cancel payment on the check," Elizabeth said.

She got the binoculars and, while her husband jumped up and down like Rumpelstiltskin, looked across the way and reported that the Irish setter had hurdled a fence and was moving into a field heading south-southwest. The weeds were tall there. The dog was jumping like an antelope to get its bearings.

"Maybe our homeowners' policy will cover it," Elizabeth hoped.

THEY SEARCHED FOR THE IRISH SETTER UNTIL 10:30 that night, driving deep into the field across the way, which didn't do the MG a lot of good. It lost a hubcap and some tough weeds wrapped themselves around the inside of a rear wheel, causing a loud, rasping sound.

They drove all the nearby section roads, shining flashlights and honking.

Andy Farmer resumed the search at sunrise and picked Elizabeth up at around 11:00 A.M.; they drove

165 miles without seeing either the dog or any evidence of where it had been.

"Something's probably eaten it by now," Elizabeth said.

The third day after the dog ran away, Andy Farmer posted some "$100 Reward" signs on the fences at surrounding intersections and he paid a crop duster named Gentry $250 to check the countryside for a week.

The afternoon of the third day after the Irish setter took off, the crop duster made several low passes over the Farmer place.

"You jackass," Andy Farmer shouted as he shook his fists. "We already looked here. Look somewhere else."

The fact that they hadn't named the dog before it ran away made the loss—be it temporary or forever—a little easier to take.

"It's not like we lost a friend," Elizabeth said. "It's like we lost... another bed or chair."

Andy Farmer nodded.

7

ELIZABETH WAS AWARE THAT THEY HAD BEEN here only a couple of weeks, and that some of the bad breaks they had experienced wouldn't happen again for years, if ever, and she was also fairly certain that some day they would look back at the $400 dog and laugh, but: She was a little concerned that they might have screwed up.

So they had a talk over grilled cheese sandwiches.

"Screwed up how?"

"Well, moving here."

She was beginning to feel vulnerable, way out in the country. These wide open spaces were a lot starker than she had expected. Sometimes when she was out walking, she felt like a target in a shooting gallery. She missed talking to her mother. She missed talking to *anybody*. Sometimes the phone worked, sometimes it didn't. She missed friends. She missed Broadway shows. She missed stores.

She made these points and shrugged; she was sorry, but there was nothing she could do about the way she felt.

"You can't miss *anything* in two weeks," Andy Farmer said.

"Maybe I'm projecting it over the course of a lifetime."

Andy Farmer scooted his plate aside and poured himself some coffee. He told Elizabeth that what had thrown her a bit off stride was the newness of the problems they had experienced here. When somebody steals your car in the city, you shrug and go on about your business. But when you dig up a body in the garden, you're shocked. But it's surprise, not terror.

"Which would you rather have, a body in the garden or a burglar in the living room?"

"That's a toughie," Elizabeth admitted. "Neither."

"The next time we dig something up," Andy Farmer said, shrugging, "we'll push it aside and move right along."

"It depends on who digs it up," Elizabeth said.

Andy Farmer's main point was: "Once we've solved a problem out here, that's it. It's not like traffic. It doesn't keep coming at you."

Elizabeth thought that over and nodded. "So, when do I get a phone that works and mail?"

Andy Farmer sighed and apologized. He said he'd take time off from working on his novel and drive into town the first thing in the morning with a list of what Elizabeth wanted fixed.

She thought about accompanying her husband, but she wasn't quite ready to go back to town so soon after the softball game. She had worn slacks and a blouse the day the attorney was blasted with the bat, and for about a half hour after their arrival at the picnic, everybody stared at Elizabeth. She wasn't going to town again until she got some boots and sweatshirts.

"Anything else?"

Elizabeth leaned back from the kitchen table and

looked into the living room. "The phone is the main thing, I guess. I'm almost *afraid* of it."

"Consider it fixed."

"Okay. Thanks."

Andy Farmer helped himself to a piece of Sarah Lee banana cake.

Elizabeth played with her spoon.

"There's nothing bothering you?"

Andy Farmer chewed cake and shook his head no.

"It's important to have talks like this, you know?"

"Very."

"Then let's do it some more."

"Fine."

They each had some fresh coffee and discussed a couple of other things that might lead to trouble if they weren't handled maturely.

For example: Elizabeth had been to the nearest grocery, a small general store nine miles away that was owned and operated by the Edwards family, *five times* in the last three days.

"What you need to do is buy larger quantities. It's more economical in the long run, and it's easier on the car."

"And what you need to do is do it yourself every once in a while," Elizabeth said.

"Agreed."

"With some of the stuff, they don't have three sizes. The store is the size of the living room. They have *one* size."

"Then buy three smalls."

"Okay," Elizabeth said. "How's the novel coming."

"Fine." Andy Farmer squinted at his wife. "*That's* one of the things bothering you?"

"It interests me."

He reminded Elizabeth that it had been a little hard to concentrate with her screaming every time a moth flew by.

"What page you on?"

Andy Farmer had a sip of coffee. "Six, seven."

"Um," Elizabeth said. "You've been working, what, ten days? Seven, eight hours a day?"

"That's right."

Elizabeth nodded.

Her husband nodded.

"Writing is hard work."

"I'm sure it is."

"I've been outlining more than I've been writing."

"Thank God," Elizabeth said.

"Meaning?"

"A page every other day." She scratched her chin. "Is it going to be a short book?"

Andy Farmer squinted.

Elizabeth stretched.

"So," she said.

"It goes faster once you've made an outline."

"You still writing about the gang that robs something?"

"You want me to put a goddamn time clock in by the typewriter? You think I'm in there working the crossword?"

"So you haven't *once* wondered if we screwed up coming here?"

"You mean, before this second?" Andy Farmer asked.

ANDY FARMER BEGAN HIS DAY OF straightening out some things— when he should have been working—by stomping into the business office of the Great Plains Telephone Company in Redbud.

The business office was a room, which appeared once to have been a drive-in eating place, as there was a tin roof over the parking lot out front.

Andy Farmer put their black table-model telephone on the counter and said, "This doesn't work worth a *damn*."

"That does it," the girl in the business office said. Her name was Judy. "I can't take any more." She began sniffling and putting things in her purse.

Andy Farmer blinked a few times and asked what she was doing.

"Leaving."

"You're going on a break?"

"No, I'm going home."

"Wait."

Judy put some keys in her purse. "There's only so much banging and screaming and swearing a person can stand." She had told her husband that very morning that if one more person barged in through the front door and slammed a phone on the counter and cussed, she was leaving—she would pick up pop bottles from along the highways to help support the family rather than be yelled or cussed at one more time.

Since Great Plains had gone computer, a steady stream of people had been in swearing. *She* didn't build or install the sorry computers. *She* didn't make calls disappear.

"I'm sorry," Andy Farmer said, slightly amazed that he was apologizing for having been cut off from most of civilization the last couple of weeks. "I didn't do anything either. All I tried to do was make some calls. Neither of us did anything."

"You're what?"

"Sorry."

Judy dried her eyes. "You must be new around here."

"We moved onto Dog Creek Road a week ago Saturday."

"Oh *God*," Judy said, rolling her eyes. "The wires out that way, they must look like one big cobweb."

"*Please* help me." Andy Farmer put a ten-dollar bill on the counter.

"What's this?"

"A tip."

Judy put the money in her purse, and put her purse back on the one desk in the room. "What seems to be the problem?"

Andy Farmer said that *everything* was the problem. Sometimes there was a dial tone, sometimes there wasn't. Sometimes operators cut in asking for money, as though the calls were being made from a pay phone.

"You're kidding," Judy said, smiling. "*That's* a new one."

"We were supposed to have a beige wall phone, not this old thing."

Judy asked where the black phone had come from.

"You people put it in."

"That's hard to believe."

"Well, maybe there's some goddamn person going around the countryside like Johnny Appleseed, only he's planting old black phones that don't work, for Christ's sake."

Judy's bottom lip quivered.

"I'd like a phone that works. *Please.*"

"It sounds to me like it's your wires, not the phone."

Judy said that all she could do was write up a Work Order. The Service Department was so backed up, it would be at least a week before anybody could get out to Dog Creek Road. "Try this one in the meanwhile," Judy said. She opened a box and produced a beige wall phone.

Andy Farmer grabbed it like it was the last item on a sale rack.

"That'll be a thirty-dollar deposit," Judy said.

"I already mailed in a deposit for that black piece of garbage."

Judy sighed and sat down at her desk and punched something into a small computer. She ducked down a little, as though she was afraid something from the screen would reach out and sock her. She sighed again.

"There's no record of you anywhere."

"Good, then I guess you can't bill me."

"This place *stinks*," Judy said. She started to get sad again. She fiddled with the computer and found that a working number for the Musselmans was still on the books.

"Eula Musselman moved to somewhere like Fort Lauderdale."

"*Shoot*," Judy said. She wiped her eyes, turned from the computer, and called somebody on an intercom. Presently a man with FRED stitched over his shirt pocket came in through the back way. Some telephone cord was draped around his neck.

Judy said, "This guy says he left a deposit for the black phone and wants a credit on a trade-in. He lives out on Dog Creek Road."

"Tough luck," Fred said. "He owes thirty more. We'll send back the deposit for the black phone later. Where'd you get it anyway?"

"You people put it in."

"Amazing."

Fred tossed the black phone into a garbage can and went out the back way.

Andy Farmer gave Judy $30.

She wrote up the Work Order.

She said a repairman named Tom would be the one to check on the wires along Dog Creek Road, whenever.

"Be nice to him," Judy said.

Andy Farmer started to ask why, but decided he didn't really want to know.

HIS NEXT STOP WAS AT THE MEMORIAL CEMETERY.

He sat in front of the office, which looked like a gingerbread house, or hut, thinking about the points he wanted to make. Tears wouldn't work this time around. He *needed* a telephone; he *didn't* need what these people had to offer.

97

The office was beside the front gate.

There should have been elves inside.

Properly rehearsed, Andy Farmer marched into the office without knocking. He stood in the doorway, glaring at Louis Pickering, the owner and manager.

"Please come in," Pickering said, putting down a brochure about headstones.

"I'm already the hell in," Andy Farmer said, setting a tone he hoped would convince Pickering he was not here to kid around. He stepped to the desk and took a statement from his back pocket. This statement was from Louis Pickering. It was a statement for the burial of one Claude Musselman, Esq. The statement was comprised of the following items:

Casket (Argentinian wood), $1,400.

Headstone (Italian marble, with 72 letters and numbers engraved on the surface), $1,200.

Rev. Cobb's sermon, $125.

Plot on Persimmon Hill, including one year of maintenance, $775.

Flowers (live), $140.

Traffic control, $25.

Hole in ground, $225.

Total due upon receipt: $3,890.

Andy Farmer dropped the statement onto Pickering's desk. Pickering smiled and looked at Andy Farmer pleasantly, hoping a check would soon be sailing his way, too.

"How did this statement get in my mailbox, *whole*?"

"The mails being what they are, I had one of my assistants drive the bill out and place it in your box."

Andy Farmer put his palms on Pickering's desk, leaned over it and said, "I hardly know where to begin."

"With what, sir?"

Andy Farmer went to an itsy-bitsy window and looked out. He picked up a glass angel from the window sill, tossed it into the air and caught it several times, and explained why he was there.

He was there because he was mad.

On the off-chance that the statement for the burial of Claude Musselman was a mistake instead of an attempt to screw him out of a lot of money, he presented a few basic facts to Pickering, who sat quietly rubbing his hands together like a weasel.

Andy Farmer didn't know Claude Musselman.

He wasn't related to Claude Musselman.

Case closed.

"I appreciate your point of view," Pickering said, pouring himself some tea. "Now please consider ours."

Andy Farmer refused a seat and leaned against a wall.

"Our attorney was struck down at an athletic event, so we've had to consult the firm of Banks, Crowbear, and Antwell in Jefferson for this opinion. A fine firm, very conservative."

The opinion, as it concerned Claude Musselman, was: You buy a place, you get what's in the ground, be it buried treasure, a hubcap, a deposit of oil, or a dead body.

"It's a law, a person had to be properly buried," Louis Pickering said, smiling. "We honor Visa and MasterCard."

"Some people were supposed to throw him in a strip pit."

Pickering shuffled through some papers on his desk.

"The sheriff brought Claude to us. We took it from there."

"Do you think," Andy Farmer said, leaning across the desk as Pickering leaned back, "I'm going to pay almost four thousand dollars to bury some bastard I've never even *seen*?"

"The law is very specific about the whys and wherefores of burials, Mr. Farmer."

"It's a nice try, but it won't work."

"You're upset with the...expense?"

"For four thousand dollars," Andy Farmer said, putting the angel back on the window sill, much to Pickering's relief, "I could have had him mounted over our fireplace."

Pickering picked up the statement and said that perhaps a point or two might be negotiable, but only to a small degree. There was no reason to get upset. The $25 for traffic control could be knocked down to $10. And possibly, something could be arranged with the casket, a switch from Argentinian wood to something less expensive—a nice ash, perhaps. Pickering said they'd dig up Claude and switch boxes, free of charge.

"Most everything is negotiable around here, Mr. Farmer," Pickering said, "but please consider this. Claude Musselman was a highly respected member of this community. His hundreds and hundreds of friends, many of whom hold positions of considerable responsibility in the city and the county, might not want him laid to rest...*too* casually."

"You can stuff him in a tree trunk for all I care," Andy Farmer said.

He took the statement from the desk, wadded it into a ball, and bounced it off Pickering's forehead.

ANDY FARMER'S FINAL STOP WAS MORE ORDERLY.

It was at the feed store.

The feed store was a tin building by some railroad tracks. It was full of huge sacks of feed and seed. The sacks of grain gave off a wonderfully natural odor. The floor of the feed store was covered with sawdust and bark.

Andy Farmer walked to the cash register and asked a clerk wearing overalls if he had any snake poison.

"You bet," the clerk said. "We've got two kinds, this and this."

The clerk put a box of shotgun shells and a can of finely ground powder on the counter and grinned.

Andy Farmer looked inside the can of powder.

"The owner invented it," the clerk said. "I wouldn't take too big a sniff."

"How does it work?"

"Like *that*."

The clerk snapped his fingers and asked what kind of snake problem they were talking about here.

"They're from a pond."

The clerk lifted a ten-pound bag of powder onto the counter.

"It's around sixty yards in diameter."

The clerk put another ten-pound bag on the counter.

"See these holes on the bag?"

There were several dozen dots along the top of each sack.

"Poke the dots and then shake the stuff out. Walk pretty fast."

Andy Farmer nodded.

"There's another thing. Keep the end of the sack pretty close to the ground so the powder won't blow off."

The powder had a bitter odor.

"After you've taken care of the snake problem, get a hose and wash the stuff off."

"What does it do to ducks?"

"I'm not sure," the clerk said, turning one of the sacks of finely ground powder, searching for a warning on it. "The owner only invented this a couple of weeks ago."

The clerk went to a telephone on a post and called the owner of the feed store and asked what the snake poison did to ducks. He listened, nodded, and hung up.

"What kind of ducks have you got?"

"Two regular ducks."

"It's liable to make them a little dizzy, that's all. Got any cows?"

"No."

"A good thing. This stuff is death on cows."

"It kills cows but not ducks?"

The clerk nodded.

"What about people?"

"I wouldn't put it on corn flakes."

Twenty pounds of the snake poison cost $85; it might have been cheaper to hire a zoologist to wade into the pond and remove the snakes by hand.

"Be sure and let us know what happens," the clerk said. "What it does to grass, trees. The owner is putting together a brochure to go inside the sacks about what all dies along with the snakes."

A small surgical mask to be worn while spreading the dust was free.

"The owner says if it gets in your eyes, get your head under a faucet, fast."

Andy Farmer carried the sacks to the MG.

The phone on the post rang.

The clerk got it.

As Andy Farmer was loading the snake poison into the trunk, the clerk stuck his head out of the door and said, "The owner says we're not responsible for any type of disaster that occurs once you're off this property."

Andy Farmer nodded and drove home.

HE SPREAD THE POWDER AROUND THE POND AT A quarter after ten that night, using a flashlight propped between some rocks on the far side of the bank by some willow trees.

Mercifully, there was no wind.

It was the first time there had been no wind since their arrival two weeks and a day ago, and it felt odd— as though somebody had put a big bowl over them.

Andy Farmer had never mentioned the snake he caught the first day. He hadn't wanted to upset Elizabeth and put another area off limits. The sheets were still nailed over the old garden. Elizabeth wouldn't walk within fifty yards of the mailbox when Petree was due. Her world had shrunk to the back porch and the clump of trees due south of the house. Andy Farmer had told Elizabeth the fish weren't biting yet this spring.

When she said she looked forward to warm weather when they could skinny-dip in the pond, he had merely paled and changed the subject.

He told her that night fishing might be better this time of year, and he spread the snake poison under that guise.

Without wind, twenty pounds of the powder was plenty.

Andy Farmer made two complete circles around the pond, spreading the most poison on the bank nearest the house.

The ducks watched from behind a bush many yards away.

Andy Farmer had a couple of pints of snake poison left over. He put it in the toolshed out back and told Elizabeth the fish still weren't biting.

THERE WERE BIG SNAKES AND LITTLE SNAKES—LONG and fat and short and thin snakes.

There were black snakes, brown snakes, green snakes, and one that was rust-colored.

A couple were halfway out of the water, with their tails still floating.

Most terrifyingly, all the snakes were pointed at the house; specifically, they were aimed at the kitchen window.

One, a black three-footer, had died no more than ten yards from the front porch.

A large catfish, perhaps a five-pounder, floated belly-up on the pond.

The ducks walked through the battleground like medics searching for survivors.

Elizabeth came upon the scene at the beginning of her morning constitutional. Leaving by the back door, she walked briskly around the corner of the house and almost tripped over a tan four-footer. She froze.

Andy Farmer found her there, ten minutes later.

He picked her up—she was stiff as a cigar store Indian—and carried her inside and brewed a fresh pot of coffee.

"YEAH, WE'RE SORRY ABOUT THAT FUNERAL," ONE OF the Criterion brothers said, pulling on some work gloves.

"Real," his brother agreed.

"What happened was, we're sailing along, headed for the strip pits, and one of the sheriff's deputies spots Claude bouncing around in the back."

"You don't see many pine boxes with bodies inside in the back of trucks."

"It was the deputy that made us take Claude to the cemetery. It was some law about corpses."

The Criterion brothers picked up snakes and slung them at their pickup truck. It became a game, like they were playing horse with a basketball. If one brother threw a snake into the pickup truck—behind his back—the other brother had to duplicate the shot or lose a buck.

"You *raise* these damn things?" one of the brothers asked.

"No," Andy Farmer said. "No."

He said he had only killed them.

"With what, a *bomb*?" a Criterion brother asked.

"Poison from the feed store."

There were twenty snakes laying dead around the pond.

The Criterion brothers recognized all the species except one—a pale snake with a long tongue. They guessed it was some kind of albino moccasin. One Criterion brother asked if he could please have this snake for his kid to take to school and get bonus points at show-and-tell.

Andy Farmer said the Criterion brothers could do anything they wished with the twenty-odd snakes, except have them buried on Persimmon Hill.

The brothers grinned and swore to God that Claude's funeral was no set-up on their end. Nobody had paid them a cent for the body. Nobody had promised them a cut of what the funeral cost. Andy Farmer wouldn't think a thing like that, would he?

"Not until now," he said.

Two, or possibly three, snakes were poisonous.

"One of them ever gets you," a Criterion brother said, "make a big cut on it and suck the poison out." This brother had to admit, twenty-some snakes was a lot for a pond this size. "I would have said it had six in it, tops."

The other Criterion brother guessed a crate of snakes on the way to some zoo must have fallen out of an airplane and into the pond at some point.

The Criterion brothers charged Andy Farmer $75 to dispose of the snakes.

They had driven by just for the hell of it, to see how everybody was hanging in there.

"How's the wife?" one of the brothers asked.

Andy Farmer looked at the house. "All right."

He put the Criterion brothers on retainer and told

them to stop by once a week, come hell or high water; and he wrote them a check for an extra $25.

Before the Criterion brothers left, they removed the two ducks from their pickup.

"They were hiding under the front seat," a Criterion brother said.

"YOU CAN COME OUT NOW, IT'S OKAY," ANDY FARMer said.

He tapped on top of the shelter with a small rock. The shelter between the house and the knoll was locked from the inside.

"I swear to God, everything is fine."

He put his ear to the shelter door.

Nothing.

"You'll pass out in there from lack of oxygen."

Nothing.

The shelter had been built back in the 1950s when everybody thought the Russians might attack; but what Elizabeth wanted to know was why the Russians would want anything around here.

The hole in the ground, which was lined with cement, also served as a tornado shelter and could, if somebody got ambitious, be put to use as a wine cellar or a place to age home-canned fruits, jellies, or vegetables.

It was also a pretty good hiding place.

"I know you're in there," Andy Farmer shouted. "Come the hell out."

"Go away," Elizabeth said.

She sat on the top step of the shelter, drinking a Coke.

"What?"

"Get lost."

"What?"

Elizabeth put her lips near the crack where the door closed, and shouted, "You could have warned me."

"I didn't know you were going to get up at *dawn*."

They sat on opposite sides of the door, which closed flat against the ground, for a few minutes.

"You want some coffee?"

"With cream and a gun," Elizabeth said softly.

"Listen, there's not a . . . reptile . . . within five miles of here, look at it that way."

"No," Elizabeth shouted.

"You use up oxygen getting excited, you'll be dead in an hour."

"*Good.*"

Andy Farmer left some coffee and a roll outside the shelter door and went to work on his novel.

Several minutes later, the door opened slowly a couple of inches. The coffee and roll disappeared. The door shut.

CLOUDS BEGAN CHURNING IN THE WEST an hour before sundown, the third Friday in May, and shortly before dusk, the Farmers witnessed their first old-fashioned country storm featuring hail, wind, lightning, and thunder.

When the storm was at its most intense, Andy Farmer moved the MG from beside the front porch to underneath the 250-year-old cottonwood tree and was almost injured by some hail; one hailstone even took a divot out of the front yard.

Strangely enough, Elizabeth enjoyed the storm.

Still stranger, the storm did wonders for the television reception. During a violent burst of lightning, the Farmers' Sony television produced a perfect picture for the first time since they arrived. And, according to a weatherman in a city sixty-five miles away, this particular storm did not contain tornadoes, at least not yet, so Elizabeth watched part of it from the front porch.

The problem with the television reception was, obviously, the antenna Andy Farmer had put on the roof. It wasn't tall enough. To pick up a couple or three signals clearly, it needed to be as tall as the World Trade Center.

After a bolt of lightning hit the field across the

road, Elizabeth ran to the beige wall phone in the kitchen and discovered a working dial tone. The new wall phone worked a little better than the black table model, but calls were still frequently disconnected. During the thunderstorm, though, Elizabeth was able to visit with her mother and a few friends back east. With the passing of the storm, the phone and television returned to their more normal states.

The phone rang and nobody was there.

The temperature in Chicago was 686,868.

Usually, the Sony television, a twenty-six-inch console that had cost $1,300, plus tax, produced pale blurred images in triplicate.

To see anything, you had to put your nose two inches from the screen, and squint.

The average sound was one big hiss.

The hail put a couple of dents on the MG. A big limb blew off the cottonwood tree. The shelter took on a foot of water. The mailbox blew over. The pond overflowed. Several shingles blew off the roof. The ducks lost more feathers. The front yard became a bog. A chunk of earth fell from the knoll out back and crashed against the rear of the house, loosening a board or two. Dog Creek Road was under water in places.

But Elizabeth was sorry to see the storm fade east— and not just because it helped the telephone and television reception.

The violent thunderstorm had been like *company*.

THE ONE-MONTH ANNIVERSARY OF their move to the country fell on a Friday, and Andy Farmer thought a movie would be a good idea.

"What'll *you* do?" Elizabeth asked.

Andy Farmer stopped the MG. They were about halfway to town. A crow landed on the hood. Dust blew in both windows.

"I don't want you to take this the wrong way," Elizabeth said. "But I'd kind of like to be alone a while, okay?"

Andy Farmer frowned.

"It's no big deal. I just don't want to see a movie. I want to shop."

Andy Farmer squinted.

"It just seems like we've been cooped up a long time."

Andy Farmer continued to frown and squint.

"It seems like everything we do is so *planned*. I want to wander around, that's all."

"You want to celebrate our one-month anniversary by yourself, fine."

Elizabeth said she hadn't realized they had been here exactly a month. She said she hadn't realized there was anything to celebrate.

Jay Cronley

"You're pissing me off," Andy Farmer said.

"Anything to keep from going to a movie," Elizabeth said.

Andy Farmer almost grinned and resumed the trip to town.

HE MAILED AN OUTLINE OF THE NOVEL HE WAS WORKing on to his agent—this material was far too important to trust to Toby's father—and obtained a complaint card from the postmaster of the Redbud post office.

This card went to the Postmaster General's office in Washington, D.C.

Petree had not been by in days.

Andy Farmer wrote: "Our mailman is an alcoholic who throws letters and packages out the window of his truck."

He signed the card and handed it to the postmaster who sat behind the counter of the Redbud post office. His name was Givens. Givens read the card and put it under the counter.

"Petree is basically a good man," Givens said. "He's got a personal problem or two."

"He's also got some *im*personal problems," Andy Farmer said. "Our letters that he throws in the ditch. What's under the counter?"

"A box," Givens said.

"I want to see it."

Givens showed Andy Farmer the *Out* box. The complaint card was the only thing in it.

"Is that a trash can?"

"No, it's a box."

112

"Then why's it lined like a trash can?"

"We're very clean people around here."

Andy Farmer had a feeling his complaint would never see the light of day.

ELIZABETH ARRIVED AT THE NEW ANTIQUE STORE IN time to see it dedicated by Mayor Barclay, who wasn't doing any cartwheels. As the owner of the furniture store, he was not entirely thrilled with the competition from Mrs. Dinges's Antique Shoppe, but who knew, maybe one place of business would stimulate the other. If somebody bought a table from Mrs. Dinges, perhaps they'd buy something to put on it—like an ashtray— from him. And genuine antiques cost a hell of a lot more than chairs made in Taiwan, so maybe this would all work out for the best.

Mayor Barclay was here to cut some ribbon stretched across the front gate.

The first thing he did was bring everybody up to date on the condition of attorney Marion Corey, Jr., who remained hospitalized in Jefferson. Marion Corey, Jr. was doing fine. He had taken a walk yesterday, and although he got lost in the basement and had to set off the fire alarm in order to be found, the doctors thought it was a good sign that he was up and around so soon after having been hit on the head with an aluminum softball bat.

Everybody was pleased.

The Mayor was a bit taken aback by the Garden Club, which he hadn't seen together as a group in a few months. The Garden Club looked like a pack of bull rhinos standing in the shade of a mimosa tree in

Mrs. Dinges's front yard. Life had been good to the Garden Club—particularly dessert. Each woman appeared to weigh around two hundred pounds. A few people around town were upset because the Garden Club hadn't done anything interesting on the Town Square lately. There was a simple explanation. The Garden Club couldn't bend over to plant anything.

The dedication of Mrs. Dinges's Antique Shoppe attracted a crowd of several dozen.

"There was a place not one *half* as charming as Mrs. Dinges's on the cover of an antique magazine last month," the mayor said before he cut the ribbon.

He then helped Mrs. Dinges hang her sign from a white post in the front yard.

The Garden Club promised to surround Mrs. Dinges's sidewalk with seasonal flowers that would bloom every month of the year.

The mayor showed what a great sport he was by going into Mrs. Dinges's shop to buy a little something. He looked around and selected an umbrella with a hand-carved duck head on the handle.

"How much is this?" he asked Mrs. Dinges, who was being hugged and congratulated by the Garden Club.

"Oh, that was John's," Mrs. Dinges said.

The mayor quickly took his hand off the umbrella.

"Yeah, now I remember," he said.

John Dinges had been one of the mayor's best friends. He had died four years ago.

The mayor took a quick look around the main part of the antique store—the living room—frowned, and beat it.

* * *

ANDY FARMER DECIDED TO KILL SOME TIME ON the Town Square.

Each time he had been to town, an old fellow named Coonfield had been sitting on the same bench, doing the same thing: reading a newspaper. Somebody said Coonfield lived in a one-room apartment over one of the shops on Main Street. He reminded Andy Farmer of the kind of person who would pass away at the age of 105, and leave behind $2 million in twenties, stuffed in the mattress, the stove, and the closet.

Andy Farmer sat next to Coonfield and asked how it was going.

"Everybody is over at the Industrial Park," Coonfield said. "There's a new business moving in that's supposed to make everybody rich. You never know."

There were six or seven cement tables on the Town Square. A few men sat at these tables, playing checkers. It was a pleasant day. Andy Farmer looked at his watch and guessed he had time for a few games before Elizabeth finished her shopping.

"Don't," Coonfield said.

"Don't what?"

"Screw with them."

"I was thinking about playing a game of checkers."

"Don't."

"Why?"

"See him?" Coonfield said, nodding at a man sitting by himself over a checkerboard. "His name is Bork."

"Is he a good player?"

"No, he's a convict."

Andy Farmer swallowed.

"On the nice days, they let the convicts sit on the Square."

"Jesus," Andy Farmer said, noticing a chain attached to Bork's leg and the base of the cement picnic table. "Isn't that a little bad for business in some of these shops?"

"Not unless one of them escapes," Coonfield said.

Andy Farmer stood up and looked around for something to do away from the Square.

"The Industrial Park is a half a mile that way," Coonfield said, nodding over a café.

Andy Farmer started to walk in that direction. He stopped after a couple of steps. "Anything else?"

"There's a red brick house behind the café. There's a collie that usually hides in the bushes out front and bites the hell out of people."

Coonfield picked up his paper.

Andy Farmer assumed he was excused.

MRS. DINGES HUGGED ELIZABETH AND TOLD HER TO come into the shop and make herself at home. The shop was the living room and dining room on the ground floor. Mrs. Dinges lived upstairs. She told Elizabeth she'd be right back with some tea and cookies, and she went to the kitchen.

Elizabeth stood at the entrance to the living room, almost afraid to move.

The place was like a museum.

Elizabeth had it to herself. After the dedication, everybody had wandered off without buying anything.

The tables in the living room were covered with

carnival glass, crystal and hand-painted vases, dishes and bowls. One cabinet was full of Art Deco treasures—most notably a Philco radio and a silver cigarette lighter in the shape of a Studebaker. There were no rusty Coca-Cola signs leaning against the walls.

Each table in the living room was covered with lace.

The dining room off to the left was full of brass—hatracks and lamps and boxes and trays—and wooden furniture that had been polished beyond belief.

The whole dining room glowed.

"This is spectacular," Elizabeth said.

"I'm glad you like it," Mrs. Dinges told her. She put some tea and a plate of cookies on a table with a marble top. They sat on a sofa. The back of the sofa was a mural in needlepoint of a pond.

Elizabeth had a sip of tea and picked up a porcelain music box that played "Meet Me in St. Louis." She looked at the bottom of the box, then inside it, for a price tag; anything less than $150 would be a steal.

"That was my sister's," Mrs. Dinges said. "She's dead."

Elizabeth said she was sorry.

"She lived one block north. Thirty years."

Elizabeth picked up her cup of tea and looked at an old sewing machine that had also belonged to the sister, and a magnificent grandfather clock that kept perfect time.

"My husband found the clock in Minnesota," Mrs. Dinges said. "It's ninety-five years old."

"How much?"

"John worked for the railroad. He loved clocks. He

picked up most of the brass in the small railroad stations when they shut down. My husband is dead."

Elizabeth nodded.

"These things happen," Mrs. Dinges said.

The Philco radio and most of the items in the tall cabinet by the fireplace, except for the china, belonged to Mrs. Dinges's son, Don. The china belonged to the sister.

"Don moved to Arizona."

Thank God, Elizabeth thought. She had almost expected to hear that his remains were in one of the vases on the mantel.

"He used to live next door. Moved to Arizona to get in some kind of insurance business. He might come home one of these Christmases. You always hope."

"How much is the radio?"

"I could never sell *that*," Mrs. Dinges said.

While Mrs. Dinges went to the kitchen for some more cookies, Elizabeth browsed through the dining room, searching for price tags, finding none. She asked about a wood-and-leather footstool and learned that it had been John's favorite; then she told Mrs. Dinges a little about herself. She was piddling around. Her husband was working on a novel.

"We're always glad to have young people move into the area."

"I'm thirty-nine," Elizabeth said.

"That's young," Mrs. Dinges told her, smiling.

Elizabeth looked at a few more things in the dining room, used the downstairs bathroom to dry a few tears out of her eyes, then she slipped two twenty-dollar bills under a brass tray while Mrs. Dinges was in the kitchen, answering the phone.

Mrs. Dinges was sorry Elizabeth had to leave so quickly.

"I'll bring my husband next time."

"Yes, please do."

Mrs. Dinges hugged Elizabeth again, and went back inside to dust off some of her antiques.

MAYOR BARCLAY, WHO WAS GOING TO NEED SOME new scissors soon, cut the ribbon at the Industrial Park and handed the microphone over to a developer named Lester Shimmerhorn.

At this point, it was a little hard to distinguish the new Industrial Park from the surrounding prairie, but all that would soon change.

"Before long, a great monument to man's ... and *woman's* ingenuity will rise from this field," the mayor said, clipping away.

Around a hundred people showed up to see the ribbon cut and to hear Lester Shimmerhorn speak.

Lester Shimmerhorn was from Chicago.

He was the president and chairman of the board of the Shimmerhorn Inland Lobster Company. His company was the first major operation to locate at the Industrial Park, but it wouldn't be the last.

"I can already tell this is going to be a great place to raise a family," Lester Shimmerhorn said to the spectators and investors. "Now all I need to do is find me a wife."

Once Lester Shimmerhorn had everybody's attention, he refreshed their memories about the dream that was going to materialize on the prairie in a few short weeks.

This was the deal:

Lobsters cost a lot, even at places next to the oceans where they lived. A dinner of lobster tails could set a family of five back $70 to $80. The reason lobsters cost a lot was because they had to be harvested from a very tricky place—the bottom of the ocean.

So Lester Shimmerhorn had come up with a plan whereby lobsters could be *raised*, not caught.

"Not many people know this," he said into the microphone, "but under the right conditions, lobsters *love* sex."

The fact of the matter was that lobsters could be raised inland at a fraction of the cost of trapping them on the bottom of the ocean. Lester Shimmerhorn and his investors were going to build some huge tanks at the Industrial Park, and haul in many thousands of gallons of salt water.

"Which is basically *free*," he shouted into the microphone.

They were going to simulate the lobsters' breeding grounds.

A dome—a plastic tent made of the finest materials—would be constructed over the tanks full of hundreds of thousands of juicy lobsters. The dome would protect the crustaceans from the elements. Once the lobsters had been bred, and once they had grown to an average size of two pounds, they would be shipped to various restaurants around the world. The first generation of lobsters would be sold for around $8 a pound, well below the prevailing market price.

According to Lester Shimmerhorn's calculations, a lobster could be raised to maturity for around *$1.29*!

Then Lester Shimmerhorn asked if there were any questions.

"If this is such a great idea, what are you doing *here*?" somebody wondered.

A couple of people booed.

"I'm a sucker for clean air," Lester Shimmerhorn said.

Everybody but the guy who had asked the question applauded.

Lester Shimmerhorn and the mayor took turns sticking a shovel into some dirt.

Thirteen prominent citizens had invested an average of $7,500 in the Inland Lobster Company. There was still room for a half dozen or so Junior Partners at $4,500 each. After a few pictures were taken, Lester Shimmerhorn passed out some brochures. He estimated that he could get the plant on its feet for around $120,000. If he came up a little short of investors, the bank had said it would proudly finance the rest.

"We're also going to build a seafood restaurant right here by the road," Lester Shimmerhorn told Andy Farmer. "Once it opens, even Junior Partners get twenty-five percent off any meal, including alcoholic beverages, for life."

Andy Farmer took a prospectus and said he'd think about a Junior Partnership.

"A lot of people are giving them as birthday presents," Lester Shimmerhorn said.

* * *

"YOU *WHAT*?" ANDY FARMER ASKED.

"The woman is so lonely, she opened an antique shop for the company, can you imagine that?"

After her shopping, Elizabeth had picked him up in front of the café across from the square.

"All the stuff belongs to dead friends and relatives and her son, who moved away and never calls. She couldn't part with any of it. Nothing's for sale. It's heartbreaking."

Elizabeth sniffed.

Andy Farmer yanked the MG around a curve.

"So I gave her forty dollars."

"This is unbelievable," Andy Farmer said. "You didn't even get a lousy ashtray?"

"I also bought a kid a bike."

Andy Farmer almost drove the MG into the right-hand ditch. He slowed down and said, "You better be kidding."

"He was dressed in rags, pulling a little red wagon that had three wheels. He was eating an old piece of bread."

Elizabeth dabbed at her eyes with a Kleenex.

"This is the worst day of my life," Andy Farmer said. "And I didn't even *do* anything."

"He hugged me."

"Christ, it's no wonder."

Elizabeth had been driving toward the center of town to pick up her husband when she had seen the little kid dragging the busted wagon along the sidewalk. The bicycle shop was next door. She took the boy inside, and that was that.

"A used bike?"

"New."

"How much?"

"One-seventy."

Andy Farmer squinted at the sun that reflected off the hood. He asked Elizabeth what else she had bought for strangers.

"Nothing."

"Thank the lord."

"But I did buy some dresses."

Elizabeth reached behind her seat for a sack. She held up a dress and began blinking back tears. "You should have seen the shop. It was dusty. The lady who owned the place said this dress was popular at Six Flags Over Texas this spring."

The dress had hundreds of tiny flowers on it. It was made of cotton so cheap it was almost transparent.

"How much?"

"Nobody had been in the shop for *days*. I had to buy *something*."

"How many?"

"Eight, no nine, dresses. And a pair of black pumps."

"How much?"

Elizabeth looked at the sales receipt. "Ninety-two."

"Dollars or hundreds of dollars?"

Elizabeth said that this was the saddest day of her life.

"LOOK OUT."

Elizabeth was wearing her seat belt. She put her right hand on the dashboard and covered her face with her left.

Andy Farmer turned the steering wheel sharply

one way and then the other. Nothing happened. *We're flying*, he thought. *Somebody moved the goddamn road.* He had driven this stretch a dozen times, and although he was still upset because Elizabeth had given away $300 to celebrate their one-month anniversary here, he had been watching the road, as long as it had lasted.

The MG sailed over a bush growing out of the bank beside Dog Creek, smashed into the creek nose first, then rolled onto its right side.

Andy Farmer's door flew open upon impact, and he was thrown several yards out of the car. He landed in a soft pile of fresh hay and rolled into some mud.

Elizabeth sat quietly a few seconds, then looked around for blood. Finding none, she unfastened her seat belt and climbed out the driver's door. The two left tires were spinning slightly. The motor hissed. The MG had flown about twenty yards.

Andy Farmer lay quietly with his limbs bent behind him at grotesque angles.

"NOW LOOK WHAT YOU'VE DONE," MARVIN SAID.

"It was your idea, you're guilty as I am," Tommy Broadstreet said.

"But you unscrewed the screws."

They stood in a field near the curve. Tommy Broadstreet had a big yellow DANGEROUS CURVE sign under his arm.

"You think we should see if anybody's dead?" Marvin wondered.

"Yeah, then we should turn ourselves in to the sheriff. *No.* Hell, they were only going twenty."

"But they were going *down* twenty."

"There was plenty of hay."

"Well, *now* what do you want to do?" Tommy Broadstreet asked his pal.

"Rip apart some pay phones?"

"Boring."

"Pull things out of the strip pits?"

"Not bad, that sounds pretty good."

They walked toward the spot where they had hidden Tommy Broadstreet's motor scooter.

"Trade you a couple of Yields for the Dangerous Curve," Marvin said.

"Forget it."

"One Bridge Out, one Yield, and a Senior Citizen Crossing."

"This Dangerous Curve is mint, it hasn't even got a bullet hole in it."

"But you haven't got a Senior Citizen Crossing."

"I'll trade you this Dangerous Curve for the Senior Citizen Crossing, the Bridge Out, and the '83 Toxic Waste Dump you got."

"Forget it," Marvin said. "F-o-r-g-e-t it."

"I can spell, you punk," Tommy Broadstreet said.

"THEY'VE DONE IT AGAIN," COTTON SAID. HE LIVED UP a hill, half a mile from the curve. He sat on his front porch with binoculars to his eyes.

"What was it this time?" Cotton's wife asked from the kitchen.

"Hard to say. Something little and red, one of them foreign jobs, I think."

Cotton told his son Bobby to get the truck.

The sheriff paid Cotton $25 a month to watch for

the high school kids who stole highway signs. As a result of this crackdown, only five Dangerous Curve signs had been stolen this quarter, as compared to nine during the same period a year ago.

"I got a feeling the brats watch us with binoculars, too," Cotton said, "and get the signs when we're not on the porch."

"Some day you should sneak up behind them," Cotton's wife said.

"Not for no twenty-five damn dollars," Cotton said.

The sheriff also paid Cotton $50 to spread hay all around the creek at the bottom of the curve, to cushion a person's fall. The highway department paid Cotton $25 a month to put up new Dangerous Curve signs. He had a supply of fifteen in his barn.

The curve produced better than some crops.

ANDY FARMER ROLLED ONTO HIS BACK.

His neck hurt.

He was afraid to move.

"Ask how much they want to tow the car up," he said quietly.

Elizabeth did that.

"Fifty dollars," Cotton said.

Andy Farmer nodded.

"It's a deal," Elizabeth told Cotton.

Miraculously, the MG came out of the accident in decent shape. It was so light, and Billy Cotton was so strong, he didn't need anybody's help to shove the car right-side up. There was a dent on the left front fender, a headlight was broken, and the right front tire was flat.

"This hay we dumped last week is like a waterbed, Daddy," Billy Cotton said.

Cotton nodded.

"Thank you," Andy Farmer said softly.

"This is our one-month anniversary," Elizabeth said.

Cotton slid down the bank, carrying a chain with a hook on the end. He explained that high school punks had stolen the Dangerous Curve sign. He put the hook on the back bumper of the MG. "Looks like one of them bumper cars at the fair," he said.

Billy Cotton climbed up the bank to the truck and took up the slack by pulling a handle and winding some chain around a spool. "What about that tree?" he asked of a small growth about halfway up the bank.

"Drag it around to the left and straight up."

"Right," Billy Cotton said, studying the situation.

He pulled the handle again, and the MG rolled slowly up the bank, which was around fifteen feet high. The drop-off from the road to the creek was steep, and Billy Cotton had to go slowly, stopping every so often to make sure he wasn't dragging the car over a sharp rock.

Andy Farmer said his spine now hurt.

The MG stopped near the top of the bank. Billy Cotton got down on his hands and knees and reported that the transmission or something was rubbing against a stump growing out of the bank.

"Pull it the hell on up," Cotton told his son. "This is no new car showroom."

"Right, Daddy," Billy Cotton said.

He pulled the handle that wound the chain around the spool. There was a brief grinding sound, then the hook flew loose from the back bumper of the MG and right at Billy Cotton. It was a big, heavy hook, the size of an anchor.

"*Hell*," Billy said, ducking.

The hook sailed over Billy Cotton's head and smashed into the rear window of the tow truck, blasting it to smithereens.

The MG fell down the bank.

Again.

But this time, it didn't fall as gracefully as before. It fell end-over-end. It bounced. It missed the hay by several feet, and missed Andy Farmer by one foot. As the MG sailed past a door flew open and crashed into Andy Farmer. The car then smashed into the trunk of a good-sized tree, spun sideways, bounced a half dozen more times, lost a door, flattened some shrubs and bushes, lost a hubcap, and came to rest on its top.

It no longer resembled a bumper car at the fair.

It resembled a wadded piece of red aluminum foil.

"Goddamn *hell*," Billy Cotton said. "Christ, *rats*."

"Watch your mouth," Cotton said to his son.

"NOW YOU TAKE IT EASY," MRS. COTTON SAID.

Elizabeth came to on a sofa. There was a cloth on her head.

"You fainted," Cotton said. "Billy took your husband to town."

Elizabeth sat up.

"We took what was left of your car around back for the insurance people to look at, if and when," Cotton said.

"The car ... my husband."

"Your husband is in better shape than your car."

"We think," Mrs. Cotton said.

Elizabeth got up, wobbled around, regained her balance, then thanked the Cottons for their help. Except for when they dropped the MG off the cliff. She walked to the front door, opened it, and wondered what she was supposed to do now.

"You're going to need some transportation," Cotton said. "For a long time."

The Cottons helped Elizabeth inside and around back, where three vehicles sat for sale. All were old. A 1978 Chevy pickup truck cost $475. Because of their bad luck on the curve, Cotton said he'd knock $50 off. The other vehicles in Cotton's backyard were ugly. The $425 truck was blue.

Elizabeth took it.

Cotton had to hold Elizabeth's hand steady and help her make out the check.

BILLY COTTON STOPPED IN FRONT OF REDBUD MEMO-rial and had a good think.

"How you doing?" he asked Andy Farmer, who was curled up in a ball on the front seat of the truck, holding his head and ribs.

"Bad," he whispered.

"We're almost there."

After a four-month run of bad luck the year before last, many people had begun calling the hospital Widow Memorial.

Dr. Leon Mayhew was the chief of staff. He was eighty-one.

Attracting competent young medical help to a rural

129

area was an on-going problem; as a result, Dr. Mayhew had climbed out of retirement four times in the last five years.

The City Commission had tried to lure a young physician to town by offering inexpensive office space and free land to build a house on. The last people to take the commission up on its offer were a young physician named Tolliver and his wife Loretta, who had blond hair that came down to her calves. Dr. Tolliver had a medical degree from the University of San Sebastian in Spain, so the story went. He and his wife arrived on the bus one September and set up shop on South Main next to a dress store. Things went fine for a while, until it was learned that Dr. Tolliver had begun writing some Class A prescriptions for his wife, who appeared to be the picture of health, except for her voice. Most days, she sat in front of the clinic with a guitar, singing stale folk songs.

Then it was discovered that Dr. Tolliver had been tattooing butterflies and flowers on some high school girls.

The City Commission took its office back and Dr. Tolliver and Loretta left the next week.

A sick person's first choice was Redbud Memorial and Dr. Mayhew. His nurse, Rue, had been in a couple of wars and was used to nursing men who crawled to her with their guts in their hands, seeking a couple of aspirin. Rue wasn't too tolerant of people whose bones weren't broken.

Billy Cotton sat in front of the tiny hospital a couple of minutes, wondering if this was one of Dr. Mayhew's good days. Sometimes, he rambled.

A light flickered in the right-hand corner of the

hospital. This was the minor surgery room. They were evidently having trouble with the wiring again.

Billy Cotton put the truck in first and decided to try Feemster's instead.

A WOMAN NAMED GRACE WORKED THE CASH REGISTER at Feemster's Pharmacy.

"Do you have an appointment?" she asked Billy Cotton, who carried Andy Farmer in his arms.

"Not hardly. This man just drove into a creek out by our place."

"You could have called from your place," Grace said.

"That costs money."

"How do you feel?" Grace asked Andy Farmer.

"Bad," he whispered.

Grace told Billy Cotton to have a seat, and she went to tell Ed Feemster there was an emergency waiting. She told Feemster it didn't look like the man had any broken bones.

ED FEEMSTER TOUCHED LENORA HORNBECK'S STOM-ach.

They were in the middle cubicle in back of the drugstore and pharmacy.

"Ouch," she said.

He touched her stomach lower.

She grimaced and said the pain was worse down there.

Ed Feemster nodded and sat back in his folding

chair and consulted Lenora Hornbeck's chart. It showed a mild history of stomach trouble, nothing serious.

"Lenora," he said, tapping his pencil against the chart. "Have you eaten anything strange lately?"

"What do you mean by strange?"

"By strange I mean something wrapped in, oh, cellophane."

"Some sandwich meat, things like that."

Ed Feemster smiled reassuringly and closed Lenora Hornbeck's chart. He said this reminded him of Helen Golden's problem.

"She came to me two months ago with a stomach ache just like yours," Ed Feemster said, putting his pencil back in his shirt pocket, as if to signify the case had been solved. "She thought her insides were falling out."

"That's *exactly* how I feel," Lenora said. "Like there's something tugging down there."

Ed Feemster winked and nodded. "Well, Helen Golden's insides were *not* falling out. I gave her a complete examination and told her she was in fine shape."

Lenora Hornbeck raised her eyebrows.

"Helen Golden had gone and swallowed a Kraft Swiss Cheese wrapper."

Lenora Hornbeck blushed.

"These wrappers," Ed Feemster said, frowning at the state of things in the modern food-packaging business, "are so lightweight and transparent, you can't always tell you've eaten one until, well, until it's *time*, Lenora. *Nature's* time."

"So you think it's a wrapper down there, not my insides falling out."

"In a nutshell."

"Thank goodness," Lenora said.

At this point in the examination, George Hornbeck opened the front screen door at Feemster's Pharmacy. He stepped inside and looked around.

Grace was on the phone.

George Hornbeck pretended to browse among some magazines. When he heard voices from the back of the store, he threw a magazine aside and marched down the aisle like an International Harvester, which is a gigantic piece of farm machinery that gobbles up everything in its path and spits it out the back.

He went to the middle cubicle and yanked the purple curtains back. When he saw his wife of twenty-five years sitting in her bra and panties, he tore the purple curtain off its track and threw it over his shoulder onto a shelf of Old Spice Cologne.

"I *knew* it," he said.

"Oh no," Lenora said.

Ed Feemster stood and pointed at his patient and said, "This is a sick woman."

"I stopped by the hospital, but the electricity was off," Lenora said. "I *swear*."

George Hornbeck was old-fashioned. He believed in the work ethic. If a person wanted to practice medicine, then he'd better by Christ have a diploma. George Hornbeck was also old-fashioned when it came to people looking at his wife in her bra and panties.

He pushed up the sleeves on his work shirt.

Damn, Feemster thought; it had begun *so* innocently. He had removed a corn from a woman's toe five years ago. Dr. Mayhew was on vacation, and Feemster was only trying to *help*. The word got around, and before Feemster knew it, he had about fifty patients, who came from as far away as Arnold, which was sixty miles north. He never did any *major* surgery, only superficial work—subcutaneous cysts and things that required a few stitches. And he was a damn *good* doctor, too.

"Look at you," George Hornbeck said to his wife.

She became embarrassed and held the sheet from the examination table in front of her.

George Hornbeck punched a hole in the wall of the cubicle. Lenora Hornbeck screamed and wrapped the sheet around her.

Grace grabbed the back of George Hornbeck's overalls and tried to pull him away from her employer.

"We better get the hell out of here," Billy Cotton said to Andy Farmer, who moaned.

There was no fight.

It was no contest.

George Hornbeck picked Feemster up and carried him to the middle of the drugstore.

Lenora Hornbeck and Grace ran out the back way, into an alley.

Billy Cotton carried Andy Farmer out the front.

George Hornbeck threw Feemster toward the soda fountain. Feemster's right foot hit a blade on the ceiling fan, which fortunately was off, and he fell onto a shelf of ice chests. The shelf holding the ice chests caved in, as did the shelf behind it, which held dozens of cans of hair spray. The shelves were glass. When Feemster hit the ice chests, it sounded like somebody had hit a window with a brick. Then, as surrounding products broke and fell on top of the druggist, it sounded like somebody had emptied a bucket of bolts onto a tile floor.

THE BLUE CHEVY PICK-UP TRUCK ELIZABETH HAD bought for $425 had no seat belt.

The front seat was slick, and Elizabeth slid around.

It seemed like there were beer cans under the front seat, instead of springs.

Worse still, the steering wheel was stiff. When Elizabeth had a turn of more than five degrees to make, she had to put both hands on top of the wheel, lift herself off the seat, and put all her weight behind it. By the time she got to town, she had blisters on her fingers. It took her an hour to make what should have been a thirty-five minute drive. The headlights were a joke. Dim, they hit the ground five yards in front of the truck. Bright, they went straight up.

By the grace of God, there was nobody downtown, so Elizabeth was able to parallel park in front of the Redbud Memorial Hospital without having to back up. By the time she got to the hospital, she felt like checking in.

The glass front doors were locked, so she banged on them and was eventually waited on by Rue, the nurse who thought that if you couldn't see a bone, it wasn't worth fussing about.

"Visiting hours are over," she said.

That was a good sign; at least there was somebody inside alive enough to visit.

"My husband, Andy Farmer, was in a car accident."

"*This* was an accident," Rue said, showing Elizabeth a picture in a book about World War II. It was a bloody picture.

"Is my husband all right?"

Rue closed her history book and said that patient Farmer had been babbling incoherently when he was brought in. Dr. Mayhew had been called at home, and he had made an examination. Dr. Mayhew had returned home for some well-deserved sleep without saying much about patient Farmer's condition.

Elizabeth asked for a few aspirin.

The nurse gave her *one*. She said Dr. Mayhew would run some tests tomorrow at noon.

"*Noon*."

The nurse locked the front door and turned off the light.

Before Elizabeth went home, she found a flashlight under the front seat of the truck and walked around behind the hospital. She looked in some windows and found her husband in a small room, stretched out near a window. Despite the shot he had received—it was probably a vitamin shot—he was thrashing around in the tiny bed.

She blew her husband a kiss.

UPON HER ARRIVAL AT THE MUSSELMAN PLACE— Elizabeth was not yet comfortable calling the place her own—she found a note taped to the front door.

It said: "I did the best I could."

It was signed: "Tom, the phone man."

Elizabeth made a quick tour of the house and discovered that the telephone repairman had broken into the house by jimmying a kitchen window. He had left other notes:

"Your television needs a new antenna."

"It smells like there's gas leaking somewhere."

"The lemon pie needs more sugar."

The repairman had removed the beige wall phone from beside the refrigerator and had installed in its place a black pay phone.

And by God, it worked.

Elizabeth spent a half hour going through drawers, looking for change, then she talked to her mother four dollars and thirty-five cents worth.

RUSS CHURCHILL WAS SO MAD AT HIS TWO SONS, he thought about cutting off their allowance and selling their dogs.

Then he thought of a much more severe punishment.

He woke them up at 7:00 A.M. on Saturday morning and marched them to the Historical Museum.

He was not going to make his sons take the guided tour, conducted by Mrs. Hodges of the Historical Society. The tour of five rooms took two hours. The tour was *too much* punishment.

Mrs. Hodges could do twenty minutes about an old doorknob.

"Daddy, *please*," Rick begged outside the Redbud Historical Museum. "I'll never fail anything again."

"I'll never fight again," Henry, the other son, promised.

"Inside," Russ Churchill said.

The Historical Museum was full of rooms depict-

137

ing early pioneer life in Matson County. It had been located in Mrs. Hodges's garage for eleven years; then business at the hospital slacked off and the Historical Society got a great deal on what had been the west wing of Redbud Memorial.

Presently, the hospital occupied the right half of the building, and the Historical Museum occupied the left.

One historical room was the re-creation of a pioneer kitchen, complete with a tin bucket for washing clothes in.

Each Churchill boy put fifty cents of his hard-earned money into a cigar box out front and took a brochure printed by the Historical Society, explaining virtually every item in each room.

The Churchill boys had to read this brochure *aloud*.

The first half hour, they learned how you churned butter and took a bath in a wooden tub.

They were so bored, they wanted to take a few steps back and butt their heads together like rams to put themselves out of their misery.

"AND THIS HERE IS A PIONEER'S BEDROOM," RUSS Churchill said, ushering his boys inside yet another of the museum's educational rooms.

"It looks like *our* bedroom, Daddy," Rick said.

"Inside."

The light was dim and the boys couldn't read the brochure, so Russ Churchill stood at the door and told his sons how the pioneers slept, and what they used for coat hangers, probably branches from trees.

"Damn, I hate this," Rick said.

"Come on," Henry said. "Let's get it over with."

"How many stupid rooms do they have here, five hundred?"

The Churchill boys went to the bed to have a look at something like a roll of straw representing a pioneer. Rick threw back the covers on Andy Farmer, who sat up and blinked.

"*Daddy*," Rich screamed. "*Help!*"

"It's *alive*," Henry yelled.

Mrs. Hodges had gone to the women's room to freshen up and go over some notes. A group of unfortunate Girl Scouts were coming in for a tour at noon, and Mrs. Hodges wanted her ad-libs polished. As a result, there had been nobody at the front desk to explain where the Historical Museum ended and the hospital began.

The Churchill family had wandered into Room 1 at the hospital, not the bedroom at the Historical Museum.

Andy Farmer was dopey. He didn't know who he was or where he was. When people began screaming, he pulled the sheet back over his head.

That scared the Churchill boys even more.

One of them ran into a chair.

"It's some kind of monster," the other one said.

Mrs. Hodges heard the racket and trotted from the ladies' room in time to turn on the overhead light and take the water pitcher from Russ Churchill. He had it over his head and was about to throw it at the bed.

Rue arrived with a thermometer, and asked what was going on.

"They took a wrong turn," Mrs. Hodges said.

"Somebody needs to put up a sawhorse so you can tell the hospital from the museum," the nurse said.

"The Society is not paying for any sawhorse," Mrs. Hodges said.

"Can you hear me?" Dr. Mayhew asked.

"Yes," Andy Farmer said.

"Well, speak up, because I can't hear you."

Dr. Mayhew, who wore a coat with huge pockets, said the fact that Andy Farmer's neck and back still hurt like hell was a very good sign. "A broken neck *doesn't* hurt," he said.

This examination was held in the back of the Chevy pickup Elizabeth had bought for $425.

Dr. Mayhew had overslept, so Elizabeth took her husband by the doctor's house. Elizabeth found him on a park bench, visiting with old Coonfield.

The reason Dr. Mayhew's pockets were so big, he said, was because patients used to pay him off with toasters. He gave Andy Farmer some pain pills.

"Some house call," he said, as Elizabeth wrapped him in blankets and got ready for the trip home.

THEY SAT ON THE PORCH THE REST OF THE AFTER-noon, rocking and holding hands.

"There's nothing like driving your new car into a creek to bring people closer together," Andy Farmer said.

The business in the MG was about all he remembered.

That and a riot in a store.

He dozed most of the afternoon.

Each time he woke up, Elizabeth fed him soup

and explained what had happened in the twenty-four hours since they'd gone over the side in the MG.

Some kids had stolen the Dangerous Curve sign.

The MG had slipped off a hook and rolled end-over-end to the bottom of the hill.

She had bought the pickup for $425.

Some townspeople thought he was a dead pioneer.

They finally had a phone that worked—a pay phone.

After a while, when Andy Farmer woke up, he pretended he was still asleep because he doubted he could take any more.

THE PLAN ANDY FARMER CAME UP WITH to resolve the problem with the mail—once and for all—was to murder Petree. He had given it a lot of thought during his convalescence. With Petree dead, any replacement on the rural route would be easier to work with.

Or he would murder the replacement, too.

Once he was up and around, he built a small tree house in a large oak on the far side of Dog Creek Road, across from the driveway. The tree house had a floor and one wall. It was painted green with flecks of brown, and it blended in perfectly with the surrounding foliage. After the tree house was in place, he began to work on a boulder. He hauled sacks of gravel and rocks to the tree house, and molded things together with cement. Working about an hour a day, he put together a monstrous boulder in a week. The boulder was five times as large as a basketball and it weighed more than a hundred pounds.

He cemented large chips of broken glass on the outside of the boulder and set up shop in the tree house one lovely Thursday, the first week in June. He dyed his jeans and shirt and ball cap leaf green, and smeared brown shoe polish on his face.

Elizabeth was concerned her husband was unstable.

PETREE HIT THE BRAKES, SKIDDED SIDEWAYS IN THE middle of Dog Creek Road, stopped, and got out.

He stopped a half a block south of where Andy Farmer knelt in his tree house, a boulder poised at the edge of the platform, his heart pounding.

Petree leaned against his truck and put some binoculars to his eyes.

"I know you're out there somewhere," he shouted. "I can feel it in my bones."

Andy Farmer pulled a branch over his head and flattened himself on the platform.

Elizabeth watched from the front porch. She was certain her husband was going to fall out of the tree into the back of Petree's truck and be crippled.

"I've seen better than you," Petree shouted. "You don't think I watch the 'Roadrunner' on television?"

Petree started a cigarette.

"Here's what I decided. I'm going to start making this run at night, at three in the morning, how the hell do you like that?"

Day, night, it made no difference, because Andy Farmer would be there. He'd begin taking meals in the tree house. He'd drag his typewriter up there.

Petree laughed and got in his truck and backed over the rise.

Andy Farmer was halfway down the tree when Petree showed himself again, going faster than he had ever gone before. He was going sixty-five miles an hour at least, and the truck was bouncing off ruts, about ready to roll. Petree was riding the horn and shaking his left fist out his window.

Andy Farmer scrambled back up the tree, yanked a brick from in front of the boulder and gave it a hard shove.

It was a hell of a shot.

Andy Farmer thought the boulder was going to land on top of Petree's head, but as the mail truck passed under the tree, it jerked suddenly right. The boulder hit the side-view mirror and snapped it off. It also grazed the left side of the truck and produced a lovely scraping sound.

Chrome flew.

The truck went out of control temporarily and began tilting from side to side.

The boulder hit the dirt road with a loud *thud* and dug a crater six inches deep.

It took Petree a while to regain control of his truck. It went into the right-hand ditch and up a bank and clipped a barbed-wire fence, uprooting a fence post. It went back into and out of the ditch and climbed onto the road a half a mile north, leaving in its wake a hubcap or two and a piece of pipe.

"I THOUGHT YOU HAD HIM DEAD CENTER," TOBY SAID.

"Six inches," Andy Farmer said, rolling the boulder into a ditch.

"There's a guy over on Swan Lake Road that's started tying letters to Coke cans full of cement and throwing them into the back of Petree's truck when he goes by. Here."

Toby handed Andy Farmer a letter.

"No envelope?"

"Nope."

Andy Farmer gave Toby an envelope to go to town with his father Saturday. It was a $1,000 check made out to the lobster company for an Associate Junior Partnership.

"Listen, you've got to hang in there," Toby said.

He got on his bicycle and pumped away without another word.

THE LETTER WAS FROM ANDY FARMER'S AGENT.

It said:

Dear Mr. Farmer:

Your outline arrived.

It's not very good.

Am I to understand that you have quit your job at the *Times* to move to the country and write a novel?

Since you are not under contract with this agency—since any work you send along will be judged on its individual merit—I would like to point out that we are under no obligation to provide advice on either a personal or a professional level.

Nevertheless, I would like to call to your attention a recent survey conducted by the Columbia School of Journalism, as it regards the writers of first novels.

On average, a writer's first novel is published four years and seven months after he or she begins work on it.

The average advance for first novels in $2,500.

Of all first novels submitted for publication, 94.5 percent are rejected.

I hope these figures will be of some use to you.

If you wish to continue to submit material to this office, please limit the initial submission to five pages.

Personally, I find the idea of a gang robbing a casino very boring.

Best wishes always,

Sam Green, the William Morris Agency, so on and so forth.

"LET ME GET THIS STRAIGHT," PECK, the dog man, said. "You *loved* the setter."

"Yes," Andy Farmer said impatiently.

"You should, it's a great dog. You should enter it in a show."

"Let's go, let's go."

"And you want *another* dog."

"That's right."

"You want a cheap dog."

"Is there a law against it?"

"I hope the hell not," Peck said. "You just don't see many people buying four-hundred-dollar dogs and two-bit dogs, that's all."

He had two cheap dogs, a Mexican hairless that was the size of a rat, and a yellow dog that had an odd look about it. It was panting.

"Believe it or not," Peck said, showing Andy Farmer the hairless, "this is a pretty good watchdog."

"What do you do, wear it around your wrist?"

"Goddamn it, Farmer," Peck said. "I don't care what people say, you're all right in my book."

"What do people say?"

"That you're hiding out."

147

That reputation was better than Andy Farmer deserved, so he let it go.

He took the yellow dog for $35.

"There's only one thing wrong with this dog, as far as I can tell," Peck said. "It's lazy."

Andy Farmer hoisted the yellow dog to its feet—it was allegedly part Labrador retriever—and dragged it to the truck. The part that was Labrador was evidently inside the dog, because it seemed ordinary—Old Yeller without any energy or acting ability.

"See you in a couple of weeks," Peck said after he helped load the yellow dog into the front of the truck.

Elizabeth thought the yellow dog was stuffed.

It got out of the truck and went to sleep on its back with its legs sticking up.

At least the yellow dog didn't run away.

It didn't roll away, either.

It didn't hardly move.

After a three-hour nap, it dragged itself to the porch and began barking for food. For dinner, it ate two pounds of ground beef.

It was slightly more active at sundown.

It barked at a rabbit hopping across the front yard. Once.

ELIZABETH LOOKED OVER A PAGE AT her husband, who sat nervously at the edge of his chair, the yellow dog dozing at his feet.

"Well?" he said.

Elizabeth smiled and said she was only on the second page.

"So how do you like it so far?"

"The *top* of the second page."

"Does the first page have a good rhythm?"

"It's hard to concentrate, sitting this close together."

Andy Farmer went to the dining room and began pacing back and forth, never taking his eyes off his wife.

"You're not laughing," he said.

"That's because you're staring at me."

Andy Farmer sat down at the dining room table, facing away from his wife.

Elizabeth took a deep breath and returned her attention to the manuscript—the start of his novel. She was actually on page fourteen. He had written around eighty pages. The start of the novel was cumbersome, to say the least. For one thing, Elizabeth despised the way her husband attributed quotes. None of the characters said *he said*.

Jay Cronley

The characters said: he said *gleefully*; or he said *furtively*; or she said *punitively*.

Elizabeth didn't get the impression she was reading spontaneous dialogue. She was of the impression she was reading something that had been bled upon.

Also:

Ten pages into this novel, she didn't know what day, week, month, year, or even *decade* her husband was writing about. The reason for the vagueness was the flashbacks. In the space of ten short pages, there had been three flashbacks, each flashing back farther than before. And, on page eight, there appeared to be a flash-sideways, where a character imagined himself in another location.

It was giving Elizabeth a headache.

She scanned the next dozen pages and said, "Honey, why don't you get us a couple of beers."

"Goddamn it, I knew it, you *hate* it," Andy Farmer said.

ELIZABETH STARTED TO SUGGEST THAT THE OPENING thirty or forty pages were too complicated.

Then she started to suggest that maybe he should only do a half a dozen pages, not *eighty*, before he sought an opinion.

She thought about saying that she wasn't qualified to comment about plot and character development because she was no editor. She also thought about saying the first twenty pages stunk to high heaven.

Unable to decide upon the right words, she put her face in her hands and began weeping softly.

"I guess this means you don't like the book," Andy Farmer said.

Elizabeth nodded.

"I guess you think it's lousy."

Elizabeth nodded again.

Andy Farmer kicked a chair and said that writing a novel was a lot of hard work; in fact, it was *terrifyingly* hard work.

Elizabeth nodded and looked up.

"It's all those flashbacks. What you need to do is start at the beginning and write a simple story, honey."

"You don't like the idea of a perfect crime?"

Elizabeth shrugged.

"So what are you saying? Should I rewrite the opening?"

Elizabeth shook her head no.

"Well, *what*?"

"Burn it."

Andy Farmer took a step toward his wife, who scooted away. He made a fist.

"Go ahead, hit me, put me out of my misery," Elizabeth said.

"You don't know what the hell you're talking about."

"Thanks."

"You don't know a damn thing about writing."

"I certainly do."

"You're a goddamn *schoolteacher*, you're no editor."

"That's obvious," Elizabeth said. "Because I read twenty pages. An editor would have read *one paragraph*."

Andy Farmer shook his fist menacingly.

"Go ahead, right here," Elizabeth said, touching her chin.

Andy Farmer took his manuscript and went to the writing room and worked four hours, until midnight.

He woke Elizabeth up and apologized for having wanted to knock her head off.

She apologized for hating his eighty pages.

He showed her the new material.

It was one page long.

Elizabeth said she loved it.

 IT TURNED HOT THE THIRD SAT-
urday in June.

The heat came out of nowhere.

One day it was seventy-five degrees, the next it
was ninety-six.

The sun appeared to be twice as large as it had
been the day before.

The yellow dog spent the day in the shallow end
of the pond.

Andy Farmer put two new tires on the blue Chevy
pickup.

Elizabeth puttered around in her tiny garden by
the clump of trees. She put about ten gallons of water
on a tomato plant. No tomato had grown larger than
a Ping-Pong ball.

When the dog climbed out of the pond at day's
end, it resembled something from a cheap horror movie.
It was coated with something green and slimy. Andy
Farmer got a hose and washed the dog off and discovered that the pond was covered by a layer of moss.
He got a rake and removed half a dozen wheelbarrows-
full of moss and dumped it down by the road. He then
got one of his nature books to see what the hell was
going on.

* * *

OVER CHEESEBURGERS, HE DETERMINED FROM THE nature book that you killed the moss on the pond with a chemical that was available at most feed stores.

He told Elizabeth he'd have somebody come out in the next week or so and pour a few gallons of the chemical into the pond, and also spray for mosquitoes.

The week after next was the target date for a number of repairs. People would come to look at the television antenna and suggest a way to improve the reception. Somebody would come to paint the house a more cheerful color than white. Somebody would come to look at the typewriter because the space bar was sticking.

"I'm glad you brought this up," Elizabeth said.

She pushed her plate aside and put their Financial Planner and her checkbook in front of her.

"Now don't get mad, but I think we need to talk about money."

"Fine," Andy Farmer said, pushing his own plate aside.

While he had been raking moss off the dog and the pond, Elizabeth had been doing some figuring and had determined that if they continued to spend money the way they had so far, they would be flat broke in less than three years; and yes, the interest they were earning on their savings—roughly 10 percent—had been programmed in.

"And what's frightening, in terms of the finances, is that nothing serious has happened yet," she said, studying some numbers. "No big pipe has busted. Things like that cost *thousands*."

Andy Farmer folded his napkin and told Elizabeth it didn't make much sense to worry about expenses that wouldn't happen again, like having a bed run over, or even painting the house.

"So how much are these repairs next week going to cost?"

"A couple of thousand. Three. Four."

Elizabeth nodded and did some figuring. If the worst happened—if their expenses, including the mortgage payments, continued to average $3,975 a month, they would be busted on or around Valentine's Day next year.

"How much have you averaged in as income?"

"Beyond the interest on our savings?"

"Yes."

"Zero."

Andy Farmer played with a knife.

Elizabeth frowned.

"That kind of pressure is very counterproductive. It's hard enough to write with a goddamn robin sitting outside your window. It's impossible with somebody standing behind you with a Financial Planner."

Elizabeth said that she was certain he would get a good book done, and that it would make them a nice sum of money; but she was only dealing with hard numbers here.

"And your point is?"

"We're spending a lot of money."

Andy Farmer made a note of that on his paper napkin.

"It doesn't worry you?"

"Not at the moment."

"Fine," Elizabeth said, closing the Financial Planner. "So. How do you like it here?"

"Very much. How do you like it here?"

"It's different," Elizabeth said. "It takes some getting used to."

"We have to make it work. That's all there is to it."

"A dog runs off, you get one that can't move."

"Right. You adapt."

"Okay," Elizabeth said.

"Is there anything else you want to talk about?"

"No, but let's start doing this every week, every Friday, how about that?"

"Fine. I have something."

"What?"

"Happy Birthday."

Andy Farmer went to a closet and got two packages and put them on the dining room table. One was a flat box containing the proof of partnership in the lobster company out at the Industrial Park.

Elizabeth examined the certificate, thanked her husband, and put the proof of partnership in the Financial Planner.

The other box was from Bloomingdale's.

Elizabeth smiled brightly at the box and tore it open.

It was a white sequined dress.

It was gorgeous.

"How in the world did you get it here in time?" Elizabeth asked.

"Federal Express. Put it on. We're going to celebrate."

Elizabeth leaned across the kitchen table and kissed her husband.

"Happy fortieth," he said.

"Christ," she said.

THE SEQUINED DRESS WAS SLIT UP THE RIGHT SIDE and it dipped daringly in the front.

Elizabeth spent two hours getting ready to celebrate her fortieth birthday. She had never been more beautiful.

Andy Farmer wore a dark suit.

He was concerned that driving to their night on the town in the beat-up Chevy pickup would take the edge off the celebration; but strangely enough, it made everything seem sexier.

When they had to wait a couple of minutes for a freight train to move out of their way, Elizabeth sat on her husband's lap.

Her right thigh was all over the place.

Had the freight train been a few cars longer, they might have missed their dinner reservation.

THEY ATE AT IVY'S CAFÉ, WHICH WAS SOUTH OF THE Square.

They sat at the counter.

It was fun.

Ivy was a huge woman with arms the size of loaves of bread. She fried everything, including the coffee, which sat on the grill next to a mound of hash-brown potatoes, which had been molded into a bust resembling Elvis Presley.

The mound of hash-browns was three feet tall.

Elizabeth had the chicken fried steak.

It was perfect.

It came with cream gravy, mashed potatoes, and okra. The chicken-fry was so large, it hung over the plate.

Andy Farmer had the Special, which was so delicious he ordered seconds and planned on thirds. The Special was a plate of lamb fries, which are small things that melt in your mouth. They were deep-fried, like french fries, and tasted something like scallops; but they were sweeter and so tender you could have sliced one with a toothpick.

The lamb fries were quite simply the best things Andy Farmer had ever eaten. It was hard to believe lamb could be so flavorful. The lamb Andy Farmer remembered had been considerably stronger, almost bitter at times.

"Another order," he said to Ivy, who shook some flour off her apron and made a notation on their check.

"There's a man who likes his lamb fries," A fellow sitting next to Elizabeth said. His name was Hall Oates. He ran a bait store out by a lake. "Excuse me." He took a biscuit from a basket that had accompanied Elizabeth's dinner.

Ivy's was a very friendly place.

People seemed to share food.

Hall Oates dunked Elizabeth's biscuit into some gravy that was in the middle of her plate.

"What's the record?" Hall Oates asked Ivy.

She scooped ten more lamb fries onto Andy Farmer's plate.

"Twenty-some."

"You know," Hall Oates said, resting his chin on the palm of his left hand as he watched Andy Farmer start on his third order of lamb fries. "It's kind of an art."

"What is?" Andy Farmer asked, sipping some milk.

"Well, about everything connected with lamb fries. Cutting them. Eating them. Most people haven't got what you would call a taste for testicles."

Elizabeth dropped her fork.

Andy Farmer stopped eating.

"Tell him why yours are so good," Hall Oates said to Ivy.

"The secret is clipping them off way up high." Ivy made a clipping motion with the first two fingers on her right hand. "They cook down about three sizes. A person doesn't have the stomach to clip them right, they fry down to the size of a marble."

Andy Farmer put his hand over his mouth and made a gagging sound.

Hall Oates frowned and scooted one seat over at the counter. "It looks to me like we've got some trouble here," he said to Ivy, who looked over her shoulder and wondered aloud why she hadn't chosen something simpler to do for a living, like driving a truck full of explosives.

"I had a hunch the way he was popping them, he didn't know what they were," Hall Oates said. "What you need to do is explain them on the menu better."

"You got any idea what it costs to print twenty-four menus?"

"So maybe you could put up one sign about how lamb fries are testicles."

Andy Farmer backed off the stool and reeled to the rest room at the back of the café, banging into tables as he felt his way.

Jay Cronley

Elizabeth paid the check and drove the truck around to the rear door. She found her husband stretched out on the rest room floor. His color was bad. He had removed his suit coat and shirt, but was now having chills.

Elizabeth wrapped him in a blanket from the truck and walked him around the field behind Ivy's Café for a quarter of an hour. He refused to go home. That would ruin Elizabeth's birthday party. He was violently ill twice more, thought about the pioneers who used to eat bats and owls, and rejoined the celebration.

WHEN ELIZABETH ENTERED THE FIGHT ARENA, THE small crowd fell silent.

She and her husband were directed to choice seats in the front row by an usher named Mike. Mike walked *very* slowly and waved the smoke away with his cowboy hat so everybody could see.

Elizabeth held her new white sequined gown from Bloomingdale's off the dirt floor.

The fight fans had never seen anything like Elizabeth. The last time a woman wore any kind of dress in here was six years ago when an undercover officer for the State Bureau of Investigation posed as a prostitute and helped raid the joint.

During the long walk to their seats, Elizabeth glanced up at the bleachers and couldn't spot another woman.

When Elizabeth sat down and crossed her legs, a couple of hundred cowboys across the way cheered and waved their hats.

"I think they like your dress," Andy Farmer said.

* * *

A GOUT OF BLOOD FLEW AT ELIZABETH AND SPLASHED against the front of her new evening gown.

"Damn it to hell," she said, ducking.

Andy Farmer removed his suit coat and wrapped it around his wife's shoulders.

"I thought you said *people* were going to fight," she said.

"I was wrong."

These were chicken fights, rooster fights—cock fights.

They were held in a big barn.

At the cock fights, two big birds are put in a pit. They have metal spurs tied to their legs. They try to kill each other.

Andy Farmer gambled with the man to his left, Pissboot Jackson, who got his nickname one year at the Grand Nationals. Seats were hard to come by at the Grand National Cock Fights. Jackson arrived four hours early and staked out a front-row seat and *never* moved, which was how he got his nickname.

Andy Farmer gambled and lost $110.

"Get rid of him and come with me," a drunk cowboy behind Elizabeth yelled.

There was an intermission after the third fight.

Many fight fans walked by Elizabeth and tried to peek down the front of her white sequined dress.

"Let's get out of here," Elizabeth said as two roosters were given last-minute instructions by their owners. She was concerned that if they stayed for the main event, several hundred drunks would follow her home.

* * *

THEY SPENT THE NIGHT, FOR A CHANGE OF PACE AND scenery, at Sid's Alpine Village, which was a series of huts numbered *A, B, C,* and *E.*

"Somebody stole *D* four years ago," Sid told Andy Farmer when he checked it.

Sid's Alpine Village was fifteen miles on the other side of town. Andy Farmer had seen it advertised on a billboard that had dozens of flashing lights. Sid had spent more on the sign than he had building his huts.

The Farmers got Cottage C.

This was the first Alpine Village Andy Farmer had ever seen built on land flat as a pancake. These were the first cottages he had ever seen that didn't have shutters, shingles, or doorknobs.

To check in, Andy Farmer signed his name and address on the back of an envelope. He was not given a key to Cottage C. He was given a doorknob. The doorknob had an orange stripe on it.

"People steal keys," Sid said. "but don't seem to have a goddamn bit of use for old doorknobs."

As Andy Farmer drove from the office to Cottage C, his headlights hit a window on Cottage A. A large man opened the front door and said, "Turn off your goddamn lights."

"Right," Andy Farmer said. He parked in front of Cottage C. When he opened the door and turned on the light, a dog ran out from under the bed. It was a collie. It ran up the hill toward the office. Andy Farmer had jumped. But as an example of how Elizabeth's birthday was going, she wasn't surprised in the least.

The bed was very soft. Andy Farmer stretched out on it and the edges curled up around him.

"You look like a hot dog," Elizabeth said.

She thought about hanging herself in the closet, but there wasn't enough room. When she turned on the water in the bathroom, the pipes rumbled, the floor vibrated, and Elizabeth felt like she was about to blast off into space.

Cottage C was—and Andy Farmer went outside at 2:00 A.M. and paced it off—exactly seven feet, two inches from State Highway 101. When a truck went by on their side of the road, Cottage C seemed to slide a little. When a big truck went by, rocks and gravel were thrown against the side of the cottage, just opposite the headboard of the bed. Between the hours of 1:00 and 3:00 A.M. nineteen big trucks went by, scattering approximately thirty-seven rocks against the side of Cottage C.

Counting trucks and rocks didn't work as well as counting sheep.

Andy Farmer left a wake-up call for 7:00 A.M.

At 6:58, the collie barked three times, just outside their door.

ANDY FARMER PULLED THE PICKUP TRUCK ONTO their property and stopped a short way up the drive as things pinged off the hood.

"It's hailing," he said. "Well, we can always use the moisture."

Elizabeth looked out of her window and said that there wasn't a cloud in the sky.

More things pinged off the hood.

"You hear that thunder?"

"How can it thunder with no clouds?"

Andy Farmer looked up. There were no clouds on his side, either.

There was another *boom* in the distance, followed by more pinging that was heavier this time. As Andy Farmer rolled slowly past the 250-year-old cottonwood tree, Elizabeth pointed and said, "*Look.*"

Hiram Penny was standing on their porch, loading a shotgun.

"He's trying to kill us," Elizabeth said. "*Stomp* it."

Andy Farmer stomped it.

The truck coughed and lurched forward.

Hiram Penny was their nearest neighbor to the south.

When he heard the truck speed up, he jammed a shell at his shotgun, missed, and picked the shell up.

"*Hurry,*" Elizabeth said.

Andy Farmer gritted his teeth, floored the gas pedal and drove hell-bent-for-leather for the left corner of their house. His plan was to drive behind the house, circle it, and run Hiram Penny into the ground.

"*Don't,*" Andy Farmer yelled.

He also honked.

Hiram Penny got a shell into each barrel and snapped the shotgun into firing position.

"It's going to be close," Andy Farmer said to Elizabeth, who had moved from the front seat to the floorboard, and was rolled up into a ball.

Hiram Penny aimed the shotgun at the truck, then led it a few inches.

Andy Farmer put his right hand in front of his face and sped for the corner of the house.

There was another explosion.

The truck disappeared behind the side of the house.

Part of the corner of the house fell off.

"YOU SHOT OUR GODDAMN *HOUSE*," ANDY FARMER yelled.

"You should have given the secret honk." Hiram Penny replied. "I thought it was criminals, not you."

"*What* secret honk."

"Two longs and a short."

"We never talked about a secret honk."

"You sure?"

"He can't see a lick," Elizabeth whispered to her husband.

"You've shot a five-foot hole in our house," Andy Farmer said.

"Yeah, well."

They had hired Hiram Penny to house-sit. There had been a couple of tractors stolen from people living in this part of the county during the last couple of weeks, so Andy Farmer had thought better safe than sorry.

He had thought wrong.

"You don't remember our blue truck?"

"*What* blue truck?"

"He's color-blind," Elizabeth whispered. "Get him out of here."

She went to get some boards to put over the hole in the house, which fortunately hadn't gone all the way through into the writing room.

* * *

Jay Cronley

"ARE WE AT THE DRIVEWAY?" HIRAM PENNY ASKED
when they reached his driveway.

Andy Farmer answered that they were.

"Honk two shorts and a long."

"I thought it was two longs and a short."

"You might be right. Honk both."

Andy Farmer honked. "I thought you lived alone."

"I paid my brother to watch my house while I
watched yours."

"How much?"

Andy Farmer had paid Hiram Penny $50.

"Fifteen dollars."

"Who watched your brother's house?"

"He pays some kid five."

It was amazing how the theft of a tractor or two
stimulated the local economy.

WHILE HER HUSBAND WAS DRIVING HIRAM PENNY
home, Elizabeth put some more numbers together and
determined that her birthday had cost them around
$1,200.

They could save a fortune by letting the place collapse around them; but on the other hand, they could
never sell the place for a profit, the thought of which
kept Elizabeth going, if they didn't keep it in decent
shape.

Elizabeth carried her sequined gown to the clothes
hamper. She carried it on the end of a yardstick, then
sat on the front porch and thought some more.

Her husband had eaten some lamb testicles.
Chickens bled on her. They had spent the night in an
outhouse. A man had shot a hole in their home.

166

The night out had been devastating.

The house and twenty-five acres no longer seemed to represent a potentially peaceful way of life—or even an investment—to her husband. It was more like a brew he, the mad scientist, had cooked up. And he was not about to hear of its dangerous side effects.

What alarmed Elizabeth the most was the casual, almost cheerful manner in which her husband had reacted to the awful birthday party. He appeared to be settling into a routine. It was as if he were being brainwashed, or building up an immunity to the country. Sometimes—when he loaded the slovenly yellow dog into the back of the banged-up truck and went shopping, with a beer can in one hand and a ball cap turned around backward—he looked exactly like a *native*.

Elizabeth was concerned that their night out was as good as it got around here.

15 THEY PUT CLAUDE MUSSELMAN DEEP in the forest to the south—several hundred yards deep.

This was on a blazingly hot Saturday, the last week of June.

The Criterion brothers didn't mind the heat at all.

"Wait until it gets summer," one of them said.

"What do you call *this*?" Andy Farmer asked.

"Late spring."

Elizabeth was very decent about the whole thing, undoubtedly because of her husband's bargaining ability with Pickering at the cemetery. He'd got Pickering down from nearly $4,000 to $770. Andy Farmer had to pay for having Claude Musselman dug up. He had to pay for a cheap casket and a headstone made out of *Michigan* marble, not Italian. This point of law stood: If it's in your ground, you own it and you're responsible for it. But you don't have to put what was buried in your ground in silk. Pickering said it was all a misunderstanding—he thought Mr. Farmer would want only the best for the previous owner of his estate.

"No, piss on him." Andy Farmer had said.

He thought that burying Claude Musselman on their property lent a certain amount of historic charm and credibility to the place, a certain amount of mystery.

LIGHTNING HIT THE YELLOW DOG.
Technically.

It hit the back of the truck the dog was riding in, causing a reaction similar to what would have happened had lightning hit the dog itself.

There was one cloud, one tiny cloud, and one bolt of lightning, which traveled sideways a mile or so.

Elizabeth saw it as a message from above.

Andy Farmer and the dog were on their way to buy some groceries.

They were halfway between the cottonwood tree and Dog Creek Road.

The lightning hit the tailgate of the pickup truck. The tailgate was up and locked. The lightning knocked the tailgate down and off. It knocked the yellow dog up and out. The dog flew six feet up and landed on its head. Andy Farmer, who guessed World War III had started, lost control of the truck, and plowed into some barbed wire by the entrance to their property.

Elizabeth trotted from the house, carrying one gunnysack.

She wondered if she should have brought two, until she saw her husband stagger out of the truck and lean against a fence post.

"Don't," Andy Farmer said as Elizabeth approached the dog with the gunnysack. "He's *alive*."

The yellow dog, stretched out on its right side with its tongue hanging out of its mouth, kicked its back legs twice.

"I think that's a reflex action," Elizabeth said. "I think he's chasing angels."

Miraculously, the yellow dog struggled to its feet like a just-born colt. It shook itself and walked up the hill as though nothing had happened. To the observant dog owner, however, it was obvious that *something* had happened, for the yellow dog walked up the hill *backward*.

"That dog has a lot of spunk," Andy Farmer said. "Here boy."

The yellow dog tried to back in a circle to its master, became confused, and wobbled on up the hill.

"It's brain is an omelet," Elizabeth said.

Andy Farmer shuffled up the hill to congratulate the dog on its display of courage. He wished others he knew were as game.

"Why don't you run backward so the damn thing won't think anything's wrong with it," Elizabeth suggested.

17 ELIZABETH PULLED THE SHEET OFF HER husband, who had been up half the night writing, and said, "The truck is missing, wake up."

Andy Farmer looked at the clock. It was a quarter of seven. He asked Elizabeth what she was doing up at this hour, trying to sneak off?

"Taking some clothes to the dry cleaners."

"How's it missing."

"Bad."

"Spark plugs. The carburetor. The lightning did it."

Andy Farmer said he'd fix the truck in a couple of hours, and he turned over and went back to sleep.

"*STOP!*" YEAKLEY SAID.

"*What?*" Sheriff Ledbetter said.

"Stop, stop *now.*"

Sheriff Ledbetter hit the brakes and slid into an intersection near Mrs. Dinges's Antique Shoppe. While skidding, Sheriff Ledbetter's foot slipped off the brake and the car lurched forward and banged into a curb.

Yeakley made a note of that.

"Rejoin traffic."

"*What* traffic?'

"Resume *driving*."

Sheriff Ledbetter did so, without signaling.

Yeakley made a note of *that*.

"Parallel park."

"Where?"

"In front of the truck."

Sheriff Ledbetter hit the curb with the right front tire and then overcorrected and parked with the right rear tire a considerable distance from the curb.

"I have to measure that," Yeakley said, getting out.

THREE WEEKS AND TWO DAYS BEFORE, SHERIFF LED-better had been called to a bar because two men were fixing to go at each other with pool cues. This dispute concerned a woman, as did the majority of disputes in Matson County bars.

What upset Sheriff Ledbetter was the "fixing to" part.

Most years, the sheriff's office was not called until *after* a pool cue had been swung. But during an election year, people took advantage of the pressure placed on an incumbent and called the sheriff every time somebody cussed in public.

A kid named Cox had announced that he would oppose Sheriff Ledbetter in this election. There was no doubt that somebody had put the kid up to making his announcement this early so the county would have the services of a nanny throughout the summer.

When Sheriff Ledbetter had arrived at the bar, which was named Barney's, a man named Delbert

Conn had a salesman in a headlock and was ramming the man's head against a wall next to the pool table.

Clovis Conn was hitting her husband with a beer tray.

Sheriff Ledbetter waded into this mess and began yanking people apart.

Glass had broken.

Tables fell.

As the sheriff stepped between Delbert Conn and the salesman, his billfold slipped out of his back pocket. A credit card and his driver's license skipped under a booth.

Sheriff Ledbetter dragged Delbert Conn off to jail.

Clovis Conn shook her substantial hips and said she was going dancing while her husband was in jail.

That night, the man who owned the bar found the driver's license under the booth.

Sheriff Ledbetter's driver's license had expired two months ago.

So he had to take the goddamn test again.

"TWO FEET, NINE INCHES," YEAKLEY, WHO ADMINIS-tered the driver's test, said, getting back in the passenger seat.

"Let me tell you the way we usually park," Sheriff Ledbetter said, glancing at the sheet of paper on which Yeakley had been scribbling with a red pen. "When we're chasing, say, a murderer, we don't always have time to goddamn *parallel* park. Sometimes we're ducking bullets, you understand what I'm saying?"

"Perfectly," Yeakley said. "Return to the base."

* * *

"How'd you do?" Jeff, the deputy, asked.

"Did he make you do a turnabout?" Wanda, the switchboard operator, asked.

"I hit some curbs," Sheriff Ledbetter said.

"You hit any people?" Wanda asked.

"No."

"Well, that should count for *something*," Wanda hoped.

Yeakley walked briskly from the office, where you bought license plates and took the written test, and handed Sheriff Ledbetter two sheets of paper. Yeakley turned and walked even faster back into the security of the building.

"Goddamn," Sheriff Ledbetter said. "I made fifty-two."

Jeff and Wanda looked at their feet.

"Maybe next time you should try for a learner's permit," Jeff said.

Wanda made a face, covered the receiver, and said to Sheriff Ledbetter, "It's *him* again."

"Tell him we're busy."

"He says that unless you get out there inside an hour, he's going to file a complaint with some sort of law-enforcement organization. He says he's a writer. He says he'll campaign for Cox. His truck is missing, remember?"

Sheriff Ledbetter pressed his fingers to his temples. "Tell him some high school kids have been stealing trucks. Not stealing them. Playing with them. Tell him the truck will turn up in some field in a day or two."

"He also wants to know if you'll bring along a couple of six packs of beer if he reads me his MasterCard number," Wanda said.

"TRUE OR FALSE," IKE SAID. "IF YOU SMELL A CARBON monoxide leak, you should get out of the car."

Ike owned and drove Ike's Cab Company.

Ike's Cab Company was a 1978 Buick four-door.

Since the sheriff's license had expired and he had been failing tests left and right, the cab business had been great. The sheriff had made a sixty-seven on the written part of the test this morning, and Ike had agreed to help him study while they pursued crime throughout the county.

"Repeat the goddamn question."

"If you smell carbon monoxide, you should get the hell out of the car."

"True."

"No, *wrong*," Ike said, laughing. "You can't *smell* carbon monoxide."

"That's a trick question," the sheriff said from the back seat of Ike's cab, which usually carried old women to and from the grocery.

"What you should do is give the guy who grades the test fifty dollars," Ike said.

THE FOUR OF THEM STOOD BY THE FRONT PORCH.

The sheriff and Ike looked at where the blue pickup truck had last been seen.

The Farmers looked at the taxi.

"What are you doing in that *cab*?" Andy Farmer asked.

"He flunked his driver's test," Ike explained.

"Any more questions?" the sheriff asked as his face turned crimson.

Ike had a map of the county. He jabbed at several places as likely spots for roadblocks. With each day of driving the sheriff to crimes, Ike had begun acting more like Sherlock Holmes. The day before yesterday, he had asked for a *gun*.

"Why doesn't he drive you in a squad car?" Elizabeth asked.

"Against some rule," Ike said. "There's no doubt they went south with your truck, seeing as how the nearest county line is that way."

Sheriff Ledbetter closed his eyes and took a deep breath.

He asked about the make and model of the missing truck, and its approximate market value.

"It's an old blue Chevy," Elizabeth said. "It's worth around ninety-five dollars."

"Ninety-five *dollars*." Sheriff Ledbetter stepped back as though he were about to draw.

"You can't put a price tag on transportation around here," Andy Farmer said, a little concerned with the sheriff's tone.

"There's a big sack of rice under the front seat," Elizabeth said. "That ought to put it over a hundred."

"Ninety-five dollars is a *misdemeanor*. You called me out here on a *misdemeanor*?"

"We're taxpayers," Andy Farmer said proudly.

Sheriff Ledbetter drew his revolver and cocked the

trigger and walked to the middle of the front yard. He stopped thirty feet from the 250-year-old cottonwood tree and pumped six rounds into its trunk.

Sheriff Ledbetter stood breathing heavily with his pistol at his side.

Then he went to the cab for a sign that said: VOTE FOR LEDBETTER.

He stuck it in the ground and left.

"We'll paint where he shot the tree," Andy Farmer said. "Brown. Put the bark back on with Super Glue. You'll never know it happened."

"I'll know," Elizabeth said.

 ANDY FARMER BEGAN DRINKING more.

Elizabeth noticed it one afternoon when he fell off the front porch.

He said he was only anemic.

He drank beer when he was working on his novel.

He drank wine, usually straight from the bottle, with and after dinner.

The drinking made him quieter; so Elizabeth let it go.

She called various information operators and learned that the nearest Alcoholics Anonymous chapter was fifty-five miles away.

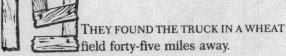THEY FOUND THE TRUCK IN A WHEAT field forty-five miles away.

It had been painted pink.

Not blush-pink.

Hot pink.

The truck almost glowed in the dark.

The outside was pink. The inside was pink. The tires were pink. The motor was pink. Even the antenna for the radio was pink.

They missed a spot behind the license plate, but that was all they missed.

People shielded their eyes when the truck went by, dogs barked, and tourists pulled over for a look.

In town, children thought it was a new ice-cream truck until Andy Farmer swore them away.

 ON SATURDAY, JULY THE FIF-
teenth, Luke Harbringer was
so hot he wanted to scream, but was afraid extra exer-
tion might cause him to pass out.

It was 106 degrees.

The sun was so big and white and hot, you felt
like ducking when it passed overhead.

As Luke Harbringer painted, it felt like a dog was
breathing on his neck—the slight breeze was *that*
unpleasant.

The sky was yellow and dirty looking.

The forecast was for more of the same.

This, Luke Harbringer decided after one hour, was
a bunch of nonsense; so he climbed down the ladder,
drank a quart of lemonade, and asked Elizabeth if she
had a towel.

She went inside and brought him a bath towel.

Luke Harbringer, of the Luke Harbringer Construction Company, wrapped the towel around his waist,
took off his clothes and threw them, along with the
ladder, paint, and brushes, into the back of his truck.

"What's going on?" Andy Farmer asked, coming
from the writing room.

"Fuck this," Luke Harbringer said.

He got in his truck and turned on the ignition.

Jay Cronley

"I think he's going home," Elizabeth said. "Home, a bar, somewhere cool."

"*Come back here!*" Andy Farmer shouted.

"You bet," Luke Harbringer said, starting his truck.

"He said he'd be back when it got cool," Elizabeth said.

"Hey you!" Andy Farmer ran a few steps toward the truck. "What if it doesn't get cool until October?"

"Then that's when I'll be back."

Luke Harbringer drove off, stealing the bath towel.

The bottom half of the south side of the house had been painted yellow.

Elizabeth had been wrong; fixing things wouldn't cost anywhere near as much as she had expected.

GALT, OF THE FIX-IT SHOPPE, WAS AN OLDER GENTLE-man, but he only weighed around 110, and the heat didn't seem to bother him too much.

He put up a television antenna that was sixty feet tall in only two hours.

"You'll be able to pick up Mars on that thing," Galt said, anchoring the antenna into the roof.

"Don't get overconfident," Elizabeth said. Mars was a little town a hundred miles west.

When Galt said, "Hit it," Andy Farmer went into the living room and turned on their Sony console and discovered a magnificent picture accented by bright and rich colors. He was able to pick up three channels perfectly, and a couple of others with only mildly annoying ghosts.

Andy Farmer embraced Galt, told him he had done a fine job, and handed him a beer.

182

"It seems a little wobbly," Elizabeth said, looking up at the $500 antenna that would pick up Mars. "A little vulnerable."

"Forget it," Galt said. "What I done was anchor the antenna into a huge block of wood up in the attic there. I put it through the roof. If the antenna goes, your whole house goes."

Galt said this particular model would withstand straight winds of up to 130 miles an hour.

"What's next?" he asked.

"GOD DOG, *WATCH IT*," GALT SAID, FOUR BEERS LATER.

Andy Farmer stood with the front door open.

Galt was carrying the IBM Selectric to the porch so he could have a look at the jammed space bar in the light of day.

Galt dropped the IBM Selectric.

It hit on its front edge and exploded.

Elizabeth shielded her eyes as tiny parts flew all over the place.

"You people got a homeowners' policy?" Galt asked, feeling his ankle where a piece of sharp steel had gouged him.

GALT PUT THE IBM SELECTRIC IN A GROCERY SACK.

The sack was so heavy, he had to drag it along the ground to get it to his truck.

He put the operator's manual in the back pocket of his overalls.

"Here, you missed one," Andy Farmer said, holding up a tiny part. He was on his hands and knees, digging around in the dust.

Galt dropped the part into the sack.

"To tell you the truth," he said, peeking into the sack as though something alive and dangerous was in there, "I never worked on this particular make and model before. Now, what is it?"

"It's an IBM Selectric that cost a thousand dollars," Andy Farmer said.

"No, no, I mean what *is* it?"

"A typewriter," Elizabeth said.

"Oh," Galt said, frowning.

"Consider this," Andy Farmer said, rising from the ground. "I want it fixed and back on the stand in the writing room in one week. You run, I'll find you."

"You don't scare me," Galt said.

Andy Farmer went inside to watch a game show.

Elizabeth got a shovel out of the toolshed and helped Galt scrape up ten or twenty pounds of dust in case he had missed two or three hundred tiny parts.

"You could always steal another one of these typewriters," Elizabeth suggested.

Galt nodded and said it would probably be easier than fixing one.

THE SHIMMERHORN INLAND LOB-
ster Plant collapsed the day the
temperature hit 108.

It was a miracle that nobody was killed.

Except some lobsters.

The plant melted.

At a quarter of one in the afternoon on the hottest
day of the summer—right after everybody was back
from lunch and feeling groggy—the top of the plastic
dome melted, just disintegrated from the intense heat,
and a number of heavy metal beams and wooden posts
crashed down about the workers, most of whom were
high school kids.

One boy almost drowned in a lobster tank.

Another boy was pinned beneath the sides of the
plastic dome, which fell once the top melted.

A girl named Henryetta was carried away by a
surge of salt water from one of the tanks and deposited
in a parking lot half a block away.

Things had not been going too well out at the
lobster company.

Even with air coolers all over the place, the water
temperature in the tanks was frequently more than
eighty degrees. Around the first of July, a few dozen

185

lobsters had heatstroke. None of the new lobsters had grown much longer than a person's finger.

All but a few of the two dozen lobster tanks were either smashed or knocked over in the accident. That created a tidal wave of the wiggly things, hundreds of which washed down a hill to Sunny Plain Estates, a relatively new housing development a block from the Industrial Park.

"You talk about a *mess* . . ." the mayor's wife said to her husband as the waves lapped against the wall in their basement game room.

"They're climbing up the walls and into closets," the banker's wife said, *they* being the salt-water waves *and* the tiny lobsters.

Roughly two thousand lobsters and God only knew how many thousands of gallons of salt water rushed into Sunny Plains Estates. Residents guessed they would be finding lobsters crawling through their walls and pipes for weeks.

"No, that's not true at all," Lester Shimmerhorn said. "They'll die in a matter of minutes."

"And start *stinking*?" the banker's wife asked.

Lester Shimmerhorn did his best. He got a shovel and tried to heave some of the tiny lobsters out of the main wall of water heading for the houses. He even stood in front of the patio entrance to the mayor's house, kicking at the water.

But he didn't have a prayer.

His next concern was for the surviving lobsters that sat baking or boiling at what was left of the plant. The workers who had almost been killed weren't too interested in picking up lobsters or covering tanks, even at time-and-a-half; most of them walked home or limped to the hospital.

AN HOUR AFTER THE COLLAPSE, A CONTINGENT OF investors and homeowners stood at the bottom of the hill.

Lester Shimmerhorn remained up with the survivors, begging for ice.

"You stay right the hell where you are, my friend," the mayor said.

One of the high school boys handed the mayor a small lobster.

"There's *plenty* more in the basement," the mayor's wife said.

"I've seen bigger sardines," the banker said. "Damn it, somebody should have gone up there to see what the hell was going on."

"What's been going on?" the mayor asked the high school boy.

"Before it caved in?"

"Before."

"Well, nothing much. The last few days, we've been putting ice in the water. It was okay at first, but when it turned hot, they kind of like quit growing, you know?"

"What are we talking about here," the mayor asked the banker.

"Assuming we can sell the tanks, I'd guess everybody is going to lose around ninety percent of his investment."

"You screwed up," Mayor Barclay shouted up the hill.

"Don't fuck with me," Lester Shimmerhorn shouted back. "I'm from Chicago."

22

"SIT DOWN," ELIZABETH SAID.

Her husband had just finished a three-hour lunch break and was thinking about returning to the writing room. He had bought an old Underwood at an office supply store in town and was pecking around on that. Galt had left the IBM Selectric in a few sacks at the edge of the driveway and moved out of the country.

"Sit in there, in the living room."

"Why?"

"I have something important to tell you."

Andy Farmer told his wife that he was at a very important place in his novel—he was changing a chapter from first person to third person—and couldn't take any terrible news at this point.

"It's great news," Elizabeth said. "It's the best news we've had since we moved to this . . . place."

"I know you hate it here, it's common knowledge."

Elizabeth led her husband to the sofa. She sat him down and backed off a few feet and removed an envelope from her jeans pocket. She opened the envelope and took out a check.

"I did it," she said. "I sold a *book*."

"A book?" Andy Farmer looked at the check, which

was made out to Elizabeth. "*What* book? We had some sort of rare book sitting around?"

"I sold *my* book. A *fiction* book. I *wrote* it."

Andy Farmer blinked.

Elizabeth beamed.

THEY HAD SOME CHAMPAGNE.

"I just wrote it on a ruled notebook, you know, a stenographer's pad."

They clicked their glasses.

"I wrote it in *longhand*, can you believe that?"

"No," Andy Farmer said.

"Can you believe a major publisher would buy something written in *longhand*?"

"What major publisher?"

Andy Farmer switched from champagne to beer.

"It's called Caliope. It's not *that* big. It's new. Somebody who used to work for one of the big houses started it. But the editor who bought my book said they own their own paperback company.

"What editor?"

"His name is Macklinberg. Is five thousand much for a first book?"

"It's all right," Andy Farmer said, crossing his legs.

"But it's a pretty good start, right? Maybe I can sell a sequel. Maybe I can get my own *typewriter*."

Elizabeth got up and began pacing around the living room, staring at the check.

"*What* goddamn book?"

"I wasn't even sure I could write," Elizabeth said.

"What book?"

Elizabeth sat back down. "It's about some animals,

mostly squirrels. It's only about three-stenographer pads long. I wonder how many pages that comes to, a hundred or so?"

"These squirrels *talk*?"

"Sure," Elizabeth said. "They're like people. It's a children's book."

"When did you do this book?"

"What's wrong?"

"Nothing's wrong. I simply didn't know you were sneaking around writing a book."

"I thought you'd be happy," Elizabeth said, putting the check in her pocket. "I wrote it at odd hours. That takes in a lot of ground around here, doesn't it. At night. On walks."

"In a notebook. In longhand."

"You want me to raise my right hand and swear?"

"Then what?"

"Well," Elizabeth said, pouring herself some more champagne. "I looked up a publishing house in a copy of *Writers' Digest*, put the book in a box and mailed it."

There wasn't much to the rest of the story.

One of Macklinberg's assistants had called several weeks ago. The assistant said they were considering the book and would let Elizabeth know.

"And then the contract and check just showed up. The phone must have been screwed up, if they tried to call. Toby brought the check just before lunch. I never thought they'd buy it. That's why I never mentioned it."

Andy Farmer took the champagne bottle and put it to his mouth and turned it upside down.

"Hey," Elizabeth said.

"Let me get this straight."

"Maybe I need an agent. What about that guy you know?"

"You wrote a book about talking squirrels."

Elizabeth smiled and nodded.

"Without telling me."

"It was like an experiment."

"How long did it take?"

"A long time. Three weeks, something like that."

Andy Farmer shook his head.

"They do things *besides* talk. They have adventures. One is from a city park. He goes to sleep in a truck to get warm and winds up in a place like . . . this."

"This squirrel is me, am I right?"

"He's funny."

"You based a fucking squirrel on me, is that what you're saying."

"At times. Not always. Who's to know?"

"What's this squirrel's name?"

"It's Andy."

"I'm a son of a bitch."

Andy Farmer shoved the coffee table back and headed for the writing room.

"When are you going to be finished in there?" Elizabeth asked.

"You may have it now," Andy Farmer said, bowing.

"Thanks."

"Congratulations."

"Thanks a lot."

"I'd like to make a reservation to use the typewriter at three in the morning a week from Tuesday."

"Don't be like that. You can use it an hour from now. I just want to type up some notes."

"What kind of cute stuff will I pull in your next book?" Andy Farmer asked, stepping out of the doorway to the writing room.

"You were run over on the last page of my first book," Elizabeth said.

23

"I GUESS YOU THINK YOU'RE pretty smart," Andy Farmer said from outside the writing room window. "But you're not smart enough."

Elizabeth had locked herself in the writing room and was hard at work on her second book. She had hidden the keys to the pink truck, having made the point repeatedly that her husband was in no condition to drive these days, the way he had been drinking.

But Andy Farmer had some *more* keys.

"Have some *clouds* talk, I haven't seen that one in a while," he said, knocking on the window.

He was out of beer and went to get some, using a set of keys Elizabeth had overlooked. These were keys to the lawnmower, which handled better than the pink truck. The lawnmower was a Toro that cost $1,000 plus tax. It was the kind you rode. Andy Farmer had mowed some weeds and grass with it once; then everything had died and turned brown. The lawnmower had sat idle for the last month.

It resembled a scaled-down tractor and attained speeds of five to ten miles per hour, full-throttle, with a tailwind.

The springs were bad, so Andy Farmer stood up during the rough stretches.

He made a left onto Dog Creek Road and drove to Cherry County, which was sixteen miles south and west. It was a relief to enter another county. The air seemed sweeter in Cherry County, the people friendlier, the heat less oppressive. The ride was reasonably invigorating, except for the 200,000 bugs that bounced off Andy Farmer's head.

He stopped at a farm to ask directions to the nearest bar, and received a grocery sack from a farmer. He cut out eye and mouth holes and completed the ride to the bar with the sack over his head as protection from the insects.

THE NEAREST BAR IN CHERRY COUNTY WAS EDGAR'S and Lou's, and it was on the outskirts of a tiny community named Elkhorn.

The bar was a small white frame building.

Several trucks with guns hanging in the rear windows sat in the gravel parking lot. This was Andy Farmer's kind of place. Although Edgar's and Lou's might have seemed dangerous-looking to the average tourist, Andy Farmer felt very secure as he parked the Toro next to a Ford pickup with a rifle hanging in a widow.

At the truly dangerous bars, *they carried the guns inside*.

The screen door at Edgar's and Lou's hung by a rusty screw. It had obviously been blown off by years of country-and-western music played unbelievably loud on the juke box.

Andy Farmer didn't care for country-and-western music.

195

Everybody whined and used strange grammar.

The men were sissies.

The female country-and-western singers sang about girls who drank tequila and danced on the bar. The male country-and-western singers sang about wimps with broken hearts who sat around sucking beer and contemplating suicide.

Andy Farmer's bottom was sore and he was thirsty.

"There's no bullshit in here," Edgar said as Andy Farmer walked inside.

"Or we'll throw you out," Lou, his wife, said.

Andy Farmer said it was nice to see them, too.

LESTER SHIMMERHORN BOUGHT THE FIRST ROUND. He *insisted*. Andy Farmer protested, but finally gave in, and said he'd buy the next round.

"Fine," Lester said.

They shook on it.

Lester Shimmerhorn paid for two beers.

"Happy Hour is over in twenty seconds," Edgar announced.

"Nice," Andy Farmer said, giving Lester Shimmerhorn a dirty look.

Beer went up a quarter a bottle during the Unhappy Hours to follow.

Lester Shimmerhorn was in a lousy mood. He wore overalls and a shirt and tennis shoes that didn't match. He said his weight was down twenty-two pounds since he'd moved to the sticks. He hadn't shaved recently.

"The sons of bitches will pay, you can mark my words on that."

He and Andy Farmer clicked their glasses together and drank to that.

"Which sons of bitches?" Andy Farmer wondered.

Lester Shimmerhorn ordered two more beers and explained what terrible shape he was in. After the collapse at the Industrial Park, they had come at him with official documents—court decrees and things like that—and impounded his house and car and personal belongings. There was going to be a big auction, with the revenue from the sale of Lester Shimmerhorn's belongings going to offset some of the losses suffered by local investors.

"All you need to do is file bankruptcy, and the hell with them," Andy Farmer said.

"You have to file in the county where you go under. Every time I go near there, they take my clothes."

They drank some more beer.

"Were you a stockholder?"

"I got my wife one of those thousand-dollar deals for her birthday."

"Jesus, I'm sorry," Lester Shimmerhorn said. "I hope you got her something else."

"A dress."

"The goddamn heat out here would melt a tank," Lester Shimmerhorn said, shaking his head. "Let's have two more beers over here."

Andy Farmer said he hadn't been living the life of Riley himself these last few months. He told Lester Shimmerhorn that they had bought the Musselman place so he could write a book, but that he had been suffering from writer's block. Furthermore, their house was in need of a number of minor repairs, and nobody could be counted on to show up for work. Andy Farmer found it easy to open up to a stranger, so he told Lester Shimmerhorn that for about a month, he frequently lay awake, wondering if they had done the right thing, moving here.

"You've got it made, friend," Lester Shimmerhorn said. "I stay awake at night wondering if there's a goddamn bat on the limb hanging over my head."

"We've got no friends. My wife hates it here."

"Sounds like a bright woman."

"I can't write, we drive an old pink truck."

"I've got to *steal* what I eat." Lester Shimmerhorn put an arm around Andy Farmer's shoulder.

"I've got a dog that's nuts." Andy Farmer put his arm around Lester Shimmerhorn. "We're going through money by the *tubs*."

"The bastards even took my cat."

"Oh Christ," Andy Farmer said.

"Oh Jesus," Lester Shimmerhorn said.

"See this," Edgar said. He pointed at a sign behind the bar. The sign said: NO CRYING.

THE DUMBEST THING THEY COULD DO, ACCORDING TO Lester Shimmerhorn, was roll over and die. They had moved to a booth away from the juke box. Lester Shimmerhorn wanted to steal them blind before they could steal him blind. He had already begun stealing chickens in Matson County and selling them in Cherry County. "The secret is, you come up behind them. You walk right up to a chicken that's looking at you, they tense up before you strangle them and the meat's tough. You come up *behind* them, that's the only way, they melt in your mouth." Lester Shimmerhorn reached out and quickly grabbed the neck of his beer bottle. "How many you want at twenty cents a pound?"

"Ten."

"Good."

They shook on that.

Lester Shimmerhorn was ready to broaden the base of his crime wave and start stealing some cows. He had staked out a couple of arthritic cows owned by a man named Copenhagen. These cows spent most of their time leaning against a fence a mile from Copenhagen's house. "We put the cows in your truck, boom, we're across the county line."

"The bottom of the truck bed has rotted out," Andy Farmer said.

He found the concept of stealing animals boring. It would be too much trouble for too little profit. But he was not all that uncomfortable with the premise of *stealing*, and as Lester Shimmerhorn finished his eighth beer of the evening, Andy made some notes on a bar napkin. He told Lester Shimmerhorn there were a couple of scenes in the novel he was working on that might be of some use. These scenes were about robbing places that had a lot of cash on hand.

"Goddamn, I love it already," Lester Shimmerhorn said.

He began thinking of places that kept money around.

"Banks."

Andy Farmer nodded.

"There's an old dirt horse-racing track twenty-five miles north where a ton of money changes hands every Sunday." Lester Shimmerhorn said he had been to the races there once. "This one brown horse comes to the starting gate wearing a long-sleeved blanket to cover the needlemarks."

Andy Farmer made a note of the race track.

"Keep thinking. Think *big*."

"You've got a hell of a way to rob something, is that what you're saying?"

"A perfect way."

"Well, the fact that you can't write a lick might turn out to be one of the luckiest things that ever happened."

"Yeah," Andy Farmer agreed reluctantly.

They got four beers to go—bringing their total to twenty-two—and set out for home.

ANDY FARMER GAVE LESTER SHIMMERHORN A LIFT ON the Toro lawnmower-tractor.

They drank the beer and sang.

They were almost run over by a truck.

Andy Farmer hadn't felt this good in months.

All a person needed was a workable project to think about, a dream, even if it was a *crime*.

Lester Shimmerhorn lived in a ratty trailer one .22 bullet and ten yards from the Malson County line.

"I walked it off myself," he said proudly. "If one of those bastards stood on the county line and shot a .22 at me, it would land there." He pointed at a bare spot on the ground.

Lester Shimmerhorn went inside his trailer and returned with a gunnysack full of chickens. Andy Farmer wrote him a check for $17.50.

* * *

"SOUP'S ON," ANDY FARMER SAID, HOLDING THE SACK of chickens up for Elizabeth to see.

She had been asleep.

"You're drunk," she said. "What's that horrible smell?"

"Me and the chickens."

"Don't put them in the freezer."

"Why?"

"It broke."

"Well, hell, what's the coldest place in this house?"

"This bed," Elizabeth said, turning over.

ELIZABETH WAS SO EXCITED, Andy Farmer guessed she had sold three more books. She was pacing around, and there was a glow on her cheeks.

"I want you to look at something," Elizabeth said.

They hadn't talked much since he had gotten drunk and driven the lawnmower to the bar, returning just before dawn with the stinking chickens. They had each continued to work on their writing. They had both begun getting up earlier and earlier because the first one up got the typewriter. Yesterday, Elizabeth got up at a quarter of six, about forty-five seconds before her husband, and ran laughing all the way to the writing room. When one of them had to eat or use the bathroom, the other snuck in and set up shop at the typewriter. They had looked for—but hadn't found—another decent typewriter within thirty-five miles.

They sat at opposite ends of the sofa.

Elizabeth handed her husband a clipping from the *Redbud Gazette*.

It said:

Dear Abby:

My husband and I recently moved to the country. We have no friends, no hobbies, no interests. I cry myself to sleep most nights. Will you please help us? I can't mention where we live because I'm afraid they might come after us. Sincerely, Stumped in the Sticks. *Dear Stumped:*

My gosh, you and your husband should be ashamed. Get out and meet people. Join clubs. *Participate*. Get your husband off his lazy duff and get out there and rejoin life. Participation *always* works. Enjoy!

Andy Farmer put the clipping on the coffee table and asked his wife when this message had been placed inside a helium balloon and released.

"About ten days after we got here."

He nodded.

"I can't take any more. All you do is lie around drunk. We have to try something."

"Or what?"

"I don't know. But I'm willing to try anything."

"Like what?"

"Acting normal."

"Okay," Andy Farmer said. "Who goes first?"

THE NEXT MORNING WAS THE THIRTEENTH OF AUGUST, a Tuesday.

A cool front had moved through the night before and, at 6:00 A.M., the temperature was only eighty-four.

They went to town.

Elizabeth let her husband off at the Highway 101 Café and wished him good luck. He wished her good luck. They were going to meet some people and do some things and act normal.

* * *

NOBODY SAID MUCH IN THE HIGHWAY 101 CAFÉ.

Mostly, everybody wolfed down huge breakfasts that included trays of biscuits and big bowls of gravy. Andy Farmer played it safe and ate food he was familiar with—orange juice and toast, for example.

The Highway 101 Café was full of fishermen.

Andy Farmer was aware that he was an outsider, and that he didn't qualify for back-slapping yet. He guessed he would remain an outsider until he earned a native's confidence either by giving him $5,000 or by dragging him from in front of a freight train.

The quieter you sat, the more you seemed to be trusted.

After what had happened out at the Industrial Park—because of the outsider from Chicago—Andy Farmer say *very* quietly.

Toby had arranged for Andy Farmer to participate in a big fishing trip to Lake Thunderbird. Toby's father, Hank, was in charge of the trip. He had maps and charts showing how deep the lake was at various points.

It was hard to tell who would fish with whom because all the tables had been pushed together in the middle of the Highway 101 Café, and a couple a dozen men were talking about which lure worked best in bright hot weather.

Andy Farmer sat between Toby's father and a man in overalls. The man in overalls had to weigh three hundred pounds. Andy Farmer hoped he wasn't going to have to ride in a boat with the fat guy.

"So you're a writer," somebody said after ten minutes.

"Yes," Andy Farmer said.

So much for the introductions.

ONCE BREAKFAST HAD BEEN MANHANDLED, EVERY-
body went outside and climbed into pickup trucks.

Andy Farmer felt like a kid who had shown up for
the big neighborhood ball game wearing a lampshade
on his head. He was the last one chosen. He rode in
the back of Hank's truck.

After he'd climbed aboard, a man with a half dozen
teeth held out a sack with a pint of bourbon in it.

Andy Farmer had a sip, handed the sack back and
wondered if he had passed his first test.

MARTHA GOODE WAS *THRILLED* TO MEET ELIZABETH.

They met at Ivy's Café.

"We always like new blood in our organization,"
Martha Goode said.

"I would have joined earlier, but we've had a little
bad luck with our cars and trucks."

"Some people thought you were stuck-up."

"No, never," Elizabeth said.

Martha Goode, who was tall and looked like an
ostrich, took an application from her purse and had
Elizabeth fill it out and come across with the membership dues of $25.

Martha Goode was the president of Citizen for a
Beautiful Redbud.

Elizabeth blinked at the stationery on which the
name of the organization was written.

"Apathy," Martha Goode said, removing a pencil from her purse.

She added an S to Citizen. She made the S a capital letter so it would stand out and mean more.

"It's nice to be plural again," she said. "We used to have four members; one died, one ran off, and one quit."

Elizabeth was asked if she had any ideas about how the organization could help make Redbud more beautiful.

She had made a few notes on the drive in and told Martha Goode that she had noticed some vacant buildings around the Square. One way to liven up a depressed block might be by painting murals on the sides of the abandoned buildings—country scenes of flowering trees, babbling brooks, and wafting clouds. A project like this could involve local and regional artists, if there were any. The CitizenS for a Beautiful Redbud could sponsor a contest to select the winning artist. It would generate a lot of publicity.

"We'll blow the Garden Club off the map," Martha Goode said.

Elizabeth was sure a project like this would be classier than wandering around the Square, picking up cigarette butts and hot-dog wrappers. She suggested that the contest and subsequent painting of murals might be preceded by a membership drive.

"To where?" Martha Goode asked.

"We need to sign up some new members."

"Oh. Fine. But there's not enough money in petty cash to drive anywhere."

Elizabeth said that anybody joining the CitizenS

could have their names painted at the bottom of the first mural.

"This is *so* exciting," Martha Goode said. "Let's work another half hour, okay?"

The way the CitizenS for a Beautiful Redbud worked was Martha Goode sipped tea while Elizabeth got a headache, trying to think up a name for their beautification project.

LAKE THUNDERBIRD WAS RED.

The land around it looked like clay.

There were six fishing boats.

They were expensive and were equipped with depth finders—sonar devices that showed how deep the water was and what was swimming under the boat. They were equipped with trolling motors and padded seats that turned in complete circles. Most of the boats had sophisticated gauges that told a fisherman the water temperature, the amount of oxygen in the water, and, Andy Farmer guessed, the number of eggs in the belly of any female fish swimming under the boat.

These people were serious fishermen. Their moods became somber once they reached the lake. They put their equipment in various boats.

"Who has to take him?" somebody asked, nodding at Andy Farmer.

"I will," Hank, Toby's father, said.

Andy Farmer climbed into Hank's fishing boat, which was metallic blue and clean, and which absolutely *reeked* of power.

Two more men followed Andy Farmer.

This was no simple joy ride.

They were fishing for good money.

They were fishing for $200 apiece. Each boat contained four fishermen. The fat man was in a red boat. Its nose pointed up. The boat that caught the most pounds of fish won 80 percent of the prize money, with the runnerup getting the rest.

Before the four boats left the shore, Hank turned and gave the members of his team some instructions.

"Use the purple worm," he said to the two men he knew.

They nodded and began tying plastic worms onto the ends of their fishing lines.

"Don't fuck up," he said to Andy Farmer.

Andy Farmer attempted to execute this command by nodding and crossing his legs.

The metallic blue fishing boat surged suddenly from the shore into open, deep water. Andy Farmer's ball cap blew off. His keys almost blew out of his pocket. He leaned forward and saw that they were going forty miles an hour over some menacing whitecaps.

THE NEXT THING ELIZABETH JOINED WAS THE PIONEER Club, which met in the president's house and then drove to the hospital.

There, the president of the Pioneer Club gave some flowers to Virginia Bloomfield, a pale woman who lay in Room 3.

"Now get up and go home," the president of the Pioneer Club said to Virginia Bloomfield, who closed her eyes and said she didn't feel up to moving around.

Elizabeth stood by the door and received an explanation from a woman named Boston.

Many years ago, many, *many* years ago, somebody had told Virginia Bloomfield she looked a little like Lana Turner. And once Virginia Bloomfield had been told that, she started *acting* like Lana Turner. Virginia Bloomfield didn't know who her father was, and assumed it was the same man who had produced Lana; maybe they were sisters. When Lana Turner changed heir hair, Virginia Bloomfield changed her hair. When Lana got a divorce, Virginia got a divorce.

"You mark my words," the Pioneer Club member named Boston said to Elizabeth, "when *People* magazine arrives this week, there'll be a story about how Lana Turner checked herself into some health spa."

Nobody could figure out how Virginia Bloomfield found out what was happening to Lana Turner so fast.

WHILE ANDY FARMER WAS TRYING TO TIE ANOTHER purple worm onto his fishing line (he had borrowed and lost nine purple worms in the first half hour), a man named Peterbrook unleashed a vicious cast from the back of the boat that sailed forward and hit a man named Brock in the neck.

Peterbrook owned a gas station.

Brock worked for the electric company.

The fishing lure, which had eight hooks dangling from its bottom, sailed between Andy Farmer and Hank. The lure whistled as it went by.

It hit the left side of Brock's neck and stuck there like a leech. At least two, and possibly as many as four, hooks appeared to have become deeply embedded, very near his jugular vein.

Blood gushed from Brock's neck.

He dropped his fishing rod and reel over the side of the boat, grabbed his neck, looked at the blood on his hands, and screamed. He fell to his knees and almost tipped the boat over.

"Brock, goddamn, I'm *sorry*," Peterbrook said.

"Jesus," Hank said of the blood spewing everywhere.

Brock fell facefirst onto the bottom of the boat.

He began kicking his feet and rolling around.

Hank jammed the boat into a forward gear and lurched ahead, but the motion caused by the rough water made Brock scream louder than anybody in Matson County had ever screamed before.

Hank stopped the boat.

It bobbed up and down.

"He's dying," Peterbrook said of his friend. "He's dying a slow death."

Brock heard that and screamed some more.

Hank knelt down to inspect the fishing lure that was stuck in Brock's neck.

"Don't pull the damn hooks," Peterbrook said. "You'll rip some veins out."

Hank stood up and shook his head.

"I have a good idea," Andy Farmer said.

NEXT, THE PIONEER CLUB STOPPED IN FRONT OF AN old frame house that needed painting.

There was a girl sitting on a rusty porch swing out front.

Her name was Theology.

She stopped swinging when she saw the Pioneer Club.

The president led the group to the porch and asked Theology to please remove her beaded headband.

"Mother," Theology said. "*Mother*."

"What's this all about?" Elizabeth asked anybody.

"The girl has been wearing a headband, pretending she's Indian, not colored," a woman said. "She's so light, she's been confusing some of the high school boys."

"Go away," Theology's mother said to the Pioneer Club.

Elizabeth stayed.

SEEING AS HOW THEY COULDN'T REMOVE THE FISHING lure from Brock's neck, for fear of killing him, Andy Farmer punched Brock in the face.

"Damn, *hell*," Brock said, trying to block the blow, a right cross, with his left arm.

Andy Farmer had studied the situation at great length and concluded that the only chance they had to save Brock's life was by knocking him unconscious so they could transport him to a doctor's office. Moving the boat had caused Brock a tremendous amount of pain.

Only Brock was a tough son of a bitch and was not easily knocked out.

Andy Farmer hit him with two quick rights and a left hook.

Brock, lying on his back in the bottom of the boat in a puddle of blood and a tangle of fishing line, ducked.

One punch caught Brock's left ear, the next hit the top of his head, the third one missed altogether.

"Bastards," Brock mumbled.

Blood was now pouring out of the left side of Brock's mouth near where Andy Farmer had slugged him the first time.

"Hold *still*," Andy Farmer said, bending over Brock with a pained expression on his face.

"He's tough," Peterbrook said.

"Somebody else take a swing," Andy Farmer said.

"Forget it," Hank said.

"At least pull his hands from in front of his face."

"No way," Peterbrook said.

Andy Farmer tried a quick left uppercut, which hit Brock on his nose.

"...*kill you* for this," Brock said as more blood appeared on his bruised face.

"This isn't working," Hank said. "You're not knocking him out. You're only beating the piss out of him."

"Damn it, *help* me," Andy Farmer said.

Peterbrook shook his head. "I only hooked him in the neck. I'm not trying to kill him."

Andy Farmer, near panic, looked around and grabbed *an oar*.

Brock opened his mouth, but didn't have any screams left.

"It's for your own good," Andy Farmer said.

He swung the oar and hit Brock's right shoulder. The oar went *whack*.

Hank and Peterbrook winced.

"This works better in those television westerns," Hank said.

Brock almost passed out, but shook himself back to consciousness and lashed out at Andy Farmer with his feet.

Andy Farmer took three more swipes at Brock with

the oar before snapping it in half on the side of the boat.

"Well, *screw* it," he said, throwing the bottom half of the oar over the side of the boat.

Peterbrook had a sip of whiskey.

Hank checked a map of the lake to see where they were.

Andy Farmer sat down and began fishing.

THEY HAD SOME COFFEE AND DOUGHNUTS IN A TINY kitchen.

"What are you doing here?" Elizabeth asked.

"Killing some time," Theology's mother, Gwen, said. "How about you."

"Just passing through, most likely."

Gwen's husband had gone somewhere four years ago.

Theology was a good basketball player and was hoping to get a scholarship to a junior college.

"Mom won't leave here as long as great-granny is alive," Theology said. "She lives next door."

"You owe your blood," Gwen said.

"How much?" Elizabeth asked.

HANK JAMMED THE BOAT INTO A FORWARD GEAR, HIT the throttle full-blast and roared, almost airborne, toward a point of land a mile away.

Peterbrook held Brock's head in his lips.

"Let's not forget who hooked you," Andy Farmer said, for what it was worth.

Hank drove the boat to a wooden pier, and the

three of them carried Brock, who tried to bite some of Andy Farmer's fingers off, up a hill to a blue house. A veterinarian named Milstead lived there. They put Brock on Milstead's dining room table. The veterinarian removed the fishing lure from Brock's neck in about thirty seconds.

"You'll need some blood and a tetanus shot," the veterinarian told Brock.

Although very weak, Brock said he was going to make Andy Farmer pay for this.

"I was only trying to help," Andy Farmer said. "If you come to get me, I'll be ready. I don't work or sleep."

As an alternative to violence, Andy Farmer offered to pay Brock's medical bills and add on an extra $200 for his trouble.

"All you do to get a hook out of somebody's skin is push down hard and yank," the veterinarian said. "The hole is already there. These kinds of injuries look a lot worse than they really are."

He bandaged Brock's face where he had been hit repeatedly.

"It *was* sort of an accident," Hank said.

"What about my shirt and pants," Brock said weakly, looking at the blood all over him.

"*And* a fishing rod and reel," Peterbrook said.

"Gas for getting the boat here, plus cleaning up the blood," Hank said.

Andy Farmer sat down and rubbed his eyes while his fishing partner added up the damages.

It came to $600 and the medical bills.

Andy Farmer wrote Brock a check and hitchhiked home, catching a ride in a station wagon full of screaming children that let him off four miles from his house.

FUNNY FARM

* * *

ELIZABETH HAD GONE TO SLEEP AT THE KITCHEN TABLE,
beside an empty wine bottle and a letter to Dear Abby,
which began "Thanks a lot for nothing."

Andy Farmer sipped bourbon in the living room.

He sipped it slowly.

He didn't want to peak too early, and he didn't
know how long that would be.

25

ANDY FARMER WENT ON A TWO-week recess from writing and drove the Toro lawnmower into a hole in the road and fell on his head.

He was on his way to Edgar's and Lou's to split a case of beer with Lester Shimmerhorn and discuss stealing some money.

The hole in the road wasn't all that deep.

But the Toro stopped and Andy Farmer continued.

He was pretty drunk, so it didn't hurt all that much.

THE LUDLUM BROTHERS—STANLEY AND MORT—stood in the middle of Dogwood Road, which led to Edgar's and Lou's, with flashlights pointed at Andy Farmer. Their ambulance, its red light flashing, was just behind them, pointed the other way.

"Say," Stanley said. "You there, in the middle of the road."

"Goddamn it," Mort said impatiently. "There's nobody else around. Let's get him, drag him and the mower over the line, nobody knows a thing, it's over, period."

"We're playing it strictly by the book," Stanley, the

conservative member of the Ludlum Brothers Ambulance Service team, said.

"What book are you talking about, the joke book?" Mort asked.

Andy Farmer opened an eye and squinted at the light and the noise.

Stanley Ludlum had drawn a line across Dogwood Road. This was the imaginary, but accurate to within a couple of feet, boundary that separated Matson and Cherry counties. The Ludlum brothers stood at this line. Stanley leaned over it as he spoke.

Andy Farmer rested on his right side, approximately twenty-five yards from the county line, and twenty-six yards from the back bumper of the ambulance.

"Can you hear me?" Stanley asked.

Andy Farmer groaned.

"You drove your goddamn lawnmower in a hole," Mort shouted.

"Help," Andy Farmer said.

"Listen very carefully," Stanley said, sitting on the back bumper of the ambulance. He explained— quickly, before Andy Farmer could black out—the state of things around here as they pertained to the health-care business.

Some people didn't pay. Some people called an ambulance, received competent emergency treatment on the way to a hospital or a doctor's, then stiffed the Ludlum brothers out of their well-deserved fee.

To get around this problem, the residents of Matson County had voted to contribute $15,000 a year to guarantee twenty-four-hour ambulance service. This bond issue passed easily. Each household had to kick

in less than three bucks. The insurance policy meant
that if a person became ill or injured in Matson County,
the Ludlum Brothers Ambulance Service would
respond and perform. If somebody tried to stiff the
Ludlums, the fee would come from the Ambulance
Fund. If indigents and deadbeats screwed the Ludlums out of more than fifteen grand during the fiscal
year, it was every injured or sick person for him or
herself.

"You're in Cherry County," Stanley Ludlum
shouted. "You've got to drag yourself across the line
here before we can touch you."

Mort Ludlum shone his flashlight into a field left
of where Andy Farmer lay. "The county line cuts that
way, not far past the fence. We could meet you there."

ANDY FARMER STAGGERED AND STUMBLED INTO SOME
holes and ditches, trying with all his might to get at
the ambulance.

Mort had turned the siren on, and Andy Farmer
tried to move toward the sound.

He felt like he was in one of those damn barrels
at the fun house where you were supposed to walk
straight through while they spun around. He couldn't
tell if he was hurt or just real drunk, and didn't particularly care.

"Over here," a voice behind him said.

Andy Farmer back-pedaled, tripped, and rolled into
a ditch.

"*Go right*, not left," Stanley Ludlum shouted.

"Now you're backing up," Mort yelled, honking the
horn on the ambulance.

Andy Farmer stumbled around with his fingers outstretched for what seemed like a couple of hours, but was probably no more than a few minutes.

Then he caught a few winks.

He caught most of the winks with his forehead when he fell and hit something.

Else.

"WHAT DO YOU THINK?" MORT LUDLUM ASKED.

He stood a short distance from the body, shining his flashlight from the field in which the body lay to the ambulance.

"He's at least four yards short," Stanley said.

Andy Farmer had fallen with both hands outstretched as though he had been trying to steal home, but had been shot by a sniper, just short.

"You've lost your goddamn mind," Mort said. "Turn your head, I'll drag him a few yards, that's that."

"If we pick somebody up in another county, we lose our license," Stanley Ludlum said. He was concerned that the man laying limp in the field might have been sent by a state agency, as a test of their scruples.

"Can I at least go through his pockets?"

"You may not."

Stanley Ludlum pitched a couple of Band-Aids and some tape and gauze from Matson County into Cherry County; then he and his brother went to pick up a calf that needed to be at the vet's first thing in the morning.

During slow periods, they moonlighted, hauling sick animals.

 "COME OUT, IT'S SERIOUS," Lester Shimmerhorn said. "Your husband has been hurt in an accident."

He turned an ear to the door of the bomb-or-storm shelter. He held a hand over his mouth so he wouldn't laugh. He had a quart of beer in his other hand.

Elizabeth, inside the shelter, had a drink of coffee, a bite of a bologna sandwich, and she turned a page in the book she was reading. She had converted the shelter into a pleasant-enough room with a table, a lamp, and a chair. She had taken to the shelter the previous day after her husband and the madman named Shimmerhorn had tried to rustle a cow. The cow had bitten both of them, and then it escaped. Elizabeth's husband had been trying to root her out of the shelter for around twelve hours, but she wasn't having any part of it. He wasn't depressed. He wasn't upset. He wasn't a happy or silly drunk. He was *dangerous*.

"We could always smoke her out," Lester Shimmerhorn said to Andy Farmer, who got on his hands and knees by the door.

"This is really pissing me off," he said. "I could have been hurt or *dead*."

Elizabeth read some more.

"We're onto something big, a way to make a fortune. Will you please come out and help us think. We're talking *thousands*."

Elizabeth turned a page.

Andy Farmer pounded on the door and screamed, "Get out of there and cook *us some goddamn dinner*."

He put an ear to the shelter door, then frowned.

"Well?" Lester Shimmerhorn said.

"She says the oven is broken."

FOUR HOURS LATER, AT 10:00 P.M., ELIZABETH OPENED the shelter door an inch, then another.

She propped the door open with the book she had been reading and sat quietly on the top step a minute or two. There was no telling where they were: They could be inside, passed out. They could be hiding in some bushes.

She listened.

She took a compact out of her purse and held it to the crack in the door to see if anybody was hiding directly behind her.

After a few more minutes, Elizabeth crawled outside, dusted herself off and looked around. A couple of lights were on in the house. The Toro was gone. Either somebody had taken it to paint it pink like the truck, or Andy Farmer and his sidekick were out partying, rustling, or stealing.

Elizabeth took the keys to the pink truck out of her purse and tossed them on its hood.

She walked around the house and glanced at the corner that had been shot off and the side that had been partially painted yellow.

She looked up at the television antenna which, several days before, had bent in half in the wind.

The front screen door was off and propped against the house.

Elizabeth looked at the clump of trees where at least one body was buried, and at the 250-year-old cottonwood tree that had been blasted by the sheriff.

She said so long to the ducks.

It was a reasonable night. It had cooled off some. Elizabeth had almost forgotten what cool air felt like. She thought about brightly colored leaves, a roaring fire, a romp through the woods with the yellow dog, deer watering at the pond, sweaters, seeing your breath, tossing a football around; maybe fall would be different.

And maybe in the morning, Tinker Bell would stop by for brunch.

27

BIG INDIANS STOOD BY THE DOORS and podium—tall, broad, serious-looking Indians—Creek Indians, somebody had said.

Several big Indians had pistols strapped to their hips.

Andy Farmer put these people out of his mind and concentrated on the business at hand, which was a bingo game called the Big T. To win, a person had to cover the top and middle lines of a bingo card, thereby forming the letter T. Andy Farmer wasn't doing worth a damn. About fifteen numbers had been called, and he had covered only two squares on the card. He didn't care much about the Big T game, since the winner got only $500.

He was here to win the blackout jackpot and the $10,000 prize.

Such a prospect made his heart beat fast; so he took a deep breath and went through the motions of playing the Big T game, while familiarizing himself with the arena in which he sat.

The bingo game put on by the Indians was a big deal—Andy Farmer had scouted it out twice, briefly, checking on the exits and avenues of escape—but he still wasn't prepared for the enormity of it all, in terms of prize money offered and bingo players in attendance. Because of the big jackpot, there were at least four thousand people in the bingo hall, probably more, most of whom were expert players. Most people played five or ten or more bingo cards at once.

The Creek Indians were making a comeback after suffering so many injustices at the hands of the greedy white man and woman.

Although playing bingo for large sums of money was illegal in this state and county, the Creek tribal leaders had put their heads together with a number of fine lawyers, and, after various laws had been studied, issued the following statement to federal, state, and local legislators and law enforcement officials: "Remember John Wayne."

During his career, he had killed about two million Indians.

According to the letter of the law, even using the white person's alphabet, state law did not apply to reservation land except when you were talking about universal law—the kind that dealt with murder, rape, burglary, and the like—*mean* things. *Gambling* laws, which varied from state to state, well, that was a gray area the Indians were fast turning green.

Reservation land was governed by federal law.

And since there was no federal law prohibiting gambling, many Indians had told the states to which they had been exiled long ago to get lost.

Nobody could argue that the Indians weren't due.

They had been driven from fertile valleys to dusty plains.

But this was a significant rally.

Andy Farmer had thrown some numbers together and guessed that these particular Indians took in around $100,000 a night on gate admissions and the sale of bingo cards, while paying out around $20,000 in prize money.

Various tribes with nearby reservation land had announced plans for horse racing tracks with pari-mutuel gambling—even *casinos* with all types of gambling. On reservation land, a person didn't have to pay state sales taxes on cigarettes or whiskey.

In the parking lot outside the bingo hall, Andy Farmer had seen cars with license plates from more than a dozen states.

The bingo game, which was played in a large tin building that looked like an airplane hangar, routinely attracted crowds of two and three thousand.

And Andy Farmer was here to rob it.

HE SAT NEAR THE BACK OF THE BUILDING, NEXT TO a woman who played twelve cards at once.

Everybody sat on folding chairs set in long rows.

The bingo cards used for the early games, which offered prizes of $500 or less, were made of cheap paper. You colored over the numbers with a felt-tipped pen that resembled a Magic Marker. The paper cards were disposable.

Hard cards and plastic chips were used for the jackpot-blackout game.

The woman to Andy Farmer's right was one great player.

When the caller at the podium read a number into his microphone, the woman could check and mark her dozen cards in a few seconds. She had the eyes of a cat burglar.

"How do you do it so fast without making a mistake?" Andy Farmer had asked.

He got dizzy playing three cards.

"Please keep quiet," she had answered.

This was no social event.

This was business.

The bingo numbers were written on Ping-Pong balls and they were rattled around in what appeared to be a popcorn machine up at the podium. A white-haired man reached into the machine and pulled out Ping-Pong balls at random and read the numbers into the microphone.

"Faster," somebody would yell after a number was called.

"Slower."

"Louder."

"Come on, come on."

"Crooked bastard."

Because of the prize money up for grabs this night, it was one tough house.

The Big T game was won by an elderly bald man sitting two rows in front of Andy Farmer.

The man yelled "Bingo" and stood and waved his card over his head.

"He's blind as a bat," somebody said. "He probably made a mistake."

"Get him a wheelchair."

"Down in front."

"He better spend the $500 this week or his heirs will get it."

Andy Farmer had expected something more akin to a church social than a floating crap game.

226

* * *

THERE WAS A FIFTEEN-MINUTE BREAK BETWEEN THE
Big T and the jackpot-blackout game.

Blackout bingo was very simple. If you covered
every space on your card within a certain limit of numbers called, you got the ten grand. If nobody covered
his or her card within the limit, the prize money dropped
to $1,000 and another thousand was added to next
week's jackpot.

Very simple.

Very emotional.

At the break, Andy Farmer got his hand stamped
by a big Indian and went out front for a breath of air.
People were milling around, trying to conjure up some
luck.

"Hi, how's it going?" Andy Farmer asked Lester
Shimmerhorn, who was fidgety.

"Not worth a damn," he said. "I need a couple of
drinks, fast."

"Later."

"Look at the size of that Indian," Lester Shimmerhorn said, nervously shifting is weight from one
foot to another. The man Lester Shimmerhorn was
referring to was a Creek who wore a colorful ribbon
shirt. Bright ribbons outlined the collar and cuffs. The
man was wearing an armband that said *Official*. He
seemed to be checking the crowd for troublemakers.

"His legs are the size of me."

"Smile, act natural," Andy Farmer said.

"Smiling is *not* natural."

Lester Shimmerhorn tried to smile, but only the
right side of his face worked.

"Look at *that*," he said of another mountain of a man who carried a blackjack in plain sight and was thumping it into the palm of his hand.

"He puts his pants on one leg at a time," Andy Farmer said.

"The hell he does. Those aren't *his* pants. He took those pants off a man he beat the hell out of for fun."

"Be quiet."

"Look at *that*."

They look at a woman who had placed her bingo card inside a Holy Bible, and was pressing the whole arrangement to her forehead.

"Look at *that*, look at *that*, look at *that*."

A woman was kissing a rabbit's foot, a man was praying, and an Official was carrying an unruly drunk toward the parking lot by the nape of the drunk's neck.

"Listen, I don't think we ought to rob these people after all," Lester Shimmerhorn said quietly. "I think we better work our way up with a few gas stations."

A bell rang.

The lights flashed.

"Let's do it," Andy Farmer said, returning to the bingo hall.

He had no doubt that he was almost rich.

Lester Shimmerhorn trotted to the bathroom.

"O-SIXTY-SIX," THE CALLER SAID.

Thousands of people lowered their heads and scanned their bingo cards.

"O-sixty-six," Andy Farmer repeated from his seat.

"Shut up," somebody said.

"Yeah," someone else chimed in.

"B-number-four," the called said.

He called a number every fifteen or twenty seconds.

He called the jackpot-blackout numbers slower than usual because people played so many cards.

"B-four, B-four," Andy Farmer whispered.

He whispered it into the collar of his shirt.

There was a tiny microphone in this collar.

"GOD HELP ME," LESTER SHIMMERHORN SAID TO HIMself.

He sat on a stool in the middle stall in the men's room.

He sat shaking and perspiring and swearing.

He sat with a tiny receiver in his left ear.

"I-nineteen," Andy Farmer said.

"Slow down," Lester Shimmerhorn said, blowing perspiration off his nose.

He wore a shower cap so the ink he was working with wouldn't run and give them away and cause them to be sent to prison.

Yes sir, Andy Farmer had thought of everything; everything except how to keep from blacking out from the pressure.

"N..." Andy Farmer said unbelievably softly.

"N *what*, goddamn it,"

"N..."

"I can't *hear* you."

"N-forty."

"That's better."

What Lester Shimmerhorn was doing in the middle stall in the men's room at the Creek Bingo Hall was printing the winning bingo card for the jackpot-blackout game.

When Andy Farmer spoke a number into the microphone in his shirt collar, Lester Shimmerhorn heard it through his receiver and printed the number under the proper column on a piece of paper that would soon become an official blackout bingo card, complete with serial number.

This had all the trappings of an organized project; or at least it had seemed to when they discussed it over some pregame beers.

Andy Farmer had stolen a real blackout bingo card two weeks ago, and they had taken it to a number of paper companies before finding one in Jefferson that could match the quality of the paper. The paper used on an official blackout bingo card was thick—almost like cardboard—and they had to tip a man in the office of the paper company $25 to come up with a big sheet in only one hour.

Then they bought a printing kit comprised of custom-made rubber numbers and a special blend of ink.

All that cost $125.

Each bingo card used for the blackout game was official because of the frame around it. The frame was brown cardboard, and it had a serial number in the upper left-hand corner. Rather than attempt to duplicate or counterfeit a cardframe, Andy Farmer had simply stolen one along with the real bingo card. Once Lester Shimmerhorn had printed the winning card, he would put it inside the official frame with Super Glue, spill a drop or two of coffee on the card to make it look good and used, and then they would proceed to the podium at the front of the hall to collect the $10,000.

That is, if Lester Shimmerhorn could hold up his end.

ANDY FARMER SAID, "*BINGO*."

The plastic chips he had covered his card with flew all over the place.

He shouted it several times.

He stood up from his folding chair and looked around. He had no idea what to expect, and was surprised by the quiet.

Nobody said a *word* for thirty or so seconds.

"*Bingo*," he yelled again.

There was a loud grumble that built in intensity like an avalanche. It seemed to originate from a fat man playing fifteen cards off to the right. Before Andy Farmer knew it, the grumble had surrounded him.

He decided to leave his row.

He had bingoed, sort of, five numbers under the limit. The odds against such a thing were astronomical. When the crowd realized that there went ten thousand down the drain, the grumble turned into a growl.

Andy Farmer side-stepped his way out of his row and bounced into the aisle to his left.

A woman on the end of his row *pushed him*.

Once in the aisle, Andy Farmer shouted, "I'm *rich*," and started working his way toward the front of the bingo hall to have his card checked by the man who called numbers.

231

Halfway there, Andy Farmer said to a man on the end of a row, "I *did* it."

"Who cares," the man said, as though Andy Farmer had insulted him.

Andy Farmer continued to wave his card and grin. He had to act very excited, but there was a limit. He couldn't rub everybody's nose in his good fortune.

As he danced his way toward the podium, the only person who seemed pleased was Lester Shimmerhorn, who stood by an entrance to the main hall, breathing heavily.

"I *won*," Andy Farmer said, hugging Lester Shimmerhorn.

"It must be pretty tough work out here, dancing around and singing."

Andy Farmer winked.

Lester Shimmerhorn gasped for breath.

Andy Farmer slipped the card he had been playing bingo with—a regular card he had bought at the door—inside Lester Shimmerhorn's jacket.

Lester Shimmerhorn slipped the card he had printed in the middle stall in the men's room inside Andy Farmer's sweater.

"A piece of cake," Andy Farmer whispered.

"A piece of cake is a lot harder to make than to eat," Lester Shimmerhorn whispered back.

"CHEAT," THE CALLER SAID. "CHEATER."

Andy Farmer thought he was hearing things.

He stopped twenty feet from the podium and looked around.

Nobody else was nearby.

The white-haired man who had been calling numbers was pointing a finger at Andy Farmer.

"*Cheat*," he said again.

"Stop that," Andy Farmer said.

He looked back at Lester Shimmerhorn, who was leaning against a wall, acting *very* nervous. He was looking right and left, like he was watching a tennis match on fast-forward.

"Don't look at *me*, goddamn it," Lester Shimmerhorn said under his breath.

The caller had a drink of water and spilled some on his shirt and pointed at Andy Farmer again as he shook the microphone, trying to get it to work.

Andy Farmer looked at the card Lester Shimmerhorn had printed. It was fine. No ink was dripping. The paper was perfectly centered inside the frame.

The caller turned the volume on the microphone at the podium way up and said onto it, "*That man is a cheat.*"

His statement bounced around and off the metal roof and walls.

"Just a damn minute here," Andy Farmer said. He held up his bingo card. "I won."

The caller began pounding on the podium with his fists.

A large man in a jump suit rose from his seat in the front row and demanded to know what was going on.

"He's out of his head," Andy Farmer said of the caller. "He's having a fit."

"He's a friend of mine," the man in the jump suit said.

Jay Cronley

Several other players in the front row stood and took steps toward Andy Farmer.

"Stay back," he said.

"Watch out, maybe he's got a gun," a woman in the third row said.

"He's a cheater," the caller said.

"He can't shoot all of us," the man in the jump suit said.

As people began creeping toward him, Andy Farmer threw his winning bingo card at the man in the jump suit. The man in the jump suit dived out of the way and fell onto some people one row back. Chairs collapsed.

"Don't throw the car keys," Lester Shimmerhorn said under his breath.

ANDY FARMER RAN PAST LESTER SHIMMERHORN AND a big Creek Indian who wore an official armband. He elbowed the Official in the stomach.

He ran outside, blinked at the darkness, then turned right and sprinted for the Dodge pickup truck Lester Shimmerhorn had "borrowed" from his neighbor.

Lester Shimmerhorn didn't know what to do. He could try playing the role of innocent bystander and sneak away after all 4,120 people had left the hall to chase Andy Farmer. But he had a feeling he appeared very guilty, particularly since Andy Farmer had shouted, "Follow me," during his exit.

So Lester Shimmerhorn ran, too.

Most of the Officials were by the podium, guarding

234

the money, the $10,000 in cash, which was in a big box.

They had a fair start.

But as Lester Shimmerhorn ran, he heard frightening sounds behind him.

He heard boots running on gravel.

He heard profanities.

He heard things whistling near the back of his head.

A beer bottle sailed past his left ear and smashed against the window of a Lincoln.

They had parked at the outermost row in the lot.

Andy Farmer had the truck started and in gear by the time Lester Shimmerhorn showed up and dived headfirst into the back. Andy Farmer gunned it, driving with the lights off through several bumpy fields before reaching a section line road a half a mile west of the Creek Bingo Hall.

THEY HAD WORN FAKE BEARDS, WHICH THEY TOOK off and tossed in a ditch.

The bingo hall was in Clay County, seventy-some miles from Andy Farmer's house.

They were going to have to abandon the truck and get the rest of the way home as best they could.

Andy Farmer stopped at a wide spot on some dirt road, turned the ignition and lights off, and sighed.

"What'd I do, screw the card up?" Lester Shimmerhorn asked.

They stared at a wheat field.

"No, the card was fine. You did a great job."

"I see."

They looked at the moon.

"I have a question."

Andy Farmer looked to his right.

"Why did I jump in the back of this goddamn truck?"

Andy Farmer rubbed some glue off his chin.

"You're telling me the guy at the podium read our minds?"

"What happened," Andy Farmer said, hardly believing it himself, "was he screwed us before we could screw him."

Lester Shimmerhorn stuck his head out his window for some fresh air. He wondered if somewhere along the way he had been drugged. "He *who*?"

"The man calling numbers."

Lester Shimmerhorn cocked his head.

"The guy calling numbers had the game fixed so somebody he knew was supposed to win the ten thousand. When he saw me coming down the aisle with the winning card, not his friend, his *accomplice*, he went off the deep end."

Lester Shimmerhorn stared unblinkingly at the darkness in front of them.

"He probably injected something into the Ping-Pong balls with a hypodermic needle, something to make certain numbers stay up and down."

Lester Shimmerhorn got out of the truck.

"It was bad luck, that's all."

Andy Farmer got out.

"We picked the wrong night. Unbelievable."

Lester Shimmerhorn walked into a cornfield.

"Where the hell are you going? Your trailer is that way."

Lester Shimmerhorn continued to walk without speaking. Cornstalks crackled under his feet. He had the slumped posture of a person who was walking into the ocean to drown himself.

"Hey," Andy Farmer shouted. "You want the rest of this whiskey?"

The noise in the field stopped.

Andy Farmer tightened the cap on the pint of bourbon and threw it near where he had last seen his pal.

The rustling resumed after a few seconds.

"Right after we got here, I bought an Irish setter for four and a quarter. The damn thing ran away. If you see it, grab it, okay?"

Lester Shimmerhorn's footsteps faded into the night.

Andy Farmer drove the Dodge pickup into a clump of trees on the other side of the dirt road, wiped the steering wheel and door handles with his shirttail and trotted toward home.

He trotted about twenty-five yards and decided to walk the last sixty-nine and a half miles.

In the morning, he would put up signs offering a $25 reward to anybody returning his good friend Lester Shimmerhorn.

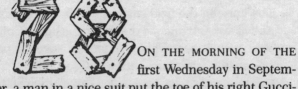 On the morning of the
first Wednesday in Septem-
ber, a man in a nice suit put the toe of his right Gucci-
clad foot against Andy Farmer's ribs, and pushed.

"Where's the person who owns this place?" the
man in the suit asked, thinking Andy Farmer was a
hired hand.

This happened on the front porch.

Andy Farmer opened his eyes and wished he
hadn't.

He could hear his eyes open. It sounded like a cat
scratching a screen door.

He didn't feel well.

His stomach felt like an empty cage with a hamster
running full speed around it. His heart was in his head,
and beating hard. His tongue seemed to have grown
recently. His lips felt rubbery.

He sat up and looked around the porch at several
jars that had contained alcohol and several bottles that
had contained beer.

"This is no good," he said.

"He is," Toby said.

"He is what?" the man in the suit asked.

"The owner of this place."

238

The man in the suit reached inside his coat for an envelope and tossed it at Andy Farmer, who ducked.

"He's been drunk the better part of a week," Toby said.

"The better part was the first seventy hours," Andy Farmer said, clearing his throat.

Toby handed Andy Farmer some Excedrin and helped him up.

"Your wife is suing you for divorce," the man in the suit said. "It's all in the envelope."

Andy Farmer stumbled around and bumped into the house and the posts that held up the front porch. He wobbled down the steps, recoiled at the sunlight, steadied himself, and said he'd be right back.

He went inside.

Doors slammed.

He called his wife's name.

The back door slammed.

The shelter door slammed.

Toby and the man in the suit stood quietly on the porch.

Andy Farmer appeared around the side of the house.

"All right, where is she?" he asked.

"New Jersey," the man in the suit said.

He got in a black car and left.

ANDY FARMER STOOD IN THE MIDDLE OF HIS FRONT yard, wearing only boxer shorts, with his arms out.

Toby hosed him off.

The yellow dog stood obediently beside its master.

Toby hosed the dog off, too.

"She's been gone quite a few days," Toby said. "More than a week."

Andy Farmer turned so Toby could water his back.

"You've been drinking too much."

Andy Farmer shivered and shook water off his head.

"Even my dad says so. He drinks *gallons*. It's something when he says that. You hungry?"

"I'm on a diet," Andy Farmer said.

"You know, if you're going to be single, I got this sister. She's a little fat. You like to meet her?"

"Only if she's flush."

"Dad says I should get your guns, you might kill yourself."

Andy Farmer dried himself off. The yellow dog rolled in the dirt and became muddy.

"Listen," Toby said impatiently. "I got some mail to deliver. Are you going to kill yourself or not?"

"No, I'm too tired," Andy Farmer said.

ANDY FARMER GUESSED IT WAS BETTER TO FIND OUT now instead of later that somebody was with you only as long as life was wonderful.

It was hard to believe you could make love to somebody around two thousand times and not have it mean a goddamn thing, though.

"I bet she doesn't ask for the house, right dog?"

The yellow dog seemed to understand their plight, and it growled.

It growled a long time.

"You can stop growling now," Andy Farmer said.

240

He reached down and grabbed the dog by its mouth and held its teeth together.

The yellow dog continued to growl, ready to defend its master against all comers.

This seemed to be the only available strategy: They wouldn't panic and would take life one microsecond at a time.

 THE NEXT FEW WEEKS WERE a joke.

ONE THURSDAY, ANDY FARMER WORKED A COUPLE of hours on his novel, which wasn't going worth a damn, then he went for a walk and discovered a bad situation at the pond.

It was dry.

That was only natural, since it hadn't rained a measurable amount in months; but it was still another depressing event that really knocked the wind out of a person.

Andy Farmer discovered one of the ducks standing in a puddle about one-inch deep. The duck seemed surprised, too. It stood in the dampness, wondering where the hell the water had gone.

The duck waded out of the puddle, shook mud off its feet and looked around for something interesting to do. Finding nothing, the duck sat down.

By nightfall—after another day of ninety-degree heat—the pond was completely dry.

Several dead catfish lay in the mud.

Andy Farmer collected the fish and offered them to the ducks, who passed. The catfish seemed deformed, due undoubtedly to the snake poison that he had spread around the pond from time to time.

Elizabeth called that night.

There was happy music playing in the background.

She didn't call to beg forgiveness. She called to tell Andy Farmer to ship her belongings to her mother's.

"You have to understand," she said. "I don't like it out there."

"I love it here," Andy Farmer said.

"You see the problem."

"Yes, you're a goddmn coward."

"Don't start," Elizabeth said.

They fell silent a few seconds.

Then Andy Farmer said, "I just don't understand how something like this could come between us."

"*Jesus*," Elizabeth said. "It's not only *between* us. It's under us and over us and *in* us."

They were quiet again.

"*Something like this*? It isn't some *point* we're talking about. It's a *way of life*."

"We've only been here..."

"Five months."

"Five months."

"You could always come home."

"To your goddamn mother's?"

The yellow dog barked.

"I *am* home."

The yellow dog continued barking.

"Then I guess my lawyer will be contacting your lawyer," Elizabeth said.

"Good."

Jay Cronley

"You *do* have a lawyer?"

Andy Farmer said of course he had a lawyer. Marion Corey, Jr., the man who'd had his brains knocked out at the softball game many months ago, had made a miraculous recovery and would be handling things on this end.

"So," Elizabeth said.

"So," Andy Farmer agreed.

"We gave it our best shot."

Andy Farmer found it laughable that his wife's best shot was a long-range missile fired from a goddamn condo in Hackensack, while he was engaged in hand-to-hand combat here in the trenches.

So he hung up.

A FEW DAYS AFTER THAT, HE RUSHED HIMSELF TO THE hospital.

Andy Farmer was almost embarrassed, but his pain more than offset the humiliation.

At the hospital, he sat on an examination table with his chin pointed up. His face, from his ears to his throat, was on fire.

"In all my years in the business," Rue, the nurse, said, "this is the lowest moment."

"Fix me," Andy Farmer told her.

Now that he was single again, he had thought that an adjustment in his lifestyle was called for. He selected for his flag of independence a beard.

He had always wanted a beard and thought it would fit nicely with the rugged surroundings. He thought it might make him feel healthier, even sexier. All it

244

did, though, was to cause a rash that was bright red and sore.

Rue, the nurse, started to shave the infected beard off without any shaving cream; but Andy Farmer demanded some Novocaine. The nurse jabbed the needle into his jaw as if she were checking a roast to see if it was done. She shaved off the beard for $100.

A FEW DAYS AFTER THAT, THE DUCKS LEFT.

They walked down the dirt driveway past the 250-year-old cottonwood tree to Dog Creek Road, where they stopped and looked both ways.

The male duck, which had bright green feathers near its wings, turned right and began walking, wearily but purposefully, down the middle of Dog Creek Road. The female, which was pale brown, followed along several yards behind.

Andy Farmer stood on the porch and watched the ducks leave.

He called after them once, and thought about chasing them.

The yellow dog howled pitifully.

"You're going *north*, you stupid damn ducks," Andy Farmer shouted. "Toward *winter*."

THE DAY AFTER THE DUCKS LEFT, AFTER A PARTICU-larly sickening day at the typewriter and a lecture from his insurance agent—"Don't even *think* about setting this place on fire, because we've got people in Dallas who can sniff out arson a block away"—Andy Farmer

called one of his favorite writers, a man who had done
about four dozen mysteries.

He was desperate for help.

He got through to the writer's editor and said he
was calling from Death Row. His last wish was to speak
with the man who had given him so many hours of
pleasure. The editor didn't buy it, and hung up.

Next, he called the town in Connecticut where
the writer lived and spoke with Information; then he
dialed the most expensive restaurant in the area.

This was a Saturday night.

He had the writer paged and, moments later, said,
"You have to help me."

Andy Farmer quickly explained that he had moved
to the country to write a novel, that his wife had left
him, and that he was having a difficult time composing
a simple sentence. The writer's block was unbearable.

"Usually," the author of four dozen mysteries said,
"a person doesn't get writer's block until after he has
published something."

The writer in Connecticut was a very nice man.

He talked about writing for a couple of minutes.

Successful writers, as far as he could tell, had only
one thing in common: talent.

"Christ," Andy Farmer said, closing the pad on
which he had hoped to take notes. "I was afraid of
that."

Furthermore, the writer of all those mysteries
doubted that talent was something you *got*. It was
probably something you were born with, then devel-
oped.

"How do you find out if you have any talent."

"You write."

"How much, how long?"

"Until you write something decent, or until you quit."

The writer said he had to finish his chocolate mousse, and he hung up.

THREE DAYS AFTER THAT—FOUR DAYS, WHO WAS counting—two odd things happened.

Around noon on Wednesday, Thursday, who the hell cared, A Federal Express courier ran up the driveway carrying a box. The box contained some canned vegetables and a couple of ideas for novels that the writer in Connecticut had made some notes about before he discarded them many years ago.

The Federal Express courier said his truck had broken down a long way off, and that he had spent the previous night in a field.

The package was a day late of the Federal Express guarantee.

"A rock knocked the transmission out of my truck," the courier said.

Andy Farmer said he wouldn't breathe a word of it.

Then in the afternoon, an old black pickup arrived.

A thin man got out and squared himself before Andy Farmer, who was rocking on his front porch. The skinny man removed his cowboy hat and wiped his brow with a sleeve and nodded.

His name was Tatum.

He said he lived in a trailer a couple of miles north and east.

He walked to the passenger door of his truck and

pulled out a dog, which was a mongrel. Tatum tied his dog to a post on Andy's front porch, then he returned to his truck and sat on the front bumper smoking a nonfilter cigarette.

Andy Farmer rocked.

After the mutt finally did its duty, Tatum untied it and led it back to the truck.

Its duty had been to relieve itself on the front porch.

"That damn yellow dog of yours has been going to the bathroom all over our steps," Tatum said.

Andy Farmer nodded.

"Fair's fair."

"Fair's fair," Andy Farmer agreed.

Tatum and his mongrel left.

THE FOLLOWING WEEKEND, ANDY FARMER DECIDED it was time for a change, so he went looking for some sex.

He met a girl named Glenda at Edgar's and Lou's Bar.

They had some beers and became friends.

"Go ahead, slug it," Glenda said after two beers.

She tensed the muscles in her rear end.

Andy Farmer doubled his fist and gave Glenda's seat a good poke. It felt like a big of sand. They laughed.

"I have the strongest bottom in the county," Glenda said.

She was a barrel racer.

At first, Andy Farmer thought she meant she pushed barrels along, like hoola-hoops, or rode in barrels, like soap-box racers. What she did, though, was ride around barrels on a horse at rodeos, for money.

Glenda was twenty-two, divorced, and she had two children.

After a couple of beers each, they got a six-pack to go and went to raise some hell.

They drank the six beers, then Glenda removed a pistol from her purse and shot the empties off some fence posts.

Andy Farmer nibbled on her neck.

Next, Glenda bet Andy Farmer $25 that old Coonfield would be sitting on his bench on the Square in Redbud, even though it was about fifty degrees, and 10:00 P.M. at night.

And sure enough, he was there.

When Andy Farmer turned the bright lights on the Square, Coonfield waved. He had been reading his newspaper with a penlight.

"You set this up," Andy Farmer said.

"He's *always* there," Glenda said, laughing as she took the $25.

They went to get some more beer.

"IT GOT TO THE POINT," ANDY FARMER SAID, PUTTING a can of beer between his legs, "where I'd sit down at the typewriter and go like this." He held his hands out in front of him, his fingers spread as though frozen. "Couldn't write a *thing*."

He brought his hands up around his neck and squeezed gently to show how he had choked.

They sat at an overlook at Lake Thunderbird, working on their third six-pack.

"You have to have talent to write," he said, drinking

half a beer. "As it turns out, I evidently have none at this point, but it's still early."

"Let me get this straight," Glenda said. She sat in the middle of the front seat of the pink pickup. She looked at the hand on her knee. "You moved here from *New York* to write *a book*?"

Andy Farmer nodded.

"You paid *how much* for that place out on Dog Creek Road?"

"Around a hundred and a quarter."

Glenda whistled. "And your wife left you?"

"You bet."

"So *now* what are you doing?"

"Not writing," Andy Farmer said, smiling.

"That's not something. That's nothing."

"You're very wrong on that point, young lady. Not writing is an art. It requires discipline and courage."

Glenda finished her beer. "So what are you going to do?"

"When?"

"Ever?"

"Have some fun," Andy Farmer said, lunging for Glenda's substantial left breast.

She knocked his hand out of the way.

He grabbed again.

"You silly son of a bitch," Glenda said. "You need to get yourself a job."

She backed up this advice with an old-fashioned asskicking.

First, she punched Andy Farmer on his nose, which knocked his head against the window on the river's side. She countered with a left uppercut.

Andy Farmer opened his door and fell backward out of the truck into some weeds.

Glenda was across the front seat and on him in a flash.

She said he was just like her worthless ex-husband, who sat around all week dreaming up get-rich schemes, then spent the weekends getting drunk.

She put the heel of her right boot on Andy Farmer's neck, said, "You men are all alike," and kicked him in the ribs.

She rolled him into some bushes and took the truck.

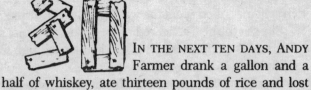 IN THE NEXT TEN DAYS, ANDY Farmer drank a gallon and a half of whiskey, ate thirteen pounds of rice and lost eleven pounds.

THERE WERE MEETINGS ALL OVER the place.

First, the lawyers met. They met in Marion Corey, Jr.'s office on Main. While that meeting was taking place, Andy Farmer and Elizabeth sat in chairs in the reception area.

Andy Farmer wore his good blue suit. Because of the weight he had lost, he had to pin the suit pants on both sides, and the seat was baggy. When buttoned, the coat still had room up front for a sack of groceries. He had cut himself shaving several times. His eyes were red, his shoes scuffed.

"Is that new?" he asked.

"Yes," Elizabeth said, trying not to look concerned because of her husband's disheveled appearance. He had globbed on a lot of cheap cologne.

Elizabeth wore a simple brown suit with a pale blouse and a chocolate scarf around her neck.

Andy Farmer thought briefly about taking the ends of the scarf and pulling, but instead told Elizabeth she looked swell, just swell.

"How's it going?" she asked, trying to make conversation. She had forgotten how it went out here.

"Pretty good," Andy Farmer said, straightening the sleeve of his suit so that it came to rest just above the

253

sleeve of his shirt, which was wrinkled. "We tried to rob a bingo game."

Elizabeth looked around for eavesdroppers.

"Right," Andy Farmer said, lowering his voice. "Only somebody screwed us before we could screw him." He said that he was no longer writing with any regularity. He was just hanging in there, basically.

Elizabeth tried to smile.

"I was thinking about getting a job," Andy Farmer said, leaning back in his chair. "Road work. Spreading tar. Field work." He shrugged.

"That's nice," Elizabeth said.

After the lawyers had met for ten minutes, Elizabeth's attorney, a man named Friedman, stepped out of Marion Corey, Jr.'s office. Friedman seemed dazed. He removed a handkerchief from his pocket and dabbed at his brow. "Will somebody please ... *explain*?" he asked.

Friedman specialized in divorce work. He was so good, the word was, the Junior League had put him on year-round retainer.

He wore an Oxxford suit and shoes undoubtedly made of something unborn. He was small, but as is sometimes the case with people who stopped growing, above it all. He had a superior air to make up for a low center of gravity.

"Explain what?" Andy Farmer asked.

Friedman peeked into the office he had just left.

"Explain my attorney?"

Friedman raised his eyebrows.

"Marion got his brains knocked out back in the spring. It's nothing to worry about, but I wouldn't get too chummy, if you know what I mean. I wouldn't sit on his lap."

Friedman took a deep breath and reentered the office.

"You didn't exactly go to Legal Aid," Andy Farmer said.

Elizabeth opened an old *Reader's Digest*.

AFTER THE FIRST MEETING, THE LAWYERS MET WITH their clients.

"I need a martini," Friedman said, sitting next to Elizabeth in the reception area.

He said that despite all odds, this might turn out to be a fascinating case.

Forget the husband, he was old news.

Although Friedman had made only a cursory inspection of the town before this session, based on what he had seen—and if all Elizabeth had told him was true—he was certain they could sue the city and the county, along with the husband, for mental cruelty.

MARION COREY, JR. WAS GOING OVER SOME NOTES from his meeting with Friedman when Andy Farmer entered the office.

"Have a cheeseburger, " Marion Corey, Jr. said.

Andy Farmer looked at his feet.

"I mean, have a seat."

Marion Corey, Jr. studied his notes, made a serious face, then said, "Basically, they want everything you have or ever will have."

"That shouldn't take long."

Marion Corey, Jr. looked at some more notes, excused himself, and went to the bay window that overlooked Main Street.

He clasped his hands behind his back and began rocking from his toes to his heels. He'd stop rocking to wave at passersby.

Although Marion Corey, Jr. had made a miraculous recovery—his attending physician in Jefferson said it would be a minor miracle if the man recovered enough to practice a game of jacks, to say nothing of the law—and was for all intents and purposes back, he wasn't *all the way back.*

Whereas Marion Corey, Jr. had won nine consecutive cases since his return to practice three weeks and four days ago, he was still at times fuzzy around the edges. Sometimes he got a word out of place. Sometimes he made funny faces.

"They like to see me here," Marion Corey, Jr. said over his shoulder, rocking from his toes to his heels, waving. "Gives them a sense of confidence."

The nine cases Marion Corey, Jr. had won were relatively minor—a couple of jaywalking tickets and a few parking violations. It was rumored that Judge Brooks simply couldn't bring himself to rule against a man who had come back from being hit with a bat, and as a result, no attorney in his right mind wanted to go up against Marion Corey, Jr.

After he had rocked the equivalent of several city blocks, he returned to his desk and picked up his notes.

"They don't care if you sell the house and property. But if you don't, they want half of its value to be paid out in equal sums, spread over a three-year period.

Very decent of them. It comes to around seventeen hundred a month, if my figuring is correct."

"Give them what they want and get them out of here," Andy Farmer said.

"Care for a game of darts?" Marion Corey, Jr. asked.

As Friedman explained the way the law regarded grandparents who passed away and left grandsons good-size amounts of money—the law regarded this windfall as community money, basically, to be shared by both partners, he said—Elizabeth rose from her seat and walked around behind her husband and straightened his hair.

A tear rolled off her cheek and landed on her husband's tie.

He looked up and blinked.

Elizabeth brushed some yellow-dog hair off Andy Farmer's suit and walked around in front of him. She straightened the lapels on his suit coat. She unrolled the cuffs on his slacks and shook some burrs out and rolled the cuffs up again.

He may be goofy, Elizabeth thought, *but he's mine*.

Friedman had seen it all before. He put his papers in a briefcase and handed Elizabeth a bill, which was due in thirty days.

The bill came to $3,500, plus travel expenses, which would be sent along at a later date.

Friedman gave Elizabeth his business card and left.

Elizabeth sat on her husband's lap and put her head against his chest.

"You think twice about getting a short haircut once you've been hit with a softball bat," Marion Corey, Jr. said. "Somebody owes me seventy-five dollars."

ANDY FARMER APPLIED FOR A job in the sports department of the *Redbud Gazette*, which was a weekly newspaper.

He applied for the job on the ninth of November, a Friday.

The *Redbud Gazette* was housed in a room behind the post office.

The newspaper was written and laid out here, then shipped to Jefferson to be printed.

Andy Farmer applied for a job with the editor and publisher of the *Gazette*, Winston Penbrook, who was a man around sixty-five years of age with a lot of white hair.

As with most of the businesses in Redbud, the *Gazette* had been owned by the same family for about forever.

Winston Penbrook was a decent sort. He was serious. In his thirty-five years as an editor and publisher, he had seen and heard it all, and was consequently leery of Andy Farmer's resumé, which include clipping of articles he had written for the *New York Times*.

Penbrook came right to the point, which he said was one of the secrets of responsible journalism: no bullshit.

It wasn't quite as sophisticated as *All the News That's Fit to Print*, but it had a certain earthy style.

"There's talk you're a lunatic," Penbrook said.

Andy Farmer explained that, as he was certain Mr. Penbrook knew, writing could be a very emotional experience. He had come here to write a novel and had become bogged down in the preliminaries. Perhaps he had been a lunatic there for a while—maybe for a month and a half—but he was making a comeback.

"You covered the Knicks and Jets and Rangers and you *quit*?"

Andy Farmer nodded.

"We'll see."

Winston Penbrook called the *New York Times* and asked to speak with the sports editor. When the sports editor came on, Penbrook identified himself and asked if a man named Andy Farmer used to work there, and if he had, what were the circumstances of his departure. Penbrook nodded a few times and said, "He's applying for a position here at the *Redbud Gazette*." He nodded some more and handed the telephone to Andy Farmer.

"What in the hell are you doing?" the sports editor of the *Times* asked.

"Looking for work."

"You finish your novel?"

"These things take time."

Andy Farmer handed the telephone back to Penbrook, who listened and nodded some more and hung up.

"He said sometimes you overdo it, write too flowery, but that you do good work."

"I try," Andy Farmer said.

"We can fix flowery." Penbrook picked up a pair of scissors and clipped some air and smiled.

AFTER BEING HIRED FOR $225 A WEEK, ANDY FARMER met the guys and gals of the *Redbud Gazette*. All but a few were Penbrooks.

Nancy Roderick was the editor of the Tempo Department, which reported the social scene at great length—who was visiting whom, and who was thinking about visiting whom, for example.

Nancy Roderick was big. She told Andy Farmer it was all-for-one and one-for-all here at the *Gazette*. If she saw some sports going on during her rounds, she let somebody know. Andy Farmer promised Nancy Roderick that if he saw anybody being social, she'd be the first to hear about it.

A man named Luft who chain-smoked cigarettes was the Sports Editor. He didn't seem to have a first name.

Luft was glad to meet Andy Farmer. He had been asking for help for years. The *Gazette* covered high school sports extensively, and some junior college when a nearby team was decent. Once or twice a year, the *Gazette* covered the major four-year school located two hundred miles away. Andy Farmer was named Outdoor Editor on the spot, and Luft was sure they'd get along fine, as long as Andy Farmer didn't write headlines that ended in a preposition or turn into a prima donna.

"What does the Outdoor Editor do?" Andy Farmer asked.

"See what's biting," Luft said. "Count dead animals."

DESPITE THE COLD THAT HAD set in, Andy Farmer rose each morning at 5:30 and ran two miles before going to work.

In the evenings, he did twenty-five push-ups and twenty-five sit-ups.

He quit drinking.

Elizabeth was proud of him. She worked on her second children's book during the day and greeted her husband each evening with large pots of soup and stew.

He mentioned one night as they sat around the fireplace that he had given some thought to the possibility of writing a nonfiction book about some of their experiences here.

Elizabeth loved that idea so much, she forced her husband into the writing room and made him try a few pages. He did ten pages about digging up a guy in the garden.

Elizabeth thought it was terrific.

In their spare time, they started some minor repairs around the house.

One day it snowed, hard.

The yellow dog kept everybody in a good mood.

During the heaviest part of the snowstorm, the

yellow dog sat barking its head off at the front door. Andy Farmer tried to explain to the dog that it wouldn't be able to go to the bathroom too comfortably in a three-foot drift, but the yellow dog would hear none of that.

"You're on your own," Andy Farmer said, swinging the front door open wide.

The yellow dog barked and ran full speed outside, just the way it always did.

It landed with a *plop* in the snow.

Andy Farmer had to bundle up and wade outside to rescue the dog from the drift.

Afterward, it hid in the closet a long while.

The *Gazette* put up a billboard downtown announcing that Andrew Farmer, formerly a writer for the *New York Times*, had joined the sports department.

These were good times, the best.

 ANDY FARMER'S FIRST AS-
signment of consequence
was covering the local football team, the Redbud Rockets, in a first-round state play-off game in the Class C
category.

The smallest schools in the state were in Class C.

The game was played on a Saturday night at Rocket
Field.

It was cold.

The kickoff was delayed fifteen minutes because
of Mariette Jankovich's pregame prayer.

Mariette Jankovich was the president of the senior
pep club. Since this was probably the last time she
would have to pray for her school in public—the Rockets were awful—she prayed and prayed.

She blessed the Rockets and their opponents, the
Tigers. She blessed the coaching staffs of both schools,
the faculties of both schools, as well as the casual
acquaintances of both schools.

"God bless *everybody*," she said four minutes into
the pregame prayer.

People cheered, thinking Mariette was finished;
but she was only warming up.

She blessed people selling food and pop.

She blessed former students back for the big game.

The Rockets had run onto the field, breaking through a circle of cardboard and streamers, some while ago; and the players were now fidgeting on the sidelines as Mariette continued with her telethon. The Rockets were so ready, their coach, Homer Jones, was concerned that the delay would take the edge off his troops. So, as Mariette Jankovich blessed the people who had painted the lovely white lines on the field, coach Homer Jones got a megaphone from a cheerleader, stepped onto his bench, aimed the megaphone at the press box, and shouted, "*Knock it off, goddamn it.*"

"Amen," Mariette whispered.

A thunderous cheer went up from both sides of the field.

The press box at Rocket Field was a wooden hut with no protection from the elements. When the wind gusted, the feeble press box shuddered.

The temperature at the kickoff was twenty-one degrees.

There was an electric heater in one corner of the press box. Since this was the warmest place in the joint, a number of freeloaders, including the band director, a science teacher, and the school nurse, had crammed themselves inside.

Andy Farmer sat in the front row, between the stadium announcer and the official statistician, a sophomore named Luke who wore glasses thick as the bottoms of Coke bottles.

The game finally started with the Tigers kicking off to the Rockets.

The Rocket standing on the goal line fumbled the football and fell on it at the one-yard line; a poor start.

Redbud's strategy was obvious from the outset.

The Rockets were not necessarily attacking their opponent's weakness; rather, they were attacking their *stadium*'s weakness. Quite a few lights had burned out on the far side, particularly around the west goal line, and the Redbud quarterback, an uncoordinated kid named Butch, continually heaved passes toward the darkened area of the field, hoping the Tigers would lose the passes in the cold night sky and crash into each other, their benches, or their coaches.

But because of the stiff wind, many of the Rocket passes went straight up and were batted around like a volleyball.

The Rocket punter kicked one backward over his head, and the Tigers had a quick 2–0 lead on the safety.

Then Butch, the quarterback, was knocked silly.

A reserve who was scared to death fumbled four straight times, the last of which was recovered by the Tigers, who tossed a long pass to score for a lead of 8–zip. The extra point was short. It was *way* short, as the Tiger kicker missed the ball entirely.

Andy Farmer had a hell of a time keeping track of who was doing what.

Both teams wore pale uniforms.

The numbers on their backs seemed to have been penciled on. Furthermore, due to the recent snow, the field was soggy and muddy, and after about two minutes, everybody was filthy and the numbers covered with goo or blood.

The stadium announcer was no help.

He announced things like: "There went Harold's

boy plunging into the line for a gain of six. No, make it one. Check that, he lost a yard."

And: "That was a complete pass from number seven to Martin's kid."

And: "Chester's grandson recovered that fumble, folks, let's give him a big hand."

"Who the goddamn hell is Harold's boy?" Andy Farmer asked once, but quickly apologized.

"You got it made, buddy," the stadium announcer said. "Wait until you have to cover a game where both teams are named the Tigers."

At the half, Andy Farmer's scorecard was a series of red question marks. He was going to have to get the essentials, like who had scored the damn points, by interviewing people after the game.

At the half, the Tigers led 14–6.

Elizabeth sat a few rows below the rickety press box.

She watched her husband work more than she watched the game, and blew him kisses every five minutes.

During the halftime ceremonies, when the Redbud band formed a pattern apparently caused by an explosion of shotgun pellets on a piece of cardboard, Elizabeth brought her husband a steaming Thermos of coffee and told him she loved him dearly.

ROCKET COACH HOMER JONES WAS MAD *AND* SAD.

It was close, and hard to believe, but he was sadder than he was mad.

"What's wrong with this country today," he said,

shaking his head as he paced slowly among his team, "is sissies."

The Rockets had expected a tantrum, but were even more afraid of their coach's strangely subdued manner.

"Gentlemen," he said. "Look up here."

Everybody looked up.

"What's going on? I asked the *gentlemen* to look up."

Everybody looked down.

"Sissies, look up here."

Everybody looked up.

"I'm not going to yell. And, if we lose this game to those sons of bitches, I'm *not going to retire*."

Earlier in the year, coach Homer Jones had said he was going to quit coaching and enter private business with his brother-in-law, who owned a car lot.

But he had changed his mind.

"I'm going to come back and coach forever and ever. I'll see you bums next spring for four-a-day-drills."

The coach smiled and went to use the bathroom.

The second he was out of sight, three quarters of the team—the underclassmen—jumped to their feet and began whooping it up. They also slapped each other around.

The seniors remained seated. They didn't particularly care what the old bastard did. But then it dawned on the seniors that many of them had brothers and cousins who would be coming up through the ranks, and sisters who would sit behind the team on the pep squad and hear streams of obscenities from Coach Jones about how they weren't cheering loud enough.

After a minute or two, the seniors got their guts up and began punching things and hollering.

They were going to kill the Tigers.

When the halftime demonstration was at its loudest, a team manager stuck his head in the door and said the captain was needed at midfield for some Most Outstanding presentation with the Senior Queen.

The captain, a halfback named Elliott, had wrenched an ankle during the first quarter and was in pain.

"Get the captain of the Special Teams," an assistant coach told the student manager.

The Special Teams unit covered kickoffs and punts.

Its captain was Eugene P. Stokes.

Eugene was black.

The Senior Queen was Judy Montgomery.

She was pert.

She was also white.

"Sam," somebody sitting one row down from Sam Montgomery said, "I hate to be the one to tell you this, but that's your daughter being kissed on the fifty yard line by a...a..."

Several black people were sitting nearby.

"By a *what*?" a black man asked.

"By a...*jujitsu*," the person one row down from Sam Montgomery said.

The black man waded into some white people behind him.

Judy Montgomery, representing the student body, gave Eugene J. Stokes, representing the football team, a little trophy for having won the conference championship for the first time in about a light year.

Judy was a good kid.

She offered her left cheek.

Eugene P. Stokes was also a good kid.

He pecked at Judy's cheek.

Sam Montgomery stood up and took a pistol from his jacket. He was a little drunk. He took aim and was going to shoot Eugene P. Stokes, but because of the fight going on in front of him, his aim was knocked off line as he pulled the trigger.

There was a *crack*.

People screamed and ducked.

People on the other side of Rocket Field stood up to see what was happening.

A black man smashed Sam Montgomery in the face, knocking him under the bleachers.

The bullet from Sam Montgomery's gun sailed over the football field and entered the press box, tearing into Andy Farmer's right arm.

The force of the bullet spun him around and almost knocked him outside.

He raked cups of steaming coffee onto the people sitting below, and came to rest hanging halfway out of the old wooden press box, unconscious.

The Redbud Rockets, inspired to unbelievable heights by the promise of their coach's retirement if they won (after the game, he promised to move out off the county if they emerged victorious from the *next* play-off game), scored thirty-five straight points while holding the Tigers to hardly anything at all, to win 43–17.

After the victory, the Rockets gathered together

for a moment of silent prayer for the man who had been shot during the riot at halftime. They also sent the game ball—autographed—home with the man's wife as a gesture of their appreciation for his support and concern for his health.

ANDY FARMER HADN'T BEEN
shot *too* much.

The bullet just tore through some muscle, that
was all, missing the bone by a good inch.

He was stitched together by Dr. Mayhew, who told
him to get plenty of rest and drink lots and lots of
orange juice.

He lay quietly on the sofa for many days, thinking.

On Wednesday around noon, he sat up and said,
"It's impossible."

Elizabeth was working on the television, trying to
get rid of the ghosts. She joined her husband on the
sofa. She had no idea how he would snap out of it,
and was prepared for anything.

"It's over."

"Well," Elizabeth said, lowering her eyes. "There's
still time. Isn't there?"

"Time?" Andy Farmer laughed and held his sore
arm. "Time for *what*?"

"To turn it around, I guess."

"Christ, they *shot* me."

Elizabeth flipped through a magazine.

"They took out a gun and *shot* me."

"I was there, remember," Elizabeth said.

Andy Farmer got up and went to the front window

273

and looked out at the place he had tried so desperately to love.

"This air isn't clean," he said solemnly. "It has *lead* in it."

Elizabeth didn't know if she should laugh or cry.

"It's over. You know it. I know it. The yellow dog knows it."

The yellow dog sat in the middle of the living room, snapping its teeth at the air.

"You know it, I know it," Andy Farmer said, correcting himself. "The goddamn yellow dog doesn't know what town it's in."

THEY HAD SOME WINE AND WATCHED A FIRE IN THE fireplace.

Andy Farmer said he wished something normal would happen. He wished a wall would fall in. But it figured, the hour after they decided to do what they could to save their lives was pleasant.

Elizabeth understood. She felt a tremendous sense of relief; but at the same time, she was genuinely sorry that the country had tried to gobble them up.

"You know what's frightening?" Elizabeth said.

Andy Farmer looked around to see if anything was crawling nearby.

"What's terrifying is that if we had it to do over again, we wouldn't do a *thing* differently."

Andy Farmer nodded.

"It's also depressing," Elizabeth said.

Andy Farmer agreed with that, too. Nobody enjoyed having pie in the sky turn into pie in the face.

"We'd have been better off moving to the Amazon,"

he said. "Where we'd have been so obviously lost, we'd have qualified for a little damn sympathy."

The sunset was a sweet-and-sour orange.

THEY LAY CLOSE TOGETHER IN BED, LISTENING TO THE wind.

Unfortunately, the fact that they had decided to bail out while they still had a pot to bail with hadn't changed a whole hell of a lot.

They couldn't write *Just Kidding* on the front of the house and catch the first bus east.

They could use some money.

"We have to get serious," Andy Farmer said,

"Right," Elizabeth agreed.

They had each brought notebooks to their bedside tables in case they got a great idea in the middle of the night.

"We need to concentrate."

"I *am*," Elizabeth said.

They had apparently dug themselves such a hole, staying was easier than leaving.

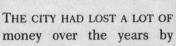THE CITY HAD LOST A LOT OF money over the years by admitting the public to commission meetings free of charge.

The city should have charged $10 a head and sold standing room.

A commission meeting was a lot more entertaining than a rooster fight, a football game, or even jackpot bingo.

The city commission was comprised of seven members, including Marion Corey, Jr., who sat down at one end of the main table.

Mayor Barclay chaired the meeting on the third Friday in November.

The Farmers sat at the back of the meeting room in the basement of City Hall, biding their time.

THE TREASURER, A MAN NAMED LUCKENBILL, OFFERED the first bit of business. You could tell it was a bad bit of business, because the mayor almost had to drag Luckenbill from his seat.

Luckenbill was a mortician.

He mumbled.

"Louder," called somebody in the crowd.

"I said, I *buried* nine hundred and thirty-five dollars and seventy cents," Luckenbill said.

The money had been earmarked for a park beautification project. Luckenbill had been preparing a few people for burial and had accidentally sealed the bag of money in with a corpse.

"If the bank stayed open past *noon*," Luckenbill said, "people wouldn't have to walk around all the time with cash."

"We're open until three P.M.," the banker said.

Luckenbill said there was no reason to panic. He had been working on only five *customers* at the time the money disappeared, only three of whom had been put in the ground. It was a simple matter of digging people up and having a look.

"Who pays for the digging?" a member of the Garden Club asked.

"He does," the mayor said, pointing at Luckenbill.

"How much interest have we lost?" somebody asked.

"For God's sake," Luckenbill said, "a *quarter*, okay?"

"A dollar sixty-one," the banker said.

Luckenbill dug a buck sixty-one out of his pocket, threw it on the podium, and went back to his seat.

NEXT ON THE AGENDA WAS A FIGHT BETWEEN SHERIFF Ledbetter and the Redbud police chief, whose name was Markham.

The way the law is enforced in a rural area is territorially. The police chief is responsible for what happens inside the city limits. The sheriff takes care of business in the country.

Chief Markham had come up with a way to save the taxpayers of this community $11,300. He wanted the city to disannex nine square blocks, thereby dumping a troublesome bar, a recreation hall where people shot dice all the time, and a house full of transients, into the county's lap.

With fewer trouble spots to cover, the chief could fire a deputy.

Sheriff Ledbetter, who had finally passed his driver's test with a resounding seventy-one and been reelected by a landslide, was in a no-nonsense mood.

"You try anything like that, I'll move the damn sheriff's office out of town, how do you like *that*."

The mayor came up with a possible compromise.

If Sheriff Ledbetter would take the recreation hall, the city would annex the drive-in movie, where the high school kids raised hell nonstop.

"The rec hall is violent," Sheriff Ledbetter said. "The drive-in is full of practical jokers."

"Question," Marion Corey, Jr. said.

The room fell silent.

A reporter from the *Gazette* turned his tape recorder on.

"When's the turkey season?" Marion Corey, Jr. asked.

"Well, Marion," the mayor said. "The bow-and-arrow season runs another week or so."

"I propose we declare a moratorium on turkey hunting Thanksgiving day."

The banker glanced at the newspaper reporter.

"Yes, well," the mayor said. "That's a nice thought, Marion, except you don't usually see too many wild turkeys here in town, do you."

"All in favor say aye," Marion Corey, Jr. said.

Eventually, the other six members of the commission raised their hands.

"All opposed?"

"There's only seven of us Marion," somebody said.

Sheriff Ledbetter said he'd think about trading the drive-in movie for the rec hall.

AFTER A FIVE-MINUTE BREAK, THE MAYOR STOOD AT the podium and presented the worst news yet: Redbud had been denied the title of Acorn Capital of the World.

People groaned.

The news had been received an hour earlier. It had come from the state senator responsible for this area.

Being the World Capital of something was very important to a small town's economic well-being. If you had more of something than any other city in the country, you could throw yourself a big festival and rake in the tourism dollars.

Finding something to be the World Capital of was difficult. It was a very competitive business. Redbud had been the Redbud Tree Capital of the World until eight years ago when a city in Florida took the lead by four hundred saplings. Most of the good stuff was already taken. There was a Wheat Capital of the World, a Pig Capital of the World—there were World Capitals for *all* the grains and *all* the animals—and there was even a Frog Capital of the World down in Louisiana. About all that was left were mosquitoes and snakes, which weren't too appealing, and acorns. As the Acorn Capital of the World, Redbud would have qualified for thousands of dollars in porkbarrel money from the state to use on a big festival. But according to the state senator, a city in Nebraska had won the acorn competition with a total of 775.

"We only got credit for a hundred and twenty-one," the mayor said. "There's a new rule you can't bring in trees from out of state and plant them within eighteen months of when you want to run your festival."

"How about sparrows?" somebody wondered.

The mayor said a city in Arkansas had 28,500, downtown.

"What the hell is left?" a concerned citizen wondered.

"From the look of things," Mayor Barclay said, holding up a brochure that showed who had what, "our best choice is crickets or timber rattlesnakes. Some city in New Mexico has two hundred thousand, seventy-nine crickets. Cogburn, Colorado, has got a natural population of fourteen timber rattlers within its city limits. Nobody has challenged either place in a number of years."

Everybody concentrated on what they could be World Capital of, but couldn't think of anything that didn't stink, or could kill you.

"Is there any other business?" the mayor asked.

"Yeah," Andy Farmer said. "Right here."

"Oh. Okay. Let's get this over with."

Andy Farmer asked for, and received, a private session with the city commission; they all adjourned to the cafeteria next door.

* * *

ANDY FARMER DECIDED TO GET RID OF HIS NOTES and ad-lib.

He tried to be brief and to the point.

"We've had it," he said, introducing his wife at the back of the room. "We're leaving."

People yawned.

"What we want to do," he said seriously, "is sell our ... the Musselman ... place."

"God rest his soul," a commission member said. "Wherever he is."

"He's in our trees," Elizabeth said.

"We're going to put an ad in the *New York Times*," Andy Farmer said. "We're going to fix the place up as best we can, but we need your help."

People stretched.

"We need to know things like where more bodies might be buried."

"Can we speed this up," the banker said.

"And for your help, and I mean for a *lot* of help, we'll give the city fifteen thousand dollars—that is, when we unload the place."

That got their attention.

The commission sat up straight.

"Continue," the mayor said.

"It's going to be a lot of hard work, because we have to make somebody believe this place is, if not paradise, at least *normal*."

"Way to go, honey," Elizabeth said from the back of the room.

What Andy Farmer proposed was this:

Could the mailman please stop throwing stuff in the ditch? Not forever. Just when a prospective buyer was around. Could people please stop bringing dogs to use his porch as their bathroom? Could people stop shooting him? Could high school kids stop stealing Dangerous Curve signs, could the law enforcement agencies quit shooting his trees, and might the nurse at the hospital quit swearing at the injured? Could criminals be kept in their cells for just a little while? Might people refrain from stealing his transportation and painting it pink?

"I don't understand exactly what you want us to do for the twenty thousand," the mayor said.

"*Fifteen* thousand. *Nothing.* That's all. Just don't do a goddamn thing for *one lousy day.*"

The majority of the city commission didn't seem to find this demand too outrageous.

"Break," the mayor said.

The commission whispered.

WHEN THE MEETING RESUMED, ANDY FARMER HAD a few more things to say.

To have any chance of selling the house and twenty-five acres for a decent price, they would have to really think *big*. They'd have to fill the pond with water. Somebody would have to truck in some brightly colored leaves and help spread them around the property.

Then, once the contract for the sale of the house was signed, everybody could go back to being their usual... *selves*.

"That's enough innuendo," the mayor said.

"How about this," a commission member—the owner of the dry cleaners, said. "My kid has a couple of pet deer. How about when somebody comes looking at your place, one of us hides in the trees and lets the deer loose and they run right across the damn front yard."

"God, that's *perfect*," Andy Farmer said.

"This sounds good," a commission member said to his neighbor. "Hell, we only sold a thousand dollars' worth of tickets for that Tree Festival before we got beat out."

"The last thing," Andy Farmer said, feeling weak, "is that we're going to need some competent help to get our house fixed up and looking nice."

"It will cost you top-dollar," the mayor said. "Cash."

"Fine."

By a vote of 7–0, it was agreed that everybody would act happy for between twelve and twenty-four hours on a date to be named later, for the sum of $15,000, which would be paid within forty-five minutes of when the Musselman-Farmer place was sold.

When the Farmers showed a prospective buyer around town—perhaps a month or so from now, at the earliest—townsmen would tip their hats, women would wave, and children would smile.

There would be no druggist practicing medicine.

Mrs. Dinges would be on a holiday.

Nobody would be beaten senseless.

This might even turn out to be *fun*.

It would be like a play—like bringing a lovely winter scene on a postcard to life.

The mayor, speaking for the city commission, said it was a deal. People in positions of authority and responsibility would take control of this project and ram it home.

Andy Farmer and the mayor shook on it.

"Now," Andy Farmer said with a smile, his wife

close at his side, "how much notice are you going to need in order to get everybody to act normal?"

The mayor considered this question, wondering if the person who had asked it was being a smart-ass.

"Forty-eight hours ought to do it," the mayor said finally.

37

THEY HAD LOOKED AT RANCHES IN Nebraska, condos in Colorado, converted barns in New Mexico, and ocean-front property around Corpus Christi. They had devoted all their vacation time to inspecting the heart and soul of this country, trying to find the perfect place to live out their years in peace, quiet, good health, and harmony. They had looked at places that straddled streams in Connecticut and pumpkin patches in Pennsylvania. But in all their travels, they had never seen anything like the place at Star Route 2, Dog Creek Road.

This, Bud Culbertson guessed, was about as close as you could get to heaven on earth.

Betsy agreed, but didn't want to get *too* excited from a distance because you never knew what the inside would look like. They had inspected an A-frame in South Carolina that was spotless on the outside, but resembled a run-down gymnasium on the inside. Still, Betsy Culbertson had to admit that the house sitting on the gentle rise with the pond on one side and the trees on the other—with a knoll in the background—met many of their requirements, at least cosmetically.

The Culbertsons stood beside their car, an Olds, and thanked God for guiding them here.

Bud Culbertson had taught English at a university

just outside New York City. He had decided that there was probably more to life one Saturday two months back as he stood inside a bush on Dog Patrol. The patrol had become a necessity when strays began attacking prospective donors who were on their way to the administration building. The most serious attack involved a woman named Dearborn, who was mauled by a great Dane not twenty-five yards from her Mercedes. Mrs. Dearborn had been on her way to the president's office to give $2.5 million for the construction of an outdoor theater. The great Dane ripped Mrs. Dearborn's mink off her back and dragged her into a flowerbed.

All told, six prospective donors had been bitten, scratched, or half scared to death by strays roaming the campus.

A university was a place of business first and a mecca of enlightenment second. You had to raise money before you could raise IQs. Therefore, the university president called all the department heads together and told them he wanted the goddamn dogs off his property. His first plan was to have some ROTC students shoot the dogs, but the ASPCA got wind of that idea and protested. A compromise was reached. The strays would be stunned with tranquilizer darts and handed over to Ralson Purina for "research."

So twice a week the faculty—lettered men and women, people quite possibly on the verge of great discoveries in medicine and aeronautical engineering—had to leave their archives and laboratories and hide in bushes to chase dogs.

The only people who enjoyed the dog patrol were

three graduate students from the science faculty who were doing some research on rabies.

That Saturday as Bud Culbertson crouched in some holly bushes by the English building with a tranquilizer gun at his side, a bulldog bit him on the ankle.

The very same week, the man who sat in front of Betsy Culbertson at the brokerage firm where she sold stocks and bonds, a man named Baker, dropped dead. He simply fell out of his seat into the aisle. Baker had been Betsy's age, thirty-eight. It started her thinking. According to the actuarial tables, women lived an average of eight years longer than men. The reason for that was fairly obvious. The average woman who lived eight years longer than the average man sat around on her can, watching soaps. Betsy Culbertson thought it would be interesting to see what the charts showed once this generation of working women plugged into the computer. She guessed that men and women with similar jobs would begin dying within hours of each other.

So after Bud Culbertson went on Dog Patrol and Betsy watched a guy her age die, they had a serious talk.

Betsy had wanted to get the hell out of town, fast.

Bud wasn't sure they had enough money.

They talked a couple of hours about what they wanted to do with the rest of their lives.

Bud was reluctant to just pack up and move.

Betsy had said terrific. One of them would die in their apartment west of Central Park. The other would get the insurance money and *then* take off.

Bud had been having some vague chest pains.

And here they were, standing by their car below the white house in the country.

"Smell that air," Bud said.

"It's sweet," Betsy said.

"Look at the rich color in the soil."

"There are *dozens* of places for a garden."

"This is the kind of place that makes a person feel lucky to be alive," Bud Culbertson said.

Betsy guessed "The Night Before Christmas" was written in a place like this.

"OH JESUS, THERE THEY ARE," ANDY FARMER SAID.

"Easy now," Elizabeth said,

They stood at their front window, holding hands and trembling.

"Did you clean out the globes over the lights?"

Elizabeth smiled and said she had.

"The dog, where's the damn yellow dog?"

"He's fine and put away."

"There's a smudge on the door and some dust on the window sill."

Elizabeth kissed her husband on the cheek and removed the smudge from the woodwork around the front door.

They were tired. They had been going at it twelve hours a day—sanding and pounding and painting and spraying poison. They had spent around $5,000 on repairs, not counting the advertising budget, which came in at around $3,500. Andy Farmer had advertised the property in the *New York Times* Sunday magazine—right in there among the multimillion-dollar villas on the ocean—and in *New York* magazine. But now that the prospective buyers had arrived, they experienced a rush of nervous energy. Elizabeth was concerned that her husband might flap his arms and fly. He was talking too fast, for one thing.

And:

"I think the pipe is a bit much, honey."

"Right, right."

Andy Farmer emptied the pipe into the fireplace.

"All you have to remember," Elizabeth said, placing her damp palms on her husband's shoulders, "is that this is all or nothing."

"We act casual."

"That's it."

"Not eager to sell."

"Precisely."

"I don't know if I'm that good an actor," Andy Farmer said, taking a deep breath.

"*Blink*, damn it," Elizabeth said.

Andy Farmer blinked. And grinned. He had been staring open-mouthed as the prospective buyers got out of their Olds.

Bud Culbertson wore a wool sport coat with a damn *shooting patch made out of leather stitched to the right shoulder*! He wore a turtleneck underneath a corduroy shirt and freshly creased slacks and penny loafers. He appeared to have just slid off the cover of *Town & Country*. His wife Betsy was resplendent in designer jeans tucked into suede boots, and a baggy and stylish sweater.

Andy Farmer almost became paralyzed.

"It's too good to be true," he whispered. "It's like they came from central casting."

"Shut up and wave."

The greetings and introductions were warm and friendly.

Everybody shook hands and grinned.

It was a glorious mid-December noon. Soft white clouds hung overhead like props. There was a nip in the air, and you could see your breath.

Andy Farmer wished there was a nip in him.

After the introductions, Bud Culbertson looked around and said, "Nice place."

He, too, had been instructed by his wife to act casual.

"It could use some tidying up," Andy Farmer said.

Elizabeth squeezed his hand.

"You haven't got a dog?" Bud Culbertson wondered.

"Yeah, we do," Andy Farmer said. "He's probably out scaring up some game."

Bud Culbertson smiled and nodded.

Elizabeth suggested that everybody go inside for a cup of coffee and a piece of pie, then the Culbertsons could have a look around on their own.

This plan was agreeable to everybody concerned.

"BUD WAS AN ENGLISH PROFESSOR," BETSY SAID, talking while glancing around the kitchen, which was spotless. "I sold stock. Bud's going to write a novel."

I'm suffocating, Andy Farmer thought. *I can't breathe*. His throat was tightening up and he couldn't get any air.

"How nice," Elizabeth said, smiling pleasantly. She did put her cup of coffee down so she wouldn't slosh any on her lap.

"How," Andy Farmer said, "how..."

He tried his coffee, some of which ran down his chin.

"A mystery," Bud Culbertson said.

"...great," Andy Farmer said. "How great. Jesus Christ, how great."

"If you don't mind," Betsy Culbertson said. "Might I ask why you're moving?"

"The service of our country," Andy Farmer said. "It's all I can say. We're being...transferred."

Elizabeth cleared her throat.

Bud Culbertson nodded.

Petree delivered the mail. He knocked on the back door. Andy Farmer froze again. Elizabeth answered the knock.

Petree was all slicked up—for him. He had shaved and had put some Murine in his eyes and chewed some gum to dull the odor of whiskey.

"Your mail, sir," he said, bowing slightly.

"Thanks," Elizabeth said.

Petree stepped around her and took the mail to the kitchen table and set it in a neat stack in front of Andy Farmer, who was making choking sounds as he tried to breathe.

"Morning folks," Petree said to the prospective buyers.

To Andy Farmer, he said, "They say the trout are running over at the river."

Petree tipped his new straw hat and left by the back door.

Elizabeth looked through the letters.

Andy Farmer excused himself from the table and said he had some bills in the other room he wanted to send with the mailman.

He caught up with Petree by the toolshed.

"You son of a bitch," he said. "I'll never forget you for this."

He stepped forward and embraced Petree warmly.

"Some people in town gave me fifty dollars to do this," he said. "For fifty a day, I'll *read* your goddamn mail to you."

"What trout? What river?"

"Thought it was a nice touch," Petree said.

THE FARMERS SAT IN THE LIVING ROOM, SPEAKING quietly.

Elizabeth had started to buckle. She said she felt guilty about presenting a false sense of security to two nice people like the Culbertsons.

The color left Andy Farmer's face. He told Elizabeth never to think anything like that again.

She crossed her legs and rocked the foot on top, which meant she was pouting.

"Listen to me. They might be a lot better at this than we are. They might goddamn *love* snakes. They might be tough. He might be a hell of a writer."

"You think?"

"Who the hell knows, there might even be oil under this place."

"Okay, okay," Elizabeth said. "You're probably right."

The conversation was broken by a scream.

* * *

"Watch it," Bud Culbertson said.

His wife jumped back and screamed again.

Bud Culbertson closed the door on the shelter.

The yellow dog had shot out, scaring the hell out of the prospective buyers.

It ran around the house and over to the 250-year-old cottonwood tree and then started running around the base, barking louder.

"Not ours," Andy Farmer said from the porch. "It belongs to a guy down the road. He's a friendly dog, though. Ours is out hunting. A setter. Cost a fortune."

"He burst out when I opened the shelter out back," Bud Culbertson said.

"I think he's cute," Betsy said.

"Why's he running around the tree like that?" Bud Culbertson asked.

"Christ," Andy Farmer said helplessly.

"He probably has a squirrel treed," Elizabeth said.

"Thanks," Andy Farmer whispered.

"See you in a little while," Bud Culbertson said, waving.

"We'll be right here," Andy Farmer told them, waving back.

The Culbertsons continued their inspection of the property.

"I thought you tied him to a tree out where Musselman is buried."

"No, I put him in the shelter," Elizabeth said.

"See what happens when you start sulking? See what happens when you think about *somebody else*?"

Elizabeth nodded.

She said she was sorry for not being more ruthless.

THE CULBERTSONS STOOD BY THE POND.

Bud tossed a rock into its middle.

"We'd need a couple of ducks," Betsy said.

Bud nodded. "So what do you think?"

"Honey, I love it. You see that kitchen."

"Yeah, the walls—the place is built like a fort."

"How much are they asking?"

"A hundred and thirty-two thousand."

"Write them a check, Bud. We'll never find anything like this as long as we live. If we don't buy it, the people from California who are coming to look tomorrow will snap it up in a second, I *know* it."

"He might be lying about that," Bud Culbertson told his wife, washing his hands in the clear pond water. "Let me work on him. You don't think this is a little *too far* out by itself?"

"Are you serious?"

"No," Bud admitted.

Their discussion was interrupted by Lester Shimmerhorn, who said, "Howdy."

He wore a sweatshirt under some overalls and carried a hoe over his shoulder.

"Hi," Bud Culbertson said, introducing his wife.

"I'm the foreman of this spread," Lester Shimmerhorn said.

Bud Culbertson nodded.

"Buy and sell produce, arrange the crops, take care of the yard, that sort of thing."

"What produce?" Bud wondered.

"Just sold a few pigs in town."

"Pigs are cute," Betsy said.

Lester Shimmerhorn bent down and picked up a handful of soil and explained things like nitrogen content and prudent fertilization, all of which would ensure a thriving garden for only pennies a day.

"IT WENT PERFECT," LESTER SHIMMERHORN SAID, accepting a fifty-dollar bill from Andy Farmer.

"You didn't overdo it?"

"You just sold some produce, some pigs and cows, that's about it."

"Pigs aren't goddamn *produce*."

"Well then, you shouldn't tell those people, should you. I ought to get a commission, not a lousy fifty."

"Get the damn dog and get him the hell out of here."

"I believe I got a shot at getting hired on as some kind of cowboy for nine hundred a month," Lester Shimmerhorn said, straightening his felt cowboy hat.

THE FARMERS TOOK THE CULBERTSONS ON A SCENIC tour before heading for town and a ten-thousand-calorie chicken-fry platter at Ivy's.

They took the scenic tour in the sparkling new Jeep that had been driven only 445 miles.

The Jeep belonged to Mayor Barclay.

"You don't actually *need* anything with four-wheel drive," Andy Farmer said, making a right onto Dog Creek Road. "But it's a lot of fun for photo safaris."

They took the Culbertsons by historic Cooperman's Bridge and stopped on top to look at a deer that the Criterion brothers had tied to a tree.

"My gosh," Betsy Culbertson said, scooting up for a look at the deer.

The deer was about fifty yards away, and it had been secured in some bushes, so you couldn't see the rope or the stake.

As the Culbertsons pressed their noses against the glass to admire the deer, Andy Farmer tapped his wife on the shoulder and called her attention to a piece of brass that was sticking up through the mud.

The brass was from *their bed*.

Elizabeth nodded and moaned slightly, remembering.

REDBUD WAS UNBELIEVABLE.

It was like a scene out of *Our Town*.

It was beautiful.

Andy Farmer parked the Jeep by the Square.

Coonfield was on his bench, same as always, but this time he wasn't reading an old newspaper; he was reading the *Wall Street Journal*.

The checker tables were occupied by nonfelons.

And, on the billboard above the Veterans of Foreign Wars' building was this message: "The Town Hall Series proudly presents Donnie and Marie, Feb. 13, all seats $10."

Elizabeth stood with her mouth open.

"Donnie and Marie Fogelman," Andy Farmer whispered into his wife's ear. "They're folk dancers."

During the walk to Ivy's, they passed the dress store. There was a stunning white sequined dress in the window. Although there was no blood on the dress, Andy Farmer recognized it immediately: It was Elizabeth's birthday dress.

"I loaned it to them," Elizabeth whispered.

Andy Farmer kissed his wife on the lips.

Dr. Mayhew was *standing* in front of his hospital.

"Evening," he said to the Culbertsons, who nodded.

Dr. Mayhew had a stethoscope hanging around his neck.

He was *tan*.

"Where'd you get that beard?" Andy Farmer asked as he walked by.

Elizabeth pulled her husband on toward the restaurant.

"It's Dr. Mayhew's brother," Elizabeth said. "They flew him in from Florida."

"Eat fast," Andy Farmer said. "This *can't* last."

IVY ABOUT BLEW IT.

She had on her menu for this special occasion: Quail, $1.95.

While the Culbertsons slid into a booth, Andy Farmer spoke with Ivy, who was wearing a new pink uniform, and told her that you couldn't sell delicacies like quail for two dollars.

"I haven't got any of it," Ivy said. "It's for show."

Although the Culbertsons noticed the bargain right off, Andy Farmer coaxed them into having the chicken-fry platters.

The dinner went perfectly.

The chicken-fry specials were so large, one would have been plenty for the four of them.

The only halfway hokey part was when one of the guys sitting at the counter started playing songs made famous by the Sons of the Pioneers—"Tumbling Tumbleweed," for example—on a guitar.

THE MEN HAD THEIR ARMS AROUND THE WOMEN.

The stars were out.

There had been one anxious moment on the way to the Jeep after dinner.

The Culbertsons had planned to spend the night at Sid's Alpine Village.

"Absolutely *not*," Andy Farmer said. "You'll stay with us in the guest bedroom."

Before heading home, they took a spin around town to show the Culbertsons such landmarks as Mrs. Dinge's Antique Shoppe, which brought a tear to Elizabeth's eye.

"I'm going to offer one-twenty," Bud whispered to his wife in the back seat of the Jeep.

"I think you're being silly," Betsy whispered back.

"We'll see. Anything under one-thirty, we'll sign the contract tonight."

"Great," Betsy said.

"EXCUSE ME," BUD CULBERTSON SAID, LEANING UP from the back seat. "What's that noise?"

Andy Farmer stopped the Jeep on the up slope of a hill, a mile outside town. He turned the radio down.

"What noise?"

"I thought I heard some sort of *roar*."

"Maybe it's the motor," Elizabeth said.

"Yeah," Andy Farmer said. "Some belt's been a little loose."

Betsy, who had her head out a back window, leaned inside and said, "No, it sounds like a train."

"Train?" Elizabeth said.

"There's no track around here," Andy Farmer said. "I'll check it out."

FIRE ENGINE 109 DIDN'T SEEM TO COME OVER THE hill in front of them.

It appeared to come up out of the earth, like one of those elevators built into the sidewalks in the city.

Suddenly, Fire Engine 109 was just *there*.

The Culbertsons screamed, grabbed each other, and hit the deck.

Elizabeth honked the horn, which didn't do her husband's ears any good, because he was leaning over the motor, checking a belt or two.

WHOOPS, JOHNNY JOHNSON THOUGHT, SHIELDING HIS eyes from the bright headlights in front of him.

Through the glare, he could see arms and legs wiggling.

He had gotten lost searching for a fire in Harold Peterson's garage. Not only had he missed the fire, he had also missed Harold Peterson's garage—and *farm*—

so he had made a circle to the south and was riding the gas pedal to make up for lost time.

Andy Farmer had left the driver's door open on the mayor's new Jeep.

A hook that held a ladder on the left side of Engine 109 caught the driver's door and dragged the mayor's Jeep dozens of yards back toward town.

A fraction of a second before the impact, Johnny Johnson had turned the siren on—better late than never—which didn't do much for morale inside the Jeep.

After Engine 109 carried the Jeep a ways, it flung it sideways into a ditch.

Engine 109 spun in a circle and somehow went from a forward gear into reverse—the transmission was in bad shape—and backed into a ditch opposite the Jeep. It as a miracle the fire truck didn't explode into flames.

"I'd have put it out in ten seconds," Johnny Johnson was to state later of that possibility.

Engine 109 came to rest with its nose pointing close to straight up.

Elizabeth was wearing her seat belt and was okay.

The Jeep landed on its left side.

Andy Farmer used a pocket knife to cut his wife out of the seat belt, which had become tangled.

He couldn't hear a thing because of the horn that had been honked six inches from his right ear.

The Culbertsons had been banged around like dice in a hot shooter's hand, and were cut, bruised, and sad.

* * *

"JESUS *CHRIST*," THE MAYOR SHOUTED AT THE TOP OF his lungs. Fifteen minutes after the accident, things— mostly chrome—were still falling off the Jeep. "What the hell happened?"

He said it looked like a meteorite had hit his goddamn Jeep.

"Don't quote me on that," he said to a reporter from the *Gazette*.

The reporter took a close-up picture of Betsy Culbertson as she lay in a ditch, and the flash in her face made her cry louder.

"Walk that line," Sheriff Ledbetter said to Johnny Johnson, who said it was not whiskey everybody smelled on him, it was gasoline from the accident.

Johnny Johnson attempted to walk the line that the sheriff had drawn with a stick in the middle of the dirt road, but he fell over backward.

"You have the right to remain silent," Jeff, the deputy, said, cuffing Johnny Johnson's hands behind his back.

"Driving under the influence, reckless driving, public intoxication, you get the drift," Sheriff Ledbetter said.

Jeff nodded.

"*Public*," Johnny Johnson said. "Where the hell? There's no law against a *private* drunk."

"You just confessed, pal," Jeff said.

"You were in a public vehicle," Sheriff Ledbetter said.

"What do you think?" Stanley Ludlum, of the Ludlum Brothers Ambulance Service, asked his brother Mort.

Jay Cronley

Mort knelt beside Bud Culbertson, who was lapsing into and out of consciousness.

"There seems to be a tender spot by his lower back," Mort said. "Odds are, it's a pulled muscle."

"Can he move his legs?"

"Not unconscious, no."

"It might be his spine," Stanley said.

"I say it's a cramp."

"All right, move him," Stanley said. "But be careful."

There was a big silver cat in the back of the Ludlum brothers ambulance. As Mort carried Bud Culbertson out of the ditch, Stanley shooed the cat up front.

"Take them to Jefferson," Andy Farmer said.

"We can't cross the county line," Stanley said. "You of all people should know that."

Mort went to fetch Betsy Culbertson. She was almost hysterical. The Ludlum brothers strapped Betsy Culbertson to a stretcher.

"It's Redbud Memorial or bust," Mort said.

THIS WAS JOHNNY JOHNSON'S STORY:

He worked for the gas company and was a volunteer fireman. He had called in sick at work and spent the afternoon in Vic's Bar, which was a block from the Square. He was sick in a way. He was sick of his wife, who sat around all day watching television. She refused to get a job, and they had been fighting almost nonstop.

A foot here, a foot there, even a few inches, Johnny Johnson could have been a star. He had been a pretty

302

good football player, back when. He even went to a junior college a semester to play linebacker.

"You're too goddamn short to get a *suntan*," his coach over at the junior college had said one lovely fall afternoon after an opposing runner *stepped over* Johnny Johnson on the way to scoring a touchdown.

Johnny Johnson quit growing at five feet, eight inches.

He had returned home to marry his sweetheart, who was a cheerleader, and here he was, virtually overnight, twenty-eight years old. And there she was, weighing 165.

Vic had limited Johnny Johnson to a beer every two hours. With prospective buyers of the Musselman-Farmer place in the area, everybody had to be on his or her toes.

All Johnny Johnson talked about was the curse of sex.

"You take somebody in high school that looks like a disaster," Johnny Johnson had said, "somebody too ugly for sex. What happens is they have other interests and get the hell out of this place. The ugly ones are the first ones out the door. You ever wonder why scientists are the ugliest sons of bitches in the world?"

Vic hadn't wondered about that.

"It's because it takes ugly people five years to have a Coke date," Johnny Johnson had said.

He had rambled on and on all afternoon about how unlucky he was because his wife had puffed up after being a knockout in high school. Vic was concerned that this depressing conversation would last into the evening, so he said, "As far as I can tell, it's got something to do with genes. A person takes the time to check it out, you probably find out that there's some-body in your wife's background big as a hog."

Johnny Johnson went to the men's room for about ten minutes after Vic made his point about genes. When he came out, his eyes were red. He said he had been crying. He was in and out of the men's room all day.

When the alarm went off at 8:30 P.M., Johnny Johnson was in the bathroom again, and he went out the window. He was gone for three minutes before Vic knew it.

Vic's bar was only half a block from the fire station.

By the time Vic got his blackjack and ran into the alley out back, Johnny Johnson was long gone.

Johnny Johnson was a member in good standing of the Redbud Volunteer Fire Department. To become a member in good standing, all you needed was the desire to serve your fellow man, and some boots; the Department, which was supported by contributions from local citizens, provided a fireproof raincoat, a fire-proof hat, and some axes.

It was a matter of economics: It took a lot of money to support a full-time fire department.

The volunteers, of whom there were twenty-some, generated a lot of civic pride whether they were swat-ting at flames with gunnysacks or marching in a parade, wearing their bright yellow rain slickers.

If you had a fire, you were at the mercy of the luck of the draw. If you had a fire during the week, there was never any problem concerning the sobriety of the volunteers who would attack your blaze. Eight hard-working businessmen and women who were volunteers worked within a two-block radius of the fire station. There were two Baptist churches within six blocks of the fire station, so Sundays were covered, too.

Saturday nights, though, when all the stores were closed—when a person liked to put his feet up and have a few cool ones—could be a problem.

You could draw a drunk.

When the alarm went off, it was first come, first drive.

Except for the Saturday late last spring when several volunteers washed the engine while splitting a case of Coors, nobody had attempted to drive a ten-ton 1955-model fire engine while drunk.

It was a miracle Johnny Johnson had even *found* the fire truck.

He'd had sixteen beers.

He had been sneaking them in the men's room at Vic's Bar.

Vic found the empties stuffed in the back of the toilet.

That was Vic's story.

Johnny Johnson was the first one to reach Engine 109.

It was bad luck.

Vic had tried to shoot out one of the tires on the fire engine as it sped by his bar on the way to Harold Peterson's garage, which unfortunately burned to the ground.

Jeff, the deputy, wrote every bit of this story down.

They wouldn't have to throw the book at Johnny Johnson.

They could drop it on his head and he'd be put away for months.

* * *

ONCE STATEMENTS HAD BEEN TAKEN AND THE INJURED had been carted away, wreckers came and went.

Nobody offered the Farmers the time of night.

Soon, they were alone.

The Farmers walked two miles to the nearest house and called Ike's Cab Company.

Ike arrived wearing a new blue suit of western cut.

He saluted the Farmers.

"Great night," Ike said, looking around for passengers.

"You can knock it off," Andy Farmer said to Ike, who hadn't heard the news and thought they were still in Act II. "It's over."

TWO DAYS LATER, LESTER Shimmerhorn stopped by with some stolen chickens. He had heard that the Culbertsons had crawled out a window at Redbud Memorial the morning after they had been dropped off there by the Ludlum brothers.

During midmorning, two days after the accident, a panel truck stopped at the driveway to the Farmer place. Two men were in the panel truck. One got out and walked to the cottonwood tree.

The man who got out of the truck said his name was Knox. He said he was a licensed private investigator. He didn't come any nearer the house. He spoke loudly and firmly. As he spoke, he kept his hand in the front pocket of his windbreaker, the way they do in all the old gangster movies.

He had come for the Culbertsons' Olds.

He told the Farmers to move into an open area between the house and the pond and keep their hands in plain sight at all times.

He got into the Oldsmobile and followed the panel truck south on Dog Creek Road.

Andy Farmer guessed this meant the deal for the house was off.

 SHE RAN OUT OF THE HOUSE, dripping blood.

Her dress had been violently torn. She had had enough, obviously, and stood at the bottom of the front steps, trying to decide which way to run.

She chose the security of the clump of trees to her left, and ran that way, stumbling and crying.

She looked over her shoulder as she ran to make sure he hadn't seen her.

He was trying to kill her.

When she was no more than five yards from the first tree—and running so hard she couldn't stop— he stepped from behind an old elm, holding a sharp ax like a ball bat.

She screamed and tried to stop running but couldn't.

He laughed like a maniac and swung the ax at her neck.

Her head flew off.

What was left of her fell and rolled.

The head sailed on into the trees.

He laughed again.

"*Cut*," the director yelled. "Goddamn, that was *tremendous*."

* * *

ANDY FARMER HAD ALWAYS HOPED HE WOULD BE ABLE to sell *something* to the movies. He had hoped it would be a novel, but it turned out to be his house.

As an assistant producer retrieved the head that had flown into the trees, Andy Farmer and Elizabeth stood by the 25-year-old cottonwood with their arms around each other, smiling like proud parents.

The head scene had gone very well. The director didn't want to cheapen the dramatic moment with a bunch of quick cuts that would come right out and say, "We faked it." He wanted one continual, flowing scene, with the head coming off at the end of a long run. To accomplish this, a short man in a dress had run toward the trees, wearing a fake head cemented on top of his own head.

The ax had been rubber.

AFTER THE CULBERTSONS ESCAPED, ANDY FARMER lowered his sights and advertised their place for sale in a number of lower-to-middle-class publications. The ad that caught the producer's eye ran in a tabloid that had a big circulation in the greater Los Angeles area.

The advertisement said: A house and 25 acres in the country, $61,500; will trade.

A photo of the house ran with the ad.

The Farmer place was just what the producer was looking for: something frightening and cheap in the middle of nowhere.

Several representatives of the film company visited the house at Star Route 2, Dog Creek Road. The man

309

in charge of sets and scenery fell in love with the place the second he saw it. In fact, the movie company didn't have to tear anything down or scuff anything up to make the house appear absolutely terrifying. A couple of carpenters actually had to *touch up* a few spots to make the Farmer place seem *believably* awful.

The movie probably wouldn't win many awards.

The story line was thin in places, but it had plenty of action.

It was about some mutants who lived next door to a nuclear weapons testing ground and gave birth to a brood of psychopaths.

The producer could have probably charged most of the budget on his Visa card.

Lester Shimmerhorn landed a bit part.

Even the yellow dog was in the film, running around the cottonwood tree nonstop.

The film company paid the Farmers $17,500 to take over their place for most of a month.

The working title of the movie was: *Hell House.*

THE FILM COMPANY, EUREKA PRODUCTIONS, WAS GOING to put the finishing touches on *Hell House* back at their studio in Los Angeles. According to the director, the ending was going to be something special. There would be a nuclear war, and the people who had been exposed to the radiation that turned them into mutants—the group of nuts living in the Farmer house—would have built up an immunity and would be the only survivors.

After the director paid Andy Farmer and Elizabeth the last installment of the seventeen-five, it took the crew the rest of the day to pack up all the gear and get their dozen or so trailers ready to roll.

Everybody left at sundown.

The Farmers waved so-long from the front porch.

The seventeen-five had solved a number of problems, at least temporarily.

It had bought them some time to poison or bulldoze or bury some more problems and further adjust themselves to the lifestyle of their choosing.

They were going to hang in there.

They hadn't discussed whether they were going to hang in there because they had to or because they wanted to; the answer might have been a little depressing, either way.

Mostly, they were ready for some privacy.

If they got luckier, they would have more than enough company during the sequels.

ABOUT THE AUTHOR

JAY CRONLEY lives in Tulsa, Oklahoma, where he writes a thrice-weekly newspaper column for the Tulsa *Tribune*. He is a frequent contributor to *Playboy* magazine and has won two *Playboy* writing awards for nonfiction. FUNNY FARM is his sixth novel.